Praise for the Popcorn Shop Mysteries

"A wry, witty voice that had me laughing out loud, a truly puzzling mystery plot and a popcorn shop setting that earns its place with clever clues aplenty. Bursting with delights."
—Catriona McPherson, award-winning author of *The Day She Died*

"Kick back, pick up a snack and enjoy . . . The heroine is delightfully sarcastic, but with a sweet spirit, and she refuses to give up on her dreams. The supporting cast runs the gamut from a potential love interest to a flaky ex-husband, and readers will be charmed by each of them."
—*RT Book Reviews*

"Popping with a protagonist full of heart and a great poodle sidekick."
—Open Book Society

"Brilliantly written with fun, quirky characters. It's got a wonderful setting, a believable crime and a smart woman with extreme determination."
—Marie's Cozy Corner

"Kristi Abbott plunges the reader headlong into a mystery that is full of red herrings, and yummy food and recipes . . . Read *Kernel of Truth*—you won't regret it!"
—Fresh Fiction

Assault
and Buttery

KRISTI ABBOTT

BERKLEY PRIME CRIME
New York

BERKLEY PRIME CRIME
Published by Berkley
An imprint of Penguin Random House LLC
375 Hudson Street, New York, New York 10014

ISBN: 9780425280935

First Edition: November 2017

Printed in the United States of America
3   5   7   9   10   8   6   4   2

Cover art by Catherine Deeter
Cover design by Sarah Oberrender

ACKNOWLEDGMENTS

I would never manage to write a book without outside help. I am lucky to be surrounded by many smart, talented and kind people who always want to lend a hand or an ear or a bit of expertise. Spring Warren, Catriona McPherson, Delilah Dawson and more, you've fed my creative soul, soothed my anxieties and cheered me on. Here's a partial list of other people who helped with this book and how:

- Katherine Pelz, for patience and thinking that of course we should use all the ideas.
- Andy Wallace, for agreeing that of course we should stop at as many missions as possible as we drove from Los Angeles to Davis and thereby discover that there was actually such a thing as popcorn soup, and also for buying a new dishwasher.

- Kris Calvin, for telling me what kinds of people run for city council.
- Beth McMullen, for listening to me whine during many, many circumnavigations of the Arboretum.
- Teresa Olson and Leslie Kuss, for suggesting I try making S'mores Popcorn.

I'm sure there are more. There always are. I always say I'm going to keep a list and then promptly forget. Please know that it doesn't mean I'm not grateful.

One

I walked over to the bars of my jail cell. "Hey! Anybody out there? I want my phone call. Don't I get a phone call?" My voice echoed down the short hallway. I could practically hear it bouncing off the door that shut the cell block off from the Sheriff's Department.

Nobody answered. I waited a few minutes, then yelled again. More echoes. Still no answers. Something made my heart flutter. Not in a good "I just saw a boy I think is cute" way. In a bad "how did I end up in this bank of four cells off a concrete hallway with a big old steel door at the end?" kind of way. I wasn't sure what it was that made the flutter, but I thought it might be fear.

Well, screw fear.

I flung myself onto my bunk and immediately regretted it. The mattress was beyond thin. The metal springs beneath it reverberated up my spine and made my head ache. I needed to come up with a plan. I needed to think. Too bad the red-hot haze of fury covered everything in my brain with a deep coat of rage. The rage did help push the fear to the far edges of my consciousness, though, so it wasn't entirely useless. I pulled my legs up crisscross-applesauce and tried to do some of the deep-breathing exercises Annie, my flower-child-in-more-than-one-way friend, had been teaching me to help deal with the stress of having my kitchen under construction again. Not cooking was hard on me. Having my business close just as I was starting to get it off the ground was even harder.

At first I sounded like a horse that had been ridden hard and put away wet. Nothing but deep snorts out of my nose. They echoed off the cement-block walls around me. After a few repetitions, however, the red haze in my head receded to a pinkish tone and then down almost to a rosy hue and my breathing became even and deep. Tension flowed out of my neck and shoulders, down my arms and out my fingertips. I wouldn't say I was at peace, but I could think in something other than expletives.

"You settling down now?" A woman lay on the bottom bunk of the cell next to mine, her arm flung up over her face. I'd been so angry about my situation and intent on letting the world know it, I hadn't even noticed her there when I'd been led in or when my cell had been locked behind me or when Sheriff Dan Cooper, my brother-in-law and the person I considered my best friend, had then walked out of the cell block and shut the door behind him.

It took me a few minutes to recognize the woman in the cell. I was used to seeing her with her hair done, her makeup perfect, her designer clothes pressed and lovely, not in an orange jumpsuit and with an inch of gray roots showing on her scalp and without so much as lip gloss. "Hi, Cathy, I didn't realize this was where you were."

"Did you think I was on a cruise to the Bahamas?" She didn't move her arm from her face. "Or perhaps spending a little time in Paris?"

I hadn't thought that. I hadn't thought much since I'd read about her arrest on the front page of the *Grand Lake Sentinel*. It had been big news. Of course, my various arrests had also been front-page news in the *Sentinel*, too. This current one hadn't appeared yet, but given time I was sure they'd get to it. I hoped they wouldn't use my mug shot this time. It never looked good. Something about the lighting was permanently unflattering. I'm on the pale side. Fluorescents totally wash me out.

The difference between the news of my various arrests and Cathy's, however, was that it looked like Cathy might actually have done what she was accused of doing. I was always innocent of all charges. Well, innocent-ish, at the very least. "No. I guess I hadn't thought about where you would be while you waited for your trial," I finally answered.

"When all your assets are seized as evidence in an investigation, it's a little tricky to make your bail." She turned on her side so her back was to me. I had been dismissed. Whatever. It wasn't like I'd be here long. It was all a mistake, a miscarriage of justice, a terrible blunder.

I went back to the bars and yelled some more. No one came until I resorted to running my comb up and down the bars and yelling, "Attica! Attica!"

The green metal door at the end of the corridor flew

open. All six foot two inches of Deputy Glenn Huerta strode in.

"Settle down," he growled at me. "Why on earth are you making a ruckus?"

"Because I haven't had my phone call." I crossed my arms over my chest and glared up at him. I'm tall, but Glenn's taller. And broader. And significantly more muscly. I didn't care. I was not backing down. I was pissed and I was pretty sure my rights were being violated in some way. Perhaps dozens of ways. The Man would not keep me down.

Glenn snorted. "You don't have a lawyer. I heard Garrett fired you as a client. Who you gonna call?"

I resisted the temptation to answer with "Ghostbusters." It wasn't a joking matter. Glenn had heard right. My boyfriend, who had also been my lawyer through a few misadventures, was part of the reason I was locked up in the first place. So I said, "I'm going to call your girlfriend."

"I don't have a girlfriend." He blushed, though.

"Yeah. Right. You don't have a girlfriend and I don't have a knife sharpener." The rage was seeping back. I took another step toward my bars to go eyeball to eyeball with Huerta. "I. Want. My. Phone. Call."

He glared, but said, "I'll see what I can do."

When I'd mentioned Glenn's girlfriend, I had been referring to Cynthia Harlen. Cynthia was a kick-ass lawyer, a real looker, and Garrett's ex. I couldn't think of a more perfect choice to get me out of my present pickle. She'd do the job and we'd piss off Garrett and Dan in the process, which suited me just fine. The two of them had pissed me off plenty. Huerta hadn't pissed me off, but it was fun to watch Cynthia and him when they were around each other. Whenever she and Huerta were in the same room together, the sexual tension was so thick I doubt I could have cut it with my sharpest knife, and I have some pretty damn sharp knives. I hadn't been joking about my sharpener.

I went back to my bunk and sat down more carefully. I'm not sure what that mattress was, but it was definitely not a pillow top. My back was going to kill me if I had to sleep on that thing. I wouldn't have to, though. Cynthia would get me out.

I looked around, but there really wasn't anything to look at. My cell had one bunk bed, one sink and one metal toilet with no seat. There wasn't even any interesting graffiti on the walls, nothing to distract myself with to make the time go faster. I twisted around so I was facing Cathy's cell.

"You've been in here the whole time? Since your arrest?" I asked her back.

There was a hesitation, then she rolled over so she was facing me. "Yep. Right here. Except for the hour each day that I get to go out and exercise. Oh, and shower time. That's always a treat." She did look pale. And haggard. Her skin looked rough and dry. Did I mention those gray roots?

I didn't feel sorry for her, though. If the accusations that were leveled against her were true—and the evidence being stacked up certainly made it look that way—she deserved it. She'd been the city comptroller for six years. One of the most trusted women in Grand Lake. She'd been the project manager for pretty much every improvement in the town. Every pothole that got filled. Every new ramada put up in a park. Every expansion to the library went through Cathy Hanover. She'd been efficient and calm and resourceful. That had been true of how she'd run those projects and also apparently true of how she'd bilked tens of thousands of dollars from the city of Grand Lake over the last six years.

It had been a clever scam, really. She'd created fake vendors, complete with bank accounts in nearby towns. Then those vendors had bid on projects being done in Grand Lake. Not big stuff. Not the renovation of the high school cafeteria that had cost thousands and thousands of dollars. Little things. Supplying paper towels or nails for other projects. A few hundred dollars here. A few there. Nothing big enough to make anyone raise an eyebrow, but plenty once it added up.

"So what are you in for?" she asked.

"Obstruction of justice."

She put her arm back over her eyes. "Amateur."

It hadn't been my intention to obstruct justice. I'd actually been seeking justice when I showed up at Lloyd McLaughlin's wake. Of course, it was mainly justice for me, although I figured Lloyd would get a little bit along the way. Call it enlightened self-interest. So enlightened, in fact, that I didn't even feel bad that he wasn't my first priority. Well, not super bad. After all, I hadn't even known who Lloyd was when he died. I'd first heard about his death at dinner with my sister, Haley; my bestie brother-in-law, Sheriff Dan Cooper; and my boo, who was at that time still my lawyer, Garrett Mills.

"You okay?" I'd asked Dan as we cleared the table.

His plate had still been half full at the end of the meal and he was usually nothing if not a good eater. It all seemed to go directly to his shoulders, which were broad and strong, but he was almost always a member of the clean-plate club, especially if I helped cook.

"I saw something today I can't seem to unsee." He'd winced. "It's actually more that I smelled something that I can't seem to unsmell."

"What happened?" That did not sound good.

"I'm surprised you don't already know." He'd crossed his arms over his chest and shot me some side-eye. "You seem to know about almost everything that goes on in this town before I do."

I knew what he meant although I didn't think he should get pissy with me about it. I didn't set out to be one of the premier stops on the gossip underground of Grand Lake. It just happened that way. Besides, it wasn't that way at the moment. "My gossip lines have dried up with the shop being closed." My gourmet popcorn shop, POPS, was closed while damage from a grease fire was being repaired. "Most of the time I heard stuff because people come in for a cup of coffee and some Coco Pop Fudge. No shop. No Coco Pop. No Coco Pop. No gossip. It's not like I go out seeking it. It comes to me. It probably helps that nobody sees me as The Man." Sharing a juicy tidbit with someone who gives you chocolate is totally different than informing on someone to the local constabulary.

"She's right," Garrett said. "No one wants to be a rat. Snitches get stitches."

I smiled at him for backing me up. And for being generally a nice guy. And for being cute. And for being a good kisser.

Dan looked down at his uniform. "I can see that." He hesitated a moment more and then blurted, "Lloyd Mc-Laughlin died."

The name hadn't rung one single bell for me, not even a tinkle of the smallest kind of bell. "Who?"

"Lloyd McLaughlin. Lives—lived—out by Highway 2 in one of the new developments. Did some kind of real estate work," Dan said.

I shook my head. "Nope. Never heard of him. I apparently didn't go to high school with him and he apparently doesn't eat popcorn." Those would be the two main ways I knew everyone who I knew here in Grand Lake. "How did he die?"

"We're not sure yet, but it didn't look natural." That pained expression passed over Dan's face. "However he died, it was messy."

I paused, mid–plate scrape. "Murder? Again?"

Dan rubbed his face. "I know. It's getting to be a little too commonplace around here for my tastes."

"Way too commonplace," Haley said. She glanced over at me from her spot at the end of the table. Baby Emily slept peacefully in her arms. Haley looked like she was about two seconds from sleep herself. "You know before you moved back we hadn't had a murder in Grand Lake since Clea Tamarack hit her husband over the head with a frying pan for forgetting to pick up milk on the way home, and there are some who still count that as accidental."

"How on earth could that be seen as accidental?" Garrett asked. He hadn't lived here long and was still learning our ways.

Haley shrugged. "She said she was waving the pan in the air to dry it and Albert's head got in the way."

Garrett stared. "And people believed her?"

Haley shifted my niece in her arms and stuck her hand out and made a *comme ci, comme ça* gesture. "Nothing's impossible and Albert was really frustrating. Still, that was the last one before you moved home." She pointed at me.

"You're blaming me?" I stared at my sister in disbelief.

She readjusted the baby in her arms. "No, but it's starting to feel weird. You know what I mean?"

I did. I didn't want to admit it, but I did. This would be the third murder in less than a year. I sat down next to Dan. "I take it the scene was pretty bad."

He leaned back in his chair and let his head loll back. "It wasn't a day on the lake, that's for sure."

I put my hand over his. I knew all too well what it felt like to stumble across a dead body. I knew how it could haunt you, popping into your mind at the most inopportune moments. I knew how it could change how you saw your life. And your food. "Anything I can do?" I asked.

He shot bolt upright. "No. There's absolutely nothing you can do. This has nothing to do with you and you need to stay out of it, Rebecca. I'm serious."

I sat back, stung. "I know that. I don't even know who this Lloyd guy is. Why on earth would I have anything to do with it?"

"All I know is that you could not—would not—keep your nose out of the last two murders in Grand Lake. You poked and prodded and you were nearly killed twice," Dan said.

"And you nearly got me killed in the process," Haley said, dabbing her mouth with a napkin. "You also nearly had me giving birth on the back porch of POPS. I'm with Dan. Stay out of it."

I looked over to Garrett for some backup, but he was sitting with his arms crossed over his chest and absolutely no smile on his lips whatsoever. He was still cute and still a good kisser, but I wasn't so sure he had my back on this one.

It didn't seem fair. I hadn't asked to be embroiled in Coco's murder or in Melanie's murder. It had been bad luck, a stupid series of unfortunate incidents, crazy mixed-up fate that had had me twisted up in unraveling what had happened to them.

On the other hand, they had a point. While I'd helped bring two murderers to justice, I'd come damn close to being a sacrifice on the altar of truth. I raised my right hand in the air. "I solemnly swear to stay out of it."

"Excellent," Dan said.

"Besides, I have my own mystery to solve," I said.

Haley cocked her head to one side. "You mean the diary?"

I did mean the diary. Days before, while Carson and I had been pulling down the remnants of the wall in what was left of my kitchen after the grease fire that had been supposed to demolish both me and POPS, we'd found a diary. Well, *find* might be exaggerating. We jumped back and squealed like kids on a roller coaster when it unexpectedly fell out of the wall at our feet. We hadn't known what it was at first. It was wrapped in an old pillowcase and had looked like a bundle of dirty clothes. Carson and I had both stared at it and then each other.

"Pick it up and see what it is," I'd said.

Carson had shaken his giant dandelion of a head—really, he had the most amazing hair—and said, "I've found some freaky-ass stuff in walls. You pick it up. It's your shop."

"Yeah, but I'm paying you to fix it," I'd pointed out.

"Not enough," he'd snapped back.

He was right. He could have charged me more. He might have been Grand Lake High's head stoner back in the day, but now he was Grand Lake's most reliable contractor. I was definitely getting the friends-and-family rate from him. Apparently, you had to pay full price to get him to deal with freaky stuff. I couldn't dispute the fairness of the arrangement.

I had taken a deep breath and poked the pillowcase with a yardstick and had been relieved that whatever was inside the pillowcase was hard, since I figured something dead would be soft. I'd crouched down, picked up the pillowcase by the tiniest part of the corner that I could pinch between my finger and thumb and shaken. A book had tumbled out.

Both Carson and I had let the air out of our lungs with a whoosh. He clutched his chest. "Oh, man, Rebecca. I thought it was going to be a dead baby." He sat down heavily on one of my spindly ice cream chairs.

"Seriously? That's the first place your mind goes? Dead babies?" I sat down next to him, my heart beating too hard for having just unearthed a book from a pillowcase, even though I swear dead babies never crossed my mind. I'd been more focused on a severed hand for some reason.

"You've had kind of a bad run with dead bodies, you know? And this was small. Definitely not a full-sized customer." Carson ran his hand through his hair, making it stand up even taller.

"I'm aware." If I hadn't noticed it myself, the constant comments from friends and family about the bodies and the murder rate would have probably clued me in. I reached down and picked up the book. The cover was a faded pink with a few water stains marring it, but not marring it enough that you couldn't read the words "My Diary" in a dark pink cursive script across the front.

"Whose diary do you think it is?" Carson asked.

"Not a clue." I pressed the button and the lock popped open. There was no name on the inside bookplate. No address. No marker. No introduction. It had just started in.

May 17
Friday

I cannot believe I am home again on a Friday evening when everyone else—EVERYONE ELSE—is out. I can see them from my bedroom window. GT, Shoop, Twinkletoes. They're all there. Walking up and down. Sitting on benches. Eating ice cream. Talking to each other like normal people.

Me? I'm inside. Reading. I hate my mother. I want to kill myself.

I gasped and showed the entry to Carson. "Do you think she really wanted to kill herself? Do you think this is like a suicide note?"

Carson took the book from my hand and leafed

through. "No. Or if she did mean it, she changed her mind. This thing goes on for another fifty or sixty pages. Plus, teenage girls are kind of into all the drama, right?"

He was right. It was probably how I sounded when I was fifteen. All drama all the time. By the time I was sixteen, I wouldn't have sat in my room whining about it to my diary. I would have gone out the window, shimmied down the porch overhang, caught on to the willow tree branches and swung myself down to the ground. Dan would have probably been waiting.

I flipped a few pages forward and read an entry from a few weeks later.

Went to the lake with Bubbles yesterday. We swam all the way out to the buoy and back, then went back to her house. Man, can she swim! Her mom made us popcorn and hot chocolate when we got to her place. Boy! That lake sure is cold.

Bubbles? I knew someone whose nickname was Bubbles. Well, I didn't really know the person. I carried her DNA.

I put my finger on the name. "I think that's my grandmother. Ella Conner. I remember Mom once telling me that Grandma's nickname in high school was Bubbles because she could stay underwater longer than anyone else by blowing bubbles. Whoever wrote this diary knew my grandmother." I barely got to know my grandmother. She died in a boating accident when I was seven. Now here she was on this diary page and she was eating popcorn! Popcorn! Maybe popcorn was in my blood.

"*Très* cool," Carson said. "I wonder what other fun factoids are in there."

"I wonder who the diary writer was," I said. I shut the diary and put it in my bag. "I'll read more tonight and see what I can figure out."

Figuring out who wrote that diary now seemed like a faraway fairy tale as I sat in my cell waiting for my lawyer. Huerta had let me out to make the call to Cynthia, who had had trouble stopping her hysterical laughter when I explained why I needed her to come to Grand Lake.

"Seriously? Dan arrested you? Again?" she'd cackled.

"Yes. But it feels different this time. This time they put me in a cell and made me put on one of those orange jumpsuits." I looked down at my new outfit. The legs were too short and the waist was too big and whoever had washed it had clearly not used fabric softener. Dan had never made me put on the jumpsuit before. I'd always gotten to wear my own clothes and been out in an hour.

"I'll be there as soon as I can," she'd said.

Sprocket, my standard poodle, arrived at my jail cell before Cynthia did, though. Less than thirty minutes after my phone call to Cynthia, Dan led him into the cell block with a pained expression on his face.

"Seriously? You're locking up my dog, too? What'd Sprocket do? Pee on the wrong fire hydrant?" I walked over to the cell bars, my eyes narrowed and my voice as sarcastic as I could make it.

"No. Or maybe. I don't know where he peed. He's been howling for hours, though. Haley said he started at almost

exactly the time we locked you in here. It's like he knew."
Dan knelt down and let Sprocket off his leash.

Sprocket trotted over to me and got up on his hind
legs. He's a big boy, and stretched out he was nearly
face-to-face with me. He whimpered. "I know, boy," I
said. "It's crazy."

He licked my face through the bars.

Dan motioned for me to stick my hands through the
bars. He handcuffed me, pulled out his keys and unlocked
my cell. I started to step out, but he held up his hand.
"Oh, no. You're staying in there. I'm going to let Sprocket
keep you company. That way if he howls, you're the only
one he's going to keep up."

"What am I? Chopped liver?" Cathy asked from the
next cell over.

Dan shot her a look, but didn't answer. Apparently she
was chopped liver.

Sprocket leapt up onto the bed and curled up. "Are
you going to bring an extra set of sheets at least?" I asked,
eyeing the top bunk.

He sighed, relocked the cell and uncuffed me. "I'll
have some brought in when they bring you your dinner."

"Who's going to walk him?" I asked, gesturing at
Sprocket with my head.

"You are." Dan leaned back against the wall, arms
crossed over his chest.

"So you're going to let me out of here four or five times
a day?" At least I wouldn't die of vitamin D deficiency
before Cynthia managed to rescue me somehow.

Dan slumped forward a little. "We will do whatever
is required."

He looked sad. I was a little glad about it. He deserved to feel sad for locking me up like this. I hoped he regretted this. I buried my face in Sprocket's sweet apricot fur and didn't look up as Dan left.

The day I found the diary, I'd gone home not too much later. There was only so much I could do to help out with the renovations. Plus, it was my goal to have at least two new products ready to go by the time we reopened POPS. Right before the grease fire that had closed me down, I'd started selling Bacon Pecan Popcorn. It had been a big hit. I wanted some companion flavors, too. I gave Sprocket a thorough brushing and then got started on some new recipes. With the butter and the sugar bubbling on the stove, I read more of the diary. Bubbles, GT, Shoop, Twinkletoes and my diary writer had quite a few adventures that seemed to mainly center on algebra tests and which boys were the dreamiest. The big excitement happened when a relative came to visit. My diary writer christened the visitor CG. CG came from Europe. My little friend had been expecting someone glamorous and worldly. Someone who had traveled and sampled the finer things in life. She'd had a rude awakening.

Ugh. CG is so gross! I can't figure out how she spends so much time in the bathroom since she's clearly not washing the four strands of hair she has on her head or brushing the seven teeth she has left in her head. To think I thought she'd be able to give me fashion tips and talk Mama into letting me wear lipstick!

CG was also prone to night terrors, apparently.

So tired today. Can barely drag my feet down the sidewalk. CG woke up at three a.m. screaming. Papa tried to wake her and she punched him. Punched him! Mama says I have to understand that CG has been through hard times. Well, I'm going through some now thanks to her. Don't know how I'll possibly stay awake through history class.

Then something really interesting happened.

CG had a fit downtown today. I was so embarrassed! Right on Main Street. She stopped in the middle of the sidewalk and pointed her long bony finger and said, "I know you!" to FW. Then she started screaming "Monster! Monster!" until Mother slapped her. I could not have been more mortified. Not in a million years. Screaming and slapping in the middle of town! My family is the absolute worst. I can't wait to graduate and get away from them. The second I cross that stage with my diploma in hand, I'm going to the bus station and getting on the next bus. I'm leaving and going as far as I can.

I recognized those sentiments. They'd pretty much been mine when I graduated from Grand Lake High, and my family hadn't been humiliating. I could only imagine what kind of impact a scene like the one she described would have on a teenage girl's reputation. Who had the monster been, though? That couldn't have been much fun, either. The timer beeped and I hopped up to stir in the vanilla and the baking soda.

I got back to the diary when I'd mixed everything together and spread it all out on the baking sheets to go into the oven.

> *CG says that FW is a Nazi! She says that he was a guard at the camp. She says she could never forget someone so hateful and cruel. She told Papa over dinner and Papa laughed so hard I thought he was going to have a heart attack. Slapping his knee and hooting while CG pulled at his hands. She gave up after a while and quieted down. Papa told her to keep her crazy to herself. That she was seeing Nazis behind every door. Apparently she thought the dentist was a Nazi, too. She said Papa would, too, if he'd lived through what she'd lived through.*
>
> *Then they were both yelling at each other, saying all kinds of hateful things.*
>
> *I asked Mama later what CG meant. She told me some things were better forgotten. She might be right, but I can tell CG sure hasn't forgotten whatever it was.*

Nazis? Right here in Grand Lake? I definitely had to figure out who this diary writer was. I guessed that the first step to figuring out who the diary writer was would be to figure out who owned my shop back in the 1950s.

I figured the best place to do that would be City Hall. I could ask in the city offices. It would give me something to do the next day. I'd been getting a little stir-crazy. There'd been times when I'd first started POPS that I would have given anything for a few days off in a row. Now that I had them, I wasn't quite sure what to do with them. Oh, sure. The first few days of sleeping until I woke up, taking Sprocket for long walks by the lake, cooking meals in my own kitchen had been luxurious. Too much luxury was apparently not good for me. I was getting antsy. I'd find out who the diary writer was and who the secret Nazi was. It would give me something to fill my time.

I finished my S'Mores Popcorn Bars and started making dinner.

Garrett walked into my apartment a few hours later bring a gust of cold air with him and said, "Smells good." He shrugged out of his coat and hung it on the coatrack by the door.

"Thanks." I knew it smelled good. Pork tenderloin wrapped in bacon with a beurre blanc sauce always smelled good. At least it did when I made it. I knew he'd take the first bite and not say anything else for several minutes because he'd be too busy eating. I knew I'd enjoy that moment of silence that every chef enjoys when she knows her meal is good. I knew Garrett would thank me afterward. He was good to cook for.

He was also, however, simple to cook for. Every once in a while, I missed the challenge of cooking for an educated and discerning palette.

People used to ask me all the time if I'd been intimidated by cooking for Antoine, my ex-husband and celebuchef of the moment. I'd tell them they clearly didn't understand what cooking for Antoine was like. Antoine loved food. Food was his passion. Food was his calling. Food was his life. He loved to eat food, to talk about food and to think about food. Cooking for him was an adventure of the senses and of the mind. It wasn't intimidating. Frankly, it was fun. Big fun. We would talk and taste and dissect and discuss. We'd tweak and tinker. I missed it a little. Only a little, but I still missed it.

I'll admit to feeling a little bit wistful as I finished the beurre blanc sauce, but then I turned around and saw Garrett sitting on the floor with Sprocket, playing tug-of-war with Sprocket's toy alligator. For a moment, the clean line of his jaw as he sat in his dress clothes on the floor with my dog took my breath away. "Dinner's ready." I set out our plates on the breakfast bar. "Wine?" I asked.

He shook his head. "I need to do some more work tonight. I'd better steer clear."

We sat side by side at my kitchen counter and ate. It wasn't the best presentation, but my apartment over the garage was small and a proper dining room table took room I didn't have. When we were done, I set my fork down and started to clear our plates.

He held up a hand to stop me. "You sit. I'll do the dishes."

I didn't argue too much. I'd spent plenty of time washing dishes. It wasn't my favorite kitchen activity. It was better than mopping the floor, but that was all the faint praise I had to damn it with. As he rolled up his sleeves— an added benefit of him doing dishes, he had marvelous forearms—I twirled the diary around on the breakfast bar. "Check out what Carson and I found hidden in a wall at POPS."

"What is it?" He ran hot water into a plastic tub in the sink.

"A diary written by a teenage girl who lived in my

shop when it was a house. I'm pretty sure she was friends with my grandmother." I ran my fingers along the edges.

He squirted in some soap. "Interesting. Anything else interesting about her?"

"She had a crazy relative visiting who thought everyone was a secret Nazi." It was a more interesting factoid than what had happened in her gym class, although that dodge ball showdown sounded epic.

"Of course. Because northern Ohio was where all those Nazis went to hide. The rumors about Brazil and Argentina were spread to put everyone off the track." He put the dishes into the hot water. "Does it say who the supposed Nazis were?"

"Not yet. She uses a lot of initials and nicknames. I think she was afraid someone might read the diary. Her parents were crazy overprotective. Plus, I've still got quite a few pages to go." I held it up to show where I'd made it to and how much was left.

"How does it end?" Garrett has a very annoying habit of reading the ends of books before he gets there. He seeks out movie reviews with spoilers. He says he likes things wrapped up neat and nice so he can relax and enjoy the journey.

I, on the other hand, am not sure I'd set out on the journey if I knew where it was going to end. "How should I know? I haven't gotten there yet."

"You haven't peeked?" He turned back to the dishes, towel slung over his shoulder.

I was momentarily distracted by the view. Is there anything sexier than a man with the sleeves of a dress shirt rolled up doing housework? I honestly don't think there is. They should totally make calendars.

"Well?" he asked.

"Huh?" I'd forgotten what we were discussing, what with the forearms and the dish-doing.

"You haven't looked at the ending? Maybe there's a big fat clue there about who she was and why she'd hide her diary." He dried the last plate and stacked it.

"Then it will still be there when I get there." I pulled the diary back toward me. "It's been there for sixty years or so. It'll wait."

He plucked it from my arms. "The ending will still be the same if I read it now or not." He walked over to the sofa and plunked down with it. I harrumphed and went to let Sprocket out for his evening yard patrol.

When I walked back into the room and unwrapped my scarf and took off my jacket, Garrett was sitting on the couch with a weird look on his face. "I think you should look at the last page," he said.

"You read it. Isn't that enough?" Although part of me wanted to know what was there, another part of me didn't.

"I did. I think you should, too." He held the diary out toward me.

"Fine." I guess that made the decision for me. I took the diary and flipped to the last page with writing on it. There were only two words on it.

I'm frightened.

Two

Cathy got up and stretched. Then she dropped to the floor and did ten push-ups. Real push-ups. No bent knees. No butt sticking up in the air.

"Impressive," I said.

"There's not a lot else here to pass the time. I'm going to finally have those Michelle Obama arms I've always wanted. Too bad I won't have a sleeveless dress to wear so people can admire them." She picked at her jumpsuit. "Life is full of irony, isn't it?"

"Life is full of unfairness." I was generally anti-exercise, but I watched Cathy with some interest. I wouldn't mind having Michelle Obama arms. "Like me being here, for instance."

She finished a set and rolled over to sit on the floor. "Let me guess. You're innocent of all charges."

"Of course I am." I scratched behind Sprocket's ears. He thumped his foot on the floor.

"So whose justice were you supposedly obstructing? Where were you sticking your nose this time?" She extended her legs out in front of her and grabbed her toes to stretch. Not only was she going to have Michelle Obama arms, she was going to be crazy limber as well.

"I wasn't obstructing justice. I was seeking it." People seemed not to understand the distinction. "My nose was in my own business. Nowhere else. Like it always is."

"Uh-huh. How's that?" She made a face that clearly said she didn't believe me.

"It's complicated." It was, too. I wasn't sure that I understood it at the moment.

"I got time," she said. Then she snorted. "In more ways than one."

Explaining it to her might let me make sense of it myself. I decided to lay it all out for her and see what she thought.

The words on the last page of the diary haunted me all night. Had something actually happened to this girl? Or had she gotten tired of keeping a diary and shoved it in the wall and forgotten about it? My desire to distract myself with the diary took on an added urgency.

I read a little bit more of it as I drank my morning coffee to see if I could figure out what was frightening her. I hit an entry that froze me.

Everybody saw the scene with CG and FW down-town. Everybody saw my mom's epic slap. Everybody was talking about it at school. Everybody wanted to know what CG had meant when she'd called FW a monster. Even HH wanted to know. When he first sat down next to me in the cafeteria, I couldn't believe it. He's never sat with me. He's never even talked to me except that one time when he wanted to borrow my history notes. But there he was. Sitting on the bench next to me. Blond hair flopping into his eyes. The leather of his letter jacket crinkling.

I hadn't explained anything to anybody. Mama and Papa had both told me to forget about it, that CG was nutso and I shouldn't worry. And I hadn't. But this was HH. And all he wanted to talk about was CG and FW. So I told him. I told him that CG said FW was a Nazi, that she'd seen him at a camp back in the old country during the war.

I think maybe Mama and Papa were right, though. I shouldn't have said anything to anyone. When I got to my locker the next morning, I found this in it.

Glued onto the page opposite the entry was a six-pointed yellow felt star. Written across it were the words "Keep your mouth shut."

I slammed the diary shut, sick to my stomach at the sight of that symbol of hatred and bigotry. Who would do such a thing? Who would threaten a young girl like that?

Had there really been a Nazi in Grand Lake? Had he been intent enough on keeping that a secret to hurt someone?

Sprocket and I headed over to City Hall with a new sense of purpose to our steps. We'd stepped out onto the stairs that led down out of my apartment over the garage and stopped for a second as the cold air nipped at both our noses.

The scent of fall was gone. The crushed leaves had been raked into neat piles and picked up by the city. The sky wasn't as gray, either. It had turned into that bright light blue that held a promise of snow in the future. I shivered, but I also grinned. I swear Sprocket smiled up at me. Our steps were light as we made our way into town. The cold chilled and thrilled me all at once. It had been ages since I'd lived in a place with snow.

City Hall rose up before us, its solid granite exterior promising stability and order. It was a whole different story once you got inside. Expansion had not been on the minds of the architects when it was built back in the twenties. Or at least not the kind of expansion we'd experienced. Plus there was modernization. Telephones and computers and all that required an infrastructure that hadn't been dreamed of. It always made me a little sad after we'd stepped through the carved lintels to hit the industrial-grade carpeting and drop ceiling.

Sprocket had gotten a little confused when we turned left toward the city offices rather than right where Dan's office was once we got into City Hall, stopping in the hallway and sitting down, head cocked to one side. Okay. Maybe not confused. Maybe blatantly skeptical of my ability to navigate my way through my own life.

"I know where I'm going," I said. "Trust me."

He hesitated, but got up and walked as I kept going. I sighed as I walked into the office. Trina was behind the counter at her desk. I'd been hoping Sally would be there.

I knew she could see me. I also knew she was ignoring

me and that she wanted me to know she was ignoring me. I considered ringing the little bell on the counter, but I doubted it would endear me to her. I doubted anything would endear me to her. Her sister, Megan, ran the diner, and I'd been stealing business from her from practically the first second I'd moved back to Grand Lake.

First it had been breakfast with my popcorn breakfast bars and coffee. Then I'd started on the lunch crowd with my Bacon Pecan Popcorn. People flocked to my shop as an alternative to what they could get from the diner.

Well, except for those few days whenever people thought I might be a murderer, and for now because some necessary renovations were going on at POPS after a fire nearly destroyed my beautiful kitchen.

I was saved from the bell when Sally walked in. "Trina," she said. "Can't you see that Rebecca is waiting at the counter?"

Trina looked up, eyes widened and mouth slightly open as if she was actually surprised. It wasn't a good look on her. It wasn't that Trina was unattractive. She really wasn't. She had a decent figure and her blond hair was always shiny. She just also always looked a little like an embryo to me, like her features hadn't quite finished forming yet. From her little blob of a nose to her squishy chin, she looked too much like uncooked bread dough. The open mouth didn't help.

"I'm so sorry. I was just so wrapped up in these requisition forms that I didn't notice her. You should have rung the bell, Rebecca."

I reminded myself of my ultimate goal in this situation. Keep it in mind, Rebecca. What will take you closer to your goal and what won't? I was pretty sure vaulting over the counter and dinging the bell against Trina's ridiculously wide forehead would not get me closer to my goal, so instead I smiled and said, "My bad."

Sally came over to the counter. "What can we help you with, Rebecca?" She smiled at me. A real smile. One that showed her slightly crooked front tooth that I found inexplicably endearing. Maybe because otherwise she'd look like a supermodel. All high cheekbones and long legs. The cardigan draped over her shoulders put a bit of a dent in the supermodel look. As did the fact that she had apparently never heard of mascara or lipstick. I suspected she kept her hair in a close-cropped afro just so she wouldn't have to brush it. Nothing could stop those luminous eyes and full lips, though.

"I want to know who owned my shop during the 1950s." I leaned my elbows on the counter like I was about to divulge a secret. "Carson and I found a diary and I want to know who wrote it."

"Where did you find the diary?" Sally leaned in, too.

"In the wall." The damage to the wall my stove was against had been pretty bad, bad enough that Carson felt it was better to take the whole thing out and start over.

"Like hidden?" Sally's eyes lit up. Who doesn't like a hidden diary, after all?

"Totally. It looks like whoever hid it put it in from the other side. It would have been a bedroom. I'm not sure exactly how. There are so many layers of paint and wallpaper on the wall it's hard to figure out what was where when." I had a vision of a teenage girl cutting a little flap into the wall behind her bed to slip her secret diary in. She would probably have had her hair up in foam rollers and been wearing floral pajamas with a Peter Pan collar.

"What's in the diary?" Sally whispered.

"Mainly stuff about school and boys and movies and clothes, but look at this." I reached into my bag and pulled the diary out and turned to the page about my grandmother. "Whoever wrote this knew my family, hung out with my grandmother, and now I'm running my shop from what was probably her bedroom. I want to know who it was and maybe find out where she is now. It would be awesome to reconnect with her."

Sprocket stood up on his hind legs and put his front paws on the counter. He gently nosed the diary toward Sally.

Sally's hand went to her heart. "Oh, Rebecca. What a crazy connection for you. When did you say the diary was written?"

I shook my head. "I'm not sure. Sometime in the 1950s?" I hadn't been able to nail down exactly when yet. I figured if I kept reading, my anonymous diary writer would mention a date or an event that I could look up or trace. So far it had been just generic enough that I couldn't be certain.

"Who were some of the boys?" she asked, turning the diary around so she could look at it herself.

"I'm not sure. She uses a lot of initials and nicknames. I only guessed that Bubbles was my grandmother because of the swimming." I gave Sprocket a look and he went back to all fours.

"Well, let's see what I've got in the records. It'll take a while. The records from back then aren't computerized yet." Sally made a face.

Trina snorted from behind her. "And won't likely ever be."

Sally turned. "You don't know that, Trina. The city could allocate funds to us at some point."

"Allocate funds for what?" I'd know that big booming baritone anywhere. The whole town would. Mayor Allen Thompson was in the house. He'd been the mayor since forever. Well, at least since I was a teenager.

"Computerizing records." Trina stood up and walked over to the counter.

"Oh, that again." Allen turned to me. "What are you and Sprocket doing here, Rebecca?" He gave Sprocket a scratch under his chin and got his hand licked in response.

I opened my mouth to answer, but before I could get a word out Sheri Denton came racing in like her hair was on fire. Well, her braid. One long, thick, fat one that came down to her waist and was currently flying behind her like a honey-blond bullwhip. "Am I late? Did I make it?" She waved a sheaf of papers in the air.

Sally looked at the clock. "You made it with five minutes to spare."

Sheri laughed and slammed the papers down on the counter. "Five minutes. Five days. Time is just a construct."

"In time for what?" I asked.

Sheri turned and hugged me. I took a step back. I was still Midwestern enough to be a little uncomfortable with spontaneous hugging. All those years in California never changed that. "Filing to run for city council. You wouldn't believe all the forms!"

I'd braced myself for a nose full of patchouli. I couldn't help it. It made me sneeze. But despite looking exactly like someone who should smell like patchouli, from her dream-catcher earrings to her Birkenstock sandals, Sheri smelled like maple syrup. I wondered if she'd been baking. My stomach growled.

Sprocket whined and lifted a paw in the air as if he was knocking on an imaginary door. He wasn't crazy about people touching me without his permission.

Sheri released me and crouched down. "No problem, Sprocket. I know she's yours. I'm just so excited I had to let my happiness out somewhere."

He licked her nose.

She laughed. "You've got a beautiful aura, Sprocket. Just beautiful. Sort of an aqua color. Very cool." She stood back up and brushed off her hands. "Now what?"

Allen glanced up at the clock. "We've got three more minutes to wait."

"Rebecca, you should ask Sheri about the diary. She did some local history research when she was writing about her grandfather," Sally said. "Edwin was alive in the 1950s. He was one of the most prominent citizens in town."

Everyone in Grand Lake knew about Edwin Vincent. His name was on park benches, water fountains, cornerstones. You name it. He'd been a huge philanthropist and, if I remembered correctly, a city council member like Sheri apparently wanted to be. Public service as a family trait. Nice.

"What diary?" Sheri asked.

"This diary I found at my shop during our repairs." I tapped it where it lay on the counter. "It's from the 1950s and there's some great stuff in it. I'd love to find the person who wrote it and find out more about some of what she talks about. She accused someone of being a secret Nazi! Then the diary ends really abruptly. It's like finding out the last chapter of a mystery novel's been ripped out of the book. I want to know how it ends."

Sheri picked the diary up and riffled through it. "Fascinating. There's nothing better than primary sources. Any chance I might borrow it? I'd love to add it to my history of Grand Lake."

Justin Cruz sauntered in. Dude had swagger. You couldn't deny that. He'd been a couple of years behind me in school. He'd stood out then in part because Grand Lake was even whiter when I was a teenager than it was now, and that's saying something. He'd also stood out because he was smart. Not so much ace-your-SATs smart. Smart about how things worked, about how people thought, about how to get things done. Okay. He was also cute. He had this dimple. I'm a sucker for dimples. Now he ran a landscaping business that took care of mostly commercial properties. Based on the watch he was wearing, it was doing okay.

He nodded to Allen. "Mayor." Then gave the rest of us a little wave. "Ladies." Then he nodded at the diary. "What do you have there, Sheri?"

"An old diary Rebecca found in her shop." She closed it and held it to her chest.

"It was hidden in a wall. I think there's something in there about my grandmother," I added.

He took a few steps forward, hand outstretched. "Can I see?"

Geraldine Richards came in, looking as always like she was stopping by here on her way to somewhere much classier. *Put together* was the term that came to mind. Her hair and skirt always looked freshly ironed. There were never food stains on her blouse or runs in her stockings. Plus, she actually wore stockings. I didn't think I'd worn a pair of pantyhose since I left Grand Lake the first time. "Are we all here yet?" she asked, glancing at her watch.

Justin still had his hand out for the diary. "I'd like to take a look at it after Sheri, if I could. It'd be so interesting to read about what was happening in Grand Lake on the down low back in the day."

Sheri made a little noise. I looked over at her. ".You know, on second thought, maybe we should leave it be. Whoever wrote it intended it to be private. We should respect that," she said.

"Whoever wrote it might not even still be alive," Justin said.

Sheri ignored him and looked straight at me. "How would you like your private teenage thoughts being pored over by strangers?"

Horrified was my unequivocal answer. "You have a point." I looked down at the diary. It had been so fascinating and there was something so exciting about finding something old and hidden like that.

Taylor Barrington came in looking like a poster for wholesome living. Rosy of cheek, smooth of skin, shiny of hair. "Are we ready?" she asked, looking around.

"Just waiting on Chris Tranhorn." Allen looked at his watch.

As if on cue, Chris strolled in and nodded to everyone.

"What's going on?" I whispered to Sally.

"It's a little tradition that Allen started a few years ago. At the deadline for filing to run for city council, all the candidates meet for a photo and for Allen to welcome them to the political process." Her voice wavered a second.

I stared at her.

"Don't give me the stink eye! It's surprisingly moving. Just you wait and see." She pulled a tissue from the sleeve of her cardigan and dabbed at the tip of her nose, which was already pinkening.

The photographer from the *Grand Lake Sentinel* came in with her ridiculously huge camera.

"That's all of us, then," Allen said. He dropped his head and took several deep breaths. After just long enough to make me wonder if he'd suddenly gone to sleep standing up, he raised his head and cleared his throat. It was a good move. Everyone was silent and completely focused on him.

"One of the greatest rights granted to us as American citizens is the right to vote. People risk their lives for this privilege and not just in foreign countries. Women died petitioning for the right to vote in this country a mere century ago. More recently than that, a voting rights act had to be passed so people of color could have fair access to their polling places. And now you five stand before me and say you are ready to go out into our community and ask people to devote their precious ballots, paid for with sweat and tears and blood by our forefathers and foremothers, to you." Allen paused and looked at each one of the candidates in turn. "Some people might laugh. They might say that this is a tiny election for a meaningless seat in a Podunk town, that the stakes are so low as to be laughable, that none of this matters. All I can say is that I'm glad that no people like that are in this room. I know why you're here. Oh, you might each have different ideas on what's important for our city. You might disagree on the issues. In fact, I hope you do. Nothing will serve our city better than open and clear-minded debate. No. Whether you think you're here because of zoning issues or recycling plans or school issues, you're here because you've been called to serve."

Despite myself and my usual ability to mock nearly everything, my heart beat a little faster. Sally was right. Allen's speech was surprisingly moving. Next to me, Sally sniffled. I looked over. Trina's lower lip was wobbling.

"You have been called to serve your city. That calling is no less important than those who feel called to serve as doctors or lawyers or priests. Whichever one of you winds up privileged enough to serve our amazing city of Grand Lake will have a sacred duty to your friends, your neighbors, your family. Are you ready for this?"

No one moved. No one breathed.

"Are you ready for this?" Allen boomed.

Sheri stepped forward. "I am! I'm ready!"

"I am, too!" Geraldine stood next to her.

Taylor, Chris and Justin all echoed them. "I am!" they cried one after the other.

Damn if I didn't have something in my eye.

I waited around until the crowd finished with their photo op and disbanded. They barreled out like football players out of the locker room after an exceptionally good half-time speech. Well, except for Sheri, who stopped to collect the recycling.

I blew my nose and said, "That was really moving, Allen."

"Surprised I had it in me, are you?" He knelt down to pet Sprocket and looked up at me with his ridiculously bright blue eyes.

He was right. He'd surprised me. I'd never been a fan of our mayor. He was too old-school with his Dockers and deck shoes. He was too corporate with his ties, both the one around his neck and the ones to the businesses in town to whom he pandered. And yes, I realize I now was one of those business interests, what with him being my landlord and all, but all the same he was too, well, too Allen.

Then he'd started dating my friend Annie. Well, I'm not sure you can call what they were originally doing dating. It was all a little more torrid than that. It had taken me too long to figure out who had put the roses in Annie's cheeks and why she'd suddenly started wearing lipstick. Once I outed them with a flower pot to the back of Allen's head, though, I'd gotten to know him a little better and had to face the fact that I'd been too quick to judge him on the basis of appearances.

I hated that. Appearances were so much easier to judge by. It just happened that most of the time judgments made that way were wrong.

"Maybe a little surprised," I admitted. "In a nice way."

Sally elbowed me. "I told you so."

Allen stood up. "So what were you doing here? Something about computerizing records? I didn't think database entry would be part of your skill set."

I made a face. Spill one mocha latte on one computer keyboard and suddenly you have a reputation as a Luddite. Whatever. "Actually, Trina was talking about computerization. I was talking about this." I slid the diary toward him.

"What is it?" He turned it over in his hands.

"A diary Carson and I found during the kitchen repairs. It was hidden in a wall!" I couldn't keep the enthusiasm out of my voice.

"And?" He arched one brow at me.

"And I want to know whose diary it is. I think she knew my grandmother. She talks about everyone using initials and nicknames, but I'm pretty sure it was her." Oh, that rising tide of excitement when she mentioned my grandmother and popcorn in the same sentence. I was looking forward to curling up with it and a glass of hot cocoa to see if there were any other mentions of my family members.

There had been a time that I couldn't wait to get away from Grand Lake. I'd wanted to cut my family ties and cauterize the ends of them so they'd never heal.

Luckily, my family was more forgiving than that. Or at least my sister, Haley, was. She was pretty much all I had left. Well, I also had Evan and Emily now that Haley was reproducing. And Dan, her husband and my old BFF from the bad old days. And Garrett. Well, I guess he wasn't actually family, but still . . .

Anyway, Haley had always been happy to be here in Grand Lake. She hadn't felt tied down by connections. She'd felt supported. Now that I'd moved back, I understood what she'd been feeling all those years. I wanted more. I hadn't thought too much about how to get it, but then this diary that talked about my grandmother literally fell into my hands from the ruins of my crispy critter of a kitchen.

Allen riffled the diary's pages. I squashed the urge to grab it out of his hands. I'd liked the way Sheri had handled it better. She'd been nearly reverential. "And you think it's from when?" Allen asked.

"Sometime in the fifties."

He shook his head. "Before my time, I'm afraid."

"If the records were computerized, we'd be able to give Rebecca that information with the touch of a few buttons," Trina said, shooting me a little conspiratorial look as if daring me to mention how uninterested she'd been a few minutes before. I guess she wasn't above making nice if it got her something she wanted. It made me respect her a little bit more.

Allen tilted his head back and laughed. "And you think I'm going to authorize thousands of dollars worth of work so Rebecca can figure out who her grandmother's friends were back in the day? Oh, Trina, you know me better than that." He leaned on one elbow against the counter and winked at her.

Trina blushed. It made her unformed baby face look almost attractive. "No. I see that."

"Good." He patted her hand. She looked at her hand like she might not wash it ever again. It was a good thing that our illustrious mayor only wanted to hold sway over Grand Lake. If he was intent on world domination I didn't think the slightly unattractive young women of the world would stand a chance.

"Who did you buy the house my shop is in from?" I asked Allen.

Allen looked upward as if consulting the fluorescent lights for guidance. "I bought that property from Marta Hansen in 2002."

That didn't go back so far. "Who did she buy it from?"

Allen shook his head. "No idea."

I'd have to ask her, then. "Any clue on where to find Marta?"

"Loving Arms Retirement Community on Willow Street," Trina said.

I knew right where that was. I didn't have the best associations with it. I wrinkled my nose but said, "Thanks."

"Good luck," Allen said.

"What does that mean?"

Trina leaned on her elbows. "It means that there's a very real possibility that she'll think you're her niece and another very real possibility that she'll think you're part of a government plot to assassinate her."

Great.

"Hey, how are things going with your kitchen repairs?" Allen asked.

"Taking way longer than I expected." And costing more, too.

He chuckled. "It always does." Then he paused. "Can you still sell anything? Anything at all?"

"I've done a few special orders out of my apartment kitchen, but it's not set up for anything big." There were certain people in Grand Lake who'd gotten accustomed to having my popcorn treats on movie nights and family game nights.

"But you can do special orders?" he pressed.

I nodded. Not sure where this was going.

"I like to send a little present to the city council candidates welcoming them to the political process. Could you do some gift baskets with that Bacon Pecan Popcorn you were starting to sell?"

I blinked. "Absolutely."

"Great." He took out his wallet and pulled out a stack of twenties. I couldn't believe anyone walked around with that much cash. I was lucky to find a crumpled-up five in my wallet and some quarters in my jeans most days. "Would this be enough?"

I didn't even bother to count it. I was hemorrhaging money into the repairs at POPS and had somewhere between nothing and zero coming in. I'd take anything I could get. "More than enough."

He leaned forward and whispered, "Make a couple of batches for Sally and Trina, too, if you don't mind. This town wouldn't run without them."

"You've got it."

Sprocket and I had made our next stop at POPS. Or what was left of POPS at the moment. The day was starting to warm up and I loosened the scarf around my neck. I turned onto Main Street and couldn't help but smile. I could hear music blasting from three doors away from my shop. Carson was at work.

I'd spent more than a few happy hours with Carson back in the day, skipping school and sipping Sloe Gin Fizzes and listening to music we thought was rebellious and reflected on our angst. Now I was a local business owner and a member of the chamber of commerce and he was the first person everyone in town turned to for a high-class renovation or remodeling job, but some things never totally changed. My man needed his tunes and he needed them cranked.

I walked in through the front of the shop. It was pretty

much intact. The fire hadn't spread this far before Eric Gladstone and his fellow firefighters had doused it. My blurry blue walls and glass shelves all still stood. My little tables with their ice cream parlor chairs were all still there. There was a little smoke damage, but most of it would be gone with a good scrubbing and a fresh coat of paint.

My heart still sank every time I walked into the kitchen, though. The wall that had sustained the worst damage was gone. That had been the one where Carson and I had found the diary. It was the least of the damage, though. There was smoke damage from the fire. Grease fires were notoriously smoky and mine had been no exception. Then there was the water damage from the firefighters putting out the fire. It wasn't a total loss, but it hurt to look at it still. I'd been content here. I'd felt as if I'd made my own place in the world that suited me and sated me. My happy places kept getting unhappy.

"Good morning, Rebecca." Carson reached over and turned the music down. "Did you find out who the diary belonged to?"

Carson had been every bit as fascinated as I had been by our find. "It's like treasure, man," he'd said. "A gem from the past."

I shook my head. "No, but I have my first lead to follow. Marta Hansen owned this place before Allen. I'll visit her and see who owned it before her."

"Right on." He glanced at his watch. "Coffee break time?"

"You bet."

I plugged in my electric kettle and set up my French press. Carson sprawled into an ice cream chair, which looked all the more spindly with his gangly frame spread over it.

"I don't suppose you're experimenting with anything?" he asked, smiling up at me. It still amazed me to see how completely angelic he could look. Lord knew it had gotten him out of more than a few scrapes back when we were in high school.

I gestured to my tote bag. He stood back up, looking nearly mechanical as he rose, rummaged through the tote bag and came up with a container. "This?" he asked.

"Mmm-hmm. It's rosemary and truffle oil with shiitake crisps." I tried to stop the smile that quirked at my lips. This was a good one and I knew it. I'd already dropped off some at Garrett's office on my way to City Hall, where I'd also filled him in on my diary discovery.

"Hot damn, girl!" Carson said through his first mouthful. "How do you make mushrooms taste like potato chips?"

I turned and bowed. "Thank you. It's a gift."

I poured our coffees and sat down next to him. "Did you find anything more in the wall?" It had only been halfway down when we'd found the diary. I hoped maybe there was something more in there that would let us identify the author.

"Nope. Did you finish reading it?" Carson asked.

"Nope. Although Garrett read the end."

"Fine pair of detectives we are."

"And maybe let's keep it that way." Dan walked into the shop. He reached into the container and took a handful of popcorn. "Is there any more coffee?"

"Enough for one cup," I said. This particular popcorn would probably go better with a nice Prosecco, but Dan was pretty relentless about not drinking on duty and I was pretty sure that day drinking was not a habit I wanted to start while my shop was closed.

"One cup is all I need." He flipped one of the chairs around and straddled it. "So what are you detecting now, Rebecca?"

"I'm trying to figure out who owned the shop around the time that the diary was written." I gave him his coffee and sat back down.

He took a sip of coffee and sighed. I wasn't sure if it was happiness over the coffee or exasperation about me and the diary. "You really can't resist a mystery, can you? Two near-death experiences weren't enough for you?"

"This is nothing like what happened to Coco or to Melanie!" I protested. Again. "Nothing at all!"

"Mmm-hmm. Let's keep it that way, shall we?" he said. "I'm not sure I'll survive another one of your adventures."

"This is a sixty-year-old diary written by an unknown teenage girl using nicknames for everyone." I tapped its cover with my index finger. "It's not any kind of adventure at all. You should be grateful. It's keeping me out of trouble while the shop is closed."

Janet Barry pushed in with her double stroller. "Oh. It's still closed? I heard the music and thought maybe . . ." Her words trailed off, but her hopeful expression spoke louder than they could have anyway.

I smiled. Janet had been one of my staunchest supporters. It might have started with allegiance to my Cashew Caramel Popcorn but it had spread to me personally. She'd helped form a stroller blockade against the press when they were hounding me and blocking the way into the shop and had been one of the first people through the door to show she believed in me despite some nasty rumors being spread. "It's more closed for some people than others."

I dug in my tote bag and pulled out another container. "For you."

Her eyes lit up as she took it. "Is it?"

"Of course." I'd made a small batch of her favorite.

She opened the container and took a small bite. "So good. You don't know how much I've missed this!"

Carson got up and held the door open for her to maneuver her Land Cruiser of a stroller out the door.

"That was nice of you," Dan said.

"I'm a nice person." Or at the very least I could pretend to be a nice person long enough to seem like one.

He snorted.

"Besides, Janet was there for me when things were down." It was good to keep people on your side. This town was fickle. One day you were up. The next you were down. No one knew that better than I did. It was best to keep as many people on your side as you could at any given moment.

I stood up and began clearing away the coffee things. "You okay here on your own today, Carson?" I wasn't much of an assistant, but I did provide some backup. I could totally hand him items as long as he was really clear about the difference between a socket wrench and an alligator wrench.

"Yep. I'm all good. What are you up to?" He sipped his coffee.

"The mayor ordered a special batch of Bacon Pecan Popcorn as welcome-to-the-political-process gifts for the city council candidates. I might as well get started on it."

Dan shook his head. "That's so Allen."

"You would have been amazed if you'd heard the speech he gave." I knew I'd been amazed.

Dan shot me a look. "You think I haven't heard that speech? The one about having a calling?"

"Oh." That was disappointing. It had been a politician's trick. All rhetoric and no substance, then. "I thought it was one of those really heartfelt expressions of his soul."

Dan patted my hand. "If it's any solace, I think he means it one hundred percent, but don't think it was unique."

It was some solace. "Whether he meant it or not, he's still willing to pay me for popcorn, and every little bit helps at the moment." The insurance was covering the repairs to the shop, or at least most of them. It was not, however, buying groceries for me or dog food for Sprocket.

Three

In the cell next to mine, Cathy shook her head. "I'm still not getting how any of this has anything to do with obstructing justice. I'm hearing nothing but popcorn, poodles and politics."

"I'm getting to it. Where's the fire?" I said, then cringed. The fire had been at my shop. Without it, I wouldn't have found the diary. Without finding the diary, I wouldn't have been at City Hall for the city council candidates campaign kickoff. If I hadn't been there, Allen might not have thought to order popcorn from me as their gift. If he hadn't ordered popcorn from me, Lloyd McLaughlin might still be alive and I wouldn't be locked up in the cell. It was a simple story. I couldn't believe Cathy couldn't sit still for it. Everyone was in such a hurry these days.

She held up her hand and lay back down on her bunk.

"You're right. It's not like I've got some place to be. At least, not some place good."

Before I could reply, Cynthia finally showed up. Huerta escorted Sprocket and me into the interview room and locked my cuffed hands to the big metal ring in the center of the table.

I'd been in this room before. Too many times, to be honest. I'd never been on this side of the table before.

"Glenn," Cynthia said in a silky voice.

"Cynthia," Huerta replied in a throaty grumble.

The air between them was so electric I would have fanned myself if I had a free hand. They'd met when Cynthia represented Antoine. I think Huerta fell in love with her when she subdued an attacker with her bare hands in the time it took me to call for help. I wasn't sure when Cynthia fell for Huerta, but the fact that the admiration was mutual was hard to miss.

Huerta pulled Cynthia's seat out for her. She smiled over her shoulder. Some kind of look was exchanged that left Huerta turning pink. Then he exited and the temperature in the room dropped about ten degrees.

"Well, Rebecca, it seems you've gotten yourself into another fine mess." She opened up her tablet and typed something. Sprocket circled the table and put his chin on her thigh. "And she's gotten you into hot water, too, hasn't she, handsome?" She scratched underneath his chin and he gave her a happy sigh.

"I didn't do anything, Cynthia. This is all some sort of craziness on Dan's part," I said. I'd seen her reduce Dan to near tears and she routinely left Garrett speechless. She'd have me out of here in no time.

"Really? So you didn't go to Lloyd McLaughlin's wake

and question mourners about their relationship with the deceased?" Cynthia looked up from the tablet.

"Well, yeah. I did do that." I twiddled with the chains locking my wrists.

She sat back in her chair and regarded me with those big hazel eyes. "And what were your purposes?"

"To find Dan some suspects in Lloyd's poisoning so people would know it wasn't me who killed him." Easypeasy. All a big misunderstanding. Nothing to see here. Everyone move along.

Cynthia sat back up and shut her tablet. "Then you're guilty."

"What? No! I'm not guilty. I was . . ." I tried to gesture with my hands, but the chains stopped me.

"Questioning potential suspects and generally getting in the way of an active police investigation." She didn't smile as she finished my sentence for me. There was no twinkle in her eyes.

"I had good reasons." It was ridiculous to think that I would sit around doing nothing while my shop and my popcorn were slandered.

"Nobody cares. Nobody cares if you did it to save orphaned kittens caught out in the rain. Nobody cares if you did it for truth and justice. They only care that you did what you're charged with doing. Intent only matters a little tiny bit." She moved her thumb and forefinger just a whisker apart.

"Nobody? Nobody at all cares why?" That hardly seemed fair.

She shook her head. "Nobody. Not even me."

I slumped into my chair. "So what now?"

"The good news is that I can probably get you out with

no more than a slap on the wrist. A fine and maybe some community service work. The bad news is that court is no longer in session and since it's Friday, it won't reopen until Monday morning. Then the priority cases will come ahead of yours. We may not be able to get you in front of a judge to set bail until Tuesday."

That straightened me right back up again. "I'm in here until Tuesday?" I counted on my fingers. "That's like four days!"

"I'm aware. I was pretty good with the whole days-of-the-week thing by the time I left preschool. Shaky on some of my colors, but days of the week I knew stone-cold." She clicked the lock of her briefcase and stood up.

Most of the time, I appreciated good sarcasm. At the moment, it wasn't making me laugh. I glared at Cynthia.

"Giving me the stink eye isn't going to change a damn thing. I suggest you get comfy for the weekend. Can I bring you anything?" she asked.

I rattled off a list. Toothbrush. Toothpaste. Pajamas. Cynthia shook her head over each one. "They're not going to let you have any of those things."

"Why not?" I asked.

"Safety issues. They'll issue all those things if they haven't already." Her eyes narrowed. "They are treating you okay, aren't they? You're not being abused?"

I wasn't being abused and they had given me all the things I'd mentioned. I just wasn't crazy about what they'd issued. I liked my cinnamon toothpaste and my electric toothbrush and my special wide-toothed comb. None of that apparently mattered to anyone but me. No one cared. No wonder prison made you hard. "Could you let people know what's going on?"

She laughed. "You really think everyone doesn't already know?"

She had a point. The gossip pipeline was pretty efficient. With Garrett's involvement, his legal secretary, Pearl, would know, and once she knew, well, everyone knew. Telegraph. Telephone. Tell a Pearl. "Could you make sure that Carson knows so he won't expect me? He's not big on gossip. He could miss the whole thing." If the music was turned up loud enough, he could miss a parade of elephants down Main Street.

"You've got it. I'll drop off some magazines and books for you, too. Do you like puzzles at all? You'll need to keep busy. It'll help pass the time." She jotted down a few notes in her phone.

"Yes, please. Do you think you can get me the diary I've been reading? It should be at my apartment on my bedside table." I could spend some time looking for more clues.

"You're keeping a diary?" She cocked her head. "As interesting as your life has been since I've known you, I don't blame you. It would probably be pretty entertaining to read."

"It's not my diary. It's one I found while Carson and I were repairing the kitchen in POPS. I'm trying to figure out whose diary it is and who some of the people in it are," I explained.

"Oh. Less fascinating," she said. "But I'll see what I can do."

Cynthia knocked on the interview room door. Huerta was there practically before her knuckles hit the metal.

"Finished, Ms. Harlen?" he asked, his voice throaty.

"Not hardly, Officer Huerta, but I'm ready to go for

now. Rest assured, I will be double-, perhaps triple-, checking that my client has been treated with the respect and dignity that her place in this community demands." She licked her lips.

"I won't disappoint," Huerta said, leaning ever so slightly forward.

"Would you two like the room?" I rattled my chains. "I'd be happy to go."

They sprang apart. "I'll be back for you and Sprocket in a minute, Rebecca. I need to escort Ms. Harlen out."

"I guess that's what the kids are calling it these days," I muttered under my breath.

Cynthia shot me a look over her shoulder, and I recalled who I was counting on to get me out of here eventually and shut my trap. "I'll be back as soon as I can," she said and then they were both gone.

Sprocket curled up on my feet under the table with a harrumph.

"They're not fooling anybody," I told him. "Not anybody at all."

Huerta finally returned to take me back to my cell after what felt like an eternity.

"That took a while," I said.

He shrugged and gestured that I should walk out of the door in front of him.

"Did you ask her out?" I asked over my shoulder.

"Ask who out?" He made a shooing gesture to keep me moving.

"Cynthia. Who else?" I sauntered down the hallway.

"Ms. Harlen and I have a strictly professional relationship." He opened the door to the cell block.

"Uh-huh. Sure." I went into the cell with Sprocket and

then stuck my hands through to have the cuffs taken off after he closed the door.

He didn't grace my remark with a reply.

"So you getting out?" Cathy asked from the next cell.

I sighed. "Not until Monday or Tuesday."

"Ooh. Hard time," she mocked me.

I settled down on my bed. Sprocket jumped up next to me. "It feels pretty hard," I whispered to him.

Cathy said, "It gets easier. Want to tell me more about what happened?"

"Sure."

I was Haley's go-to babysitter and had been since I'd moved back to town. Not that Haley had been awake enough to go out much since Emily was born, but still, if she did, I was the one to take over. Once Allen's order for the city council candidates was ready, Sprocket and I loaded up the fold-up wagon that Haley had bought to haul toys and kids back and forth from playground to beach to car to house with Bacon Pecan Popcorn in POPS tins. Well, I loaded the tins. Sprocket chased Evan around the front yard while Haley sat on the front porch nursing Emily, a blanket thrown over them both. The circles under Haley's eyes looked like purple half moons.

"Are you getting any sleep at all?" I asked.

"Define sleep," she said.

"It's that thing you have when your head is on a pillow and your eyes are closed," I explained, since I was pretty sure she had forgotten what it was.

"Oh, I remember that. That was good stuff." She leaned her head back against the railing. "The answer is no."

I winced. "Anything I can do?"

"Take Evan to the park this afternoon? Emily seems to nap longest around two. Maybe I can sleep while she sleeps if little man there is occupied." She nodded at Evan, who was now rolling across the lawn and giggling wildly as Sprocket licked his ears.

I smiled. "Consider it done."

"Thanks, sis." She looked like she might cry.

I finally convinced Evan and Sprocket to stand still long enough for me to get the leash on Sprocket and a kiss on Evan. Then we were off to City Hall with promises to return for the afternoon outing. The sky was a bright hard blue and the sun shone, although it didn't seem to be casting much warmth. "Lighthouse?" I asked Sprocket.

He picked up his pace, which I took to be a yes.

We took the detour up Marina Road to the shore of Lake Erie where the lighthouse stabbed into the cold blue sky. It had been built from metal melted down out of Civil War cannons. It was where my father proposed to my mother and where I used to make out with boyfriends in high school and where Sprocket got shot. It used to be my happy spot. Now I had mixed emotions. It was still gorgeous, though, and despite the trauma he experienced there, Sprocket seemed to like to stand on the dock and give the lake air a good hard sniff on a pretty routine basis.

"Rebecca!" a voice called to me as I looked out over the choppy gray waters of Lake Erie.

I turned. "Dario!"

Dario ran toward me down the path. He had been working in the kitchen at POPS until our recent problems. He'd been a lifesaver in so many ways.

"What are you doing out here, girl?" he asked, running up to us. He bent over and rested his hands on his thighs to catch his breath. Sprocket took the opportunity to lick his face. He laughed and scratched Sprocket behind the ears.

"Walking like a sane person," I said, eyeing his running shoes.

"And that?" He pointed at the wagon.

"Special order for the mayor. Apparently he likes to give gifts to the city council candidates. He took pity on me and special-ordered some popcorn." I looked over at the tins stacked up, liking the way they glinted in the sun.

"I saw the article about the council elections in the *Sentinel*. That's quite a slate." He kicked at the ground with his toe. "Any word on when POPS is going to reopen for real?"

I sighed. "I wish I knew. Carson is doing the best he can, but we keep running into problems. There was more damage to the electrical than he thought there was at first. We're still waiting for cabinets. The ones that match my original ones were out of stock. Frankly, it's a nightmare."

"Renovations always are. Eric and I know three different couples who ended up splitting up because of renovation projects. People are much more committed to wood-front cabinets versus glass-front cabinets than you'd think." He shook his head. "Let me know when you're close to done. That is, if you still want help."

"I think I'll need even more when we reopen." Trying to re-create what I'd had sometimes seemed daunting. It would be a lot easier with Dario by my side. He had an amazing way of knowing what I wanted before I even knew.

He waved good-bye and took off trotting down the

path. I sighed. I missed Dario. I missed drinking strong coffee with him in my kitchen. I missed having a kitchen to drink coffee with Dario in.

Sprocket and I walked the rest of the way to City Hall, but some of the spring had left my step.

We wound our way up the wheelchair ramp into City Hall and down the corridor to the mayor's office. I knocked on the doorjamb as I walked in. "Special delivery," I sang out.

Allen's personal assistant, Otis Hanson, looked up from his computer. "Rebecca, was Allen expecting you?" The smile was friendly; I wasn't sure about the words. Otis liked to keep Allen on schedule. Unexpected people dropping in was not conducive to that end.

"Nope, and I don't need to talk to him. I'm dropping off his popcorn order." I pointed to the pile of tins in my wagon.

"Popcorn order?" Otis's brow creased.

"For the city council candidates. His welcome-to-the-political-process presents." Leave it to Allen to forget that he'd special-ordered the popcorn from me.

Understanding dawned on Otis's face. "Oh, yes." He pointed to a credenza on the far wall. "Stack them up there. I'll call the messenger service."

I paused. "Do you want me to deliver them? It wouldn't be that much extra trouble."

Otis shook his head. "Oh, no. I've had the service scheduled for weeks. I just didn't know exactly what they'd be delivering until now."

"Okay, then." I stacked the tins up—with the exception of the ones Allen had ordered for Sally and Trina—and made my way down the hall to the city offices.

Just my luck. Trina was behind the desk. Again. I put the tin on the counter. She stared at me. "What do you want, Rebecca?"

"To drop this off." I stared back. I was perfectly prepared to not blink for the next ten minutes if necessary.

Luckily, that wasn't necessary. She blinked first. I felt a not-so-proud sense of satisfaction. "The tin is cute," she said.

For a second, I thought I'd misheard. Trina saying something nice to me? For no reason? "Thanks. I had them designed especially for the shop. They're new. They just came in."

She grunted. "So that's for us?"

"Yep. Allen wanted to give one to you and one to Sally. He said the city would grind to a halt without you two." That whole giving-credit-where-credit-was-due was another side of Allen I hadn't really seen before.

A little smiled played on Trina's thin lips. I considered quoting her a French adage about flattery that Antoine used to say all the time, which roughly translated to "Every flatterer lives at the expense of the one who listens to him." I decided just to leave my popcorn and go. Why ruin someone's moment of happy? Even Trina's.

"Who's ready for the park?" I asked as I came in the front door.

Evan stuck his arms out like an airplane and ran at me making a buzzing noise. "Me! I am!"

"Great. Go get your coat and your shoes." It was one of those wonderful sunny fall afternoons. He'd probably ditch the coat within five minutes of getting to the playground, but I thought I should at least look responsible until we got out of the house. I would be keeping my coat on. It was chilly outside.

He scampered off.

Haley was draped on the couch with Emily asleep on her chest. It almost looked like the baby had no bones. If the circles under my sister's eyes got any darker, however, she'd look like a raccoon.

"Want me to put Emily in her crib?" I offered. I wasn't even sure how Haley would be able to sit up from the position they were in.

Haley shook her head. "Setting her down in her crib seems to be about the same as dropping her in a vat of ice water. She's screaming by the time she hits the sheets. We're going to nap right here on the couch. If I don't move, she might stay asleep for more than an hour."

"What if you have to pee?" I could see any number of logistical issues with the plan.

"Hush. I don't need any power of suggestion making me need to get up. Take Evan and go. Don't come back for two hours." Her eyes started to close before she got all the words out.

"Two? You said one." Two hours might be a long time at the playground unless there were other kids around. I'd have to come up with some other plans to stretch our playdate. It was a little cold for ice cream.

Haley sighed. "No need to cut anything short."

I watched her breathing slow. How tired do you have to be to fall asleep midsentence? "You got it," I whispered, draping a blanket over the two of them.

Evan and I walked over to Neil Armstrong Park. It was far enough that normally I probably would have driven, but I figured the walk would eat up extra time. Sprocket was more than happy to get a little more exercise and Evan seemed very happy to alternate between buzzing like an airplane and jumping from sidewalk square to sidewalk square in a pattern that I couldn't quite discern. He took off at a run when the swing set came within view.

I caught up with him and pushed him on the swings for a while. Then he was ready to take on the roller slide. I started to climb up after him, but Sprocket whined. "It's okay, boy. It's just a slide."

He barked and whined some more.

"Fine. I'll come back down. Fraidy-cat." Sprocket and I walked over to one of the benches and sat down. The cold started to seep up through my jeans almost instantly.

A minivan pulled up in the parking lot. The side door slid open and three little blond girls came tumbling out. Sheri came around the front of the van. "Go ahead, girls. Enjoy the sunshine. I'll be right there." She gestured to the bench where I was sitting.

"I thought we had to go to the grocery store," the tallest of the three said, huddling by the van while her two younger sisters made wild dashes for the monkey bars.

"We do. Let's get a little exercise first. The groceries will still be there when we're done." Sheri smiled an extra bright smile at her daughter.

The girl gave her mother a funny look, but then apparently decided to not look gift horses in the mouth and claimed the middle swing and started pumping her legs like she meant to kick the sky.

"Hi, Rebecca. What are you doing at the playground?" Sheri asked, settling down next to me.

"Getting Evan out of Haley's hair for the afternoon so she can get some sleep. Emily is not great about the whole sleeping-through-the-night thing." I leaned forward to keep Evan in view as he chased around the slide.

Sheri sighed. "I remember those days. Ada didn't sleep through the night until she was three. I don't actually remember large portions of her babyhood."

I laughed. "I can only imagine."

"So what are you doing to keep yourself busy while your shop is under repair?" she asked.

"Worrying. It takes a surprising amount of time." At least, it seemed to at around two o'clock in the morning.

"I hear that." She glanced over at the playground. "Brigitte, don't twist the swing up like that! You'll kick Cecilia."

"Three is a lot to juggle," I said. Two were kicking Haley's butt at the moment and Haley was pretty together.

Sheri shrugged. "You get used to it, then you don't know how you ever did anything without them."

I snorted. "You did it when you wanted to, how you wanted to and why you wanted to. That's how."

She laughed. "I suppose so."

We sat in silence while we watched the kids play. Ada had engaged Evan in a game of what might have been tag and might have been just chasing each other around in arabesques and figure eights while avoiding being kicked by Brigitte on the swing.

"Did you make any headway in figuring out who wrote the diary you found?" she asked.

I shook my head. "I'm working my way backward, trying to find out who owned the house in the 1950s."

"How are you going to do that?" Sheri asked.

"Marta Hansen owned my shop before Allen did. I

figured I might stop over at the nursing home in the next few days and talk with her. Maybe she'll remember something." It seemed like the best way to start.

"She'll remember something. How accurate it might be is another question," Sheri said. "I was surprised how inaccurate people's memories were when I was trying to find information about Grandpa Edwin. They'll think they're one hundred percent right and not even be close."

"Really? That's too bad. I'm not sure where else to find out information about the place." Evan threw himself into the sandbox. I braced for a scream, but he came up giggling.

"When was your place built?" Sheri asked.

It took me a second to clue back into what she was talking about. "In the twenties."

She nodded. "Our place, too. My grandfather bought it in the late 1940s and it's been in the family since."

I smiled. I lived in my family home, too. Sort of. Over the garage counted as in, didn't it? "Did you get your popcorn yet?" I asked.

"My what?" Sheri asked.

"Oh. Maybe I shouldn't have said anything. Allen had me make some special popcorn batches for the city council candidates. I dropped them at the office this morning. Otis was going to messenger them out."

"For all the candidates?" Sheri smiled. "That's so sweet."

I nodded. "Yep."

"Interesting. I'll look forward to it." She pulled some packets out of her purse. "Girls, do you want a snack?"

All three came barreling toward us with Evan in hot pursuit. "Do I have snack, Auntie Becca?" he asked.

Oops. "How about we go get a snack? We can go downtown."

"I want to snack here." His pudgy little face started to crease up.

"Here. You can have some of mine." Ada held out a package of crackers. "I like to share."

I looked over at Sheri. "How did you train her to be like that? Most six-year-olds I know would rather watch someone burst into flames than share their cinnamon bunny crackers."

Sheri dropped a kiss on her daughter's head. "Lucky. It's pretty much who she was since she was born."

"Lucky is right."

"They really are who they are right from the moment they're born, you know. You can nudge them in one direction or another. You can make sure they have the veneer of civilization on them. You really can't do much else." She brushed Ada's hair back behind her ears.

"Then you must come from excellent stock." I pulled a tissue out of my pocket to wipe off Evan's face. At least I knew to bring those along. I added *snack* to my mental list of good things that aunties had in their pockets on a playdate, though.

"I like to think so," Sheri said. She glanced at her watch. "It is definitely time for the grocery store, though! Come on, girls. Back to the van!"

Evan watched them go, a sad look on his face. "It was nice to have those girls to play with, wasn't it?" I said.

He nodded, then turned to hug my legs. "You're nice, too, Auntie Becca."

I felt warm all the way down to my toes.

* * *

After the park, we walked over to the shop. Carson helped Evan hammer a nail into a board and pronounced him his top assistant. Evan's eyes went wide and I swear he got a little taller.

"Did you hear anything about the cabinets?" I asked.

Carson shook his head. "Called the guy this morning. I'm guessing it's not good news since he hasn't called me back."

My heart sank. "How stuck are we?"

"Pretty stuck." Carson didn't look nearly as depressed as those words made me feel.

The idea was too depressing to contemplate, so Evan and I walked over to Garrett's office to pay him a visit.

"Who's this?" Pearl asked as we walked in. Pearl was Garrett's secretary. He hadn't actually ever hired her. She'd simply walked in one day and taken over. I couldn't decide if he felt too lucky or too frightened to complain. She was formidable in a lot of ways.

"I'm Evan, Pearl," Evan replied, hands fisted on his hips. "I'm me."

"No. You couldn't possibly be Evan. Evan's a little tiny boy. You're great big." Pearl shook her head. "No. Can't be Evan."

"I am! I am Evan! I grew!" He pulled himself up to his full three feet and four inches.

She peered at him as if really examining him. "Oh, so you are. You're definitely Evan. How are you today?"

"I'm having a playdate with Auntie Becca so Mommy and Emily can finally get some sleep."

My eyebrows went up. I hadn't known how much of

all that he'd been listening to and absorbing. I was going to have to be careful what I said around my nephew or it was going to get repeated back verbatim.

"Then we met three girls in the park and we played tag," he said.

"Sounds fantastic."

"Then we went to Auntie Becca's shop and I helped builded it."

Pearl looked up at me.

"He was hammering nails with Carson. I'd say it counts as buildeding it." I'd take all the help I could get at this point.

Garrett came out of his office. "You're a builder now?" he asked Evan.

Evan nodded. "I'm a natral."

"I'm not surprised. Your mom's pretty handy, too," Garrett said. It was true. Haley was amazing with DIY. She kept the house from falling apart around everyone's ears in a million different ways. He looked over at me now. "Having a good day?"

"Totally. Delivered the city council gifts and had a hot date." I smiled over at Evan.

Garrett smiled, too. "Want another one tonight?"

Heat flooded my face and I know my smile matched his. "You mean, when we have dinner with my sister and brother-in-law? That kind of hot date?"

"I'll take what I can get," he said.

"Get a room, you two," Pearl said and made a shooing gesture with her hands.

"I'll walk you out," Garrett said.

We walked out into the bright afternoon sunlight. The air felt chilly after the overheated office and I knelt down to zip up Evan's jacket for him. I looked up to find Garrett watching us with a funny look on his face. "What?"

"Hmm? Oh, nothing. Just thinking."

I stood up and gave him a kiss, one that lingered a few seconds longer than our usual public displays of affection. "There. That should give you something to think about for the rest of the afternoon."

"Don't you know it," he said.

Four

I woke up Saturday morning stiff and cramped. My first night in jail hadn't been much fun. The mattress was thin and the blanket was scratchy. Thank goodness I had Sprocket to keep me warm. I wasn't sure how Cathy was handling it at all.

Actually, I was sure. Sometime in the dark hours after Vera came in and told us it was time for lights-out and before our breakfasts (such as they were) arrived, I heard her crying. The sound was so small, so tiny, that I hadn't been sure what it was at first. It was like a squeak. Then I realized it was her whimper.

I'd pulled Sprocket closer to me and buried my face in his fur and squeezed my eyes shut tight to keep my own tears from leaking out.

Now, post powdered eggs and white-bread toast, the door to our cell block creaked open. Cathy and I both looked up. I cannot stress enough how boring it is to be locked in a cell. The door opening and closing was like hearing the theme music to a much-anticipated television show. Entertainment would be forthcoming.

We weren't disappointed. Vera walked through. Haley marched in behind her with Emily and Evan.

"Hey, sis." I bounced off my bunk over to the bars and crouched down. "Hi, Evan. What's up?"

Evan stared at me and the bars and the ceiling and then back at me. "Why are you in a zoo, Auntie Bec?"

"It's a very good question, Evan. I think you should ask your daddy. He's the one who put me in here." I was not above fighting dirty. If I had to enlist every toddler in town in my case, so be it.

Haley made a noise in her throat. I looked up at her. "What? Tell me I'm wrong about that one. Go ahead. Try it."

She shook her head. "I don't want to get between you and Dan on this one, Rebecca. It's a lose-lose situation for me."

I stood up. "So what brings you here? Doing a little scared-straight moment for my nephew?"

"No." She pressed her lips together hard like she did when she was annoyed. "You were supposed to babysit today. It's Evan's day to go to gymnastics."

I gestured around the cell. "Sorry, sis. I'm kind of tied up at the moment."

She took another step toward the bars. "Are you, though?"

"What do you mean?" I wasn't sure I liked the glint in her eye. I didn't see it very often these days. It had been a staple of my teenage years, but I earned it less in my thirties than I had at seventeen.

"I mean, it's not like Emily needs space to run around. She only started rolling over this morning." Haley gestured to the baby carrier.

"She rolled over?" Damn it. I'd missed her rolling over. I'd missed Evan rolling over, too, and that had been my fault. I'd been too caught up in life with Antoine to be there for all the special and wonderful milestones. But now I was here. I'd made the choice to be present and I'd still missed it. Dan was so going to get it.

"Yes. She rolled over once. She's not going far. You could totally still watch her," Haley said.

I gestured at the cell. "From here?"

"Why not?" Her chin went up like she was expecting to take one on it.

I was not in any state to be throwing punches. "I dunno. Because I can't imagine that isn't breaking the rules somehow."

"Rules are meant to be broken."

My jaw dropped. That was not something I ever thought I'd hear Haley say. If you could divide the world into rule-followers and rule-breakers, our house would have been a mixed household. I had been squarely in the breaking camp until I'd learned the advantages of following the rules while baking. When had Haley learned not to follow them?

"I've got everything you need here." She lifted up her diaper bag. "Bottle, bottle warmer, diapers, wipes, a change of clothes, some rice cereal already mixed up."

I looked over at Vera. She shrugged. "It's fine with me."

Vera gestured me over to the bars. I stuck my wrists through and she handcuffed me.

"Is that totally necessary?" Haley asked.

"All prisoners must be handcuffed when their cell doors are open. I'll uncuff her once we get the baby in there." Vera waited for me to withdraw my hands and step back and then unlocked the cell door.

Haley walked in with Emily in her carrier and the diaper bag, set it all down, and then kissed Emily on the head. "Be good for Auntie Rebecca, okay?"

Evan leaned down and kissed Emily on the head, too. "Bye, baby. Have fun at the zoo!"

Then they were gone. Vera shut the cell door, uncuffed me, and left right after them.

"Your family is crazy," Cathy said. "Certifiably loony tune, whackadoodle, off-their-rockers crazy."

It was a hard point to argue.

I'd felt like I was the crazy one when Dan had called me into his office saying he had something he wanted to talk to me about. I'd thought he wanted to plan Haley's birthday celebration. I'd brought a sample menu of what I thought we should serve.

"Remember that guy I told you about? Lloyd McLaughlin?" he asked.

"Who?" The name didn't mean anything to me.

"The guy who was poisoned?" he prompted.

"Oh, yeah! The one who ruined your dinner the other night." I remembered now. He had told us about it at dinner.

"You'll never guess what he was poisoned with." Dan leaned back in his chair, watching my face intently.

"Okay. If I'll never guess it, how about you just tell me?" It seemed like a reasonable response.

"Your popcorn," Dan said flatly.

"What do you mean Lloyd McLaughlin was poisoned with my popcorn?" I'd demanded, leaning over Dan's desk.

"I mean that the medical examiner identified a container of Bacon Pecan Popcorn as the source of the pesticide that killed Lloyd," he'd replied. He didn't sound happy. "Know anyone else in town making Bacon Pecan Popcorn?"

I shook my head.

"I thought not." His jaw clenched.

"How did he get any of my popcorn?" I had no idea who this guy was. Even after Dan had showed me his photo, I hadn't recognized him as one of my customers. I hadn't recognized him as anything at all. Granted, he was kind of a generic white guy with brown hair, but still!

Dan ran his hand over his face. "I'm assuming he got it the way everyone else in town got it. He bought it. You do have a shop, you know."

He was right. It had been one of my bestsellers for the few days I'd been able to make it and sell it. It might have even been a better seller than the pumpkin-spice popcorn bars had been back in October. On the other hand, no one could have bought popcorn from my shop since October. "So it was old popcorn? The shop hasn't been open since the fire."

"I have no way of gauging the freshness of the popcorn, Rebecca. It was poisonous. I'm not going to taste it to see if it's stale," he said.

"Fine. He bought popcorn from me before the fire and someone poisoned it." I sat down. Sprocket rested his chin on my knee and I scratched him behind his ears. The only other batches I'd made of that popcorn since the shop closed had gone to the city council candidates. I'd seen all of them and this guy wasn't one of them.

Dan shook his head. "Are you listening to yourself, Rebecca?"

I sat back in my chair. I didn't always think before I spoke. Actually, I rarely thought before I spoke. Words seemed to tumble from my lips of their own accord. It wasn't a great way to communicate. I was working on it. I pressed my lips together to keep any other words from escaping unbidden and went over what he'd said and what I'd said. I still didn't see anything wrong with it. "What? What did I say?"

"Rebecca, were you acquainted with Lloyd McLaughlin? Were there any bad feelings between the two of you?" He opened up his little notepad and picked up a pen.

I blinked. Sprocket whined. "Dan, are you questioning me?"

He squinted his eyes. "I'm doing my job."

Dan's job was to be the sheriff. His job was to arrest criminals.

"I'm not saying another word without my lawyer present." I stood up to go to the door, but Dan stood, too, and held up his hand.

"Then call him," he said.

I pulled my phone from my pocket and called Garrett.

"Dan is questioning me regarding Lloyd McLaughlin's murder," I told him.

He laughed. "Good one, Rebecca. Now, what do you want?"

"No. Seriously. He's questioning me and I said I wasn't going to say another word without my lawyer. You're still my lawyer, aren't you?" I looked over at Dan, who had started working through paperwork on his desk.

"Of course. I'll be right there."

He came right away. He always did. It still felt like an eternity of sitting and not talking to Dan until he got there.

Garrett skidded in, his shoes slipping on the tile floors. "Dan, you've got to be kidding me. Why on earth do you think Rebecca is involved with this?"

"It was my popcorn," I said. "He said Lloyd ate poisoned popcorn."

"You're not the only person in the world who makes popcorn." Garrett sat and leaned back in his chair and looked at Dan through squinted eyes.

"No, but she's pretty much the only person around here who makes Bacon Pecan Popcorn." Dan mirrored Garrett's pose.

I wondered which one was going to draw on the other one first.

"Is that the only reason you're questioning my client?" Garrett asked, not moving.

"At the moment," Dan answered, equally still.

Garrett was silent for a few seconds and then said, "Proceed."

"How did you know Lloyd McLaughlin?" Dan asked.

"I don't." Even though it felt like I knew everyone in town, I didn't. If I didn't go to high school with a person and if that person didn't eat popcorn, I didn't know them. I didn't know anything about Lloyd McLaughlin. Nothing. Nada. Zilch. Zero. I'd never even heard his name before he had the bad form to die after eating my Bacon Pecan Popcorn.

"How did Mr. McLaughlin come to have your popcorn in his home?" Dan asked.

"I have no idea." I couldn't come up with any scenario that had my popcorn in his house. "Maybe somebody else bought it and gave it to him."

"Have you had any dealings with Mr. McLaughlin? Business or social?" Dan asked.

We'd been over this. I rolled my eyes. "Not that I know of and I definitely didn't have any reason to poison him."

Garrett made a funny noise in his throat. I looked over and he shook his head. Right. Answer the question asked and nothing else.

Dan made some notes on the papers in front of him. "When was the last time you saw Mr. McLaughlin?"

"Never as far as I know." As far as I knew, I also hadn't had an opportunity to poison him.

After a few minutes of this, Dan finally shrugged and said, "You're free to go. Please contact me if you think of anything, though."

"You'll be the first," I said.

We walked out of Dan's office and Garrett suggested we have lunch.

I agreed even though I knew what that meant.

"I don't know why you hate the diner so much," Garrett said as he held the door open for me.

We'd dropped Sprocket off at his office to hang out with Pearl. Sprocket loved Pearl. I suspected Pearl shared more than a few snacks with my dog when I wasn't looking. He got that dreamy-eyed look in his eye when he saw her that was usually reserved for sources of hamburger, turkey, or other forms of edible flesh.

Megan, however, was not a big Sprocket fan. Well, that wasn't true. She probably loved Sprocket. She was definitely not, however, a big Rebecca fan and was not above using my own dog against me. She'd laid down the law and told me that unless Sprocket was a service dog, he wasn't allowed in her diner. As tempting as it was to get him some kind of fake service dog certification, I couldn't bring myself to do it. There were people who actually needed their dogs with them. Faking the certification seemed like it might get in their way and I didn't want to twist up my karma that much.

"I don't hate the diner. I just know how much better it could be if they made a few changes. It offends the restaurateur in me." I had no intention of opening a restaurant of my own, but that didn't mean I didn't know how it should be done, and Bob's Diner was not doing it how it should be done.

"Fancy words coming from a woman who sells poisoned popcorn," he said, signaling to Megan that we wanted a booth for two.

"Rebecca," she said as she ushered us to the corner booth. I knew we were getting the good spot in the corner because Garrett was there. If I'd come in on my own, I'd have gotten the table in the back where you could get smacked in the back by the door every time anyone went in and out of the bathroom. Well, I didn't actually have proof of that since I pretty much never came in unless I was being dragged by Garrett or Dan, and Megan liked them both more than she hated me, but I still suspected.

"Megan," I said.

"Hear you're having some trouble." She slapped menus down in front of us as we slid into the booth. A smile quirked at the corner of her mouth. Apparently my trouble was pleasing to her.

"Nothing that I can't handle. Carson'll have POPS up and running again in short order," I said with a confidence I didn't actually have. We couldn't put in the stove until we had the flooring and we couldn't put in the flooring until we had the cabinets and the cabinets were on back order for at least another two weeks.

"Oh, I wasn't talking about your fire damage. Renovations are a pain, but they get done. Plus, Carson is doing the work. Everyone knows how good he is. I was talking about how your customers are dying." She poured us each a cup of coffee while the mean little smile spread over her whole face. Schadenfreude much?

My face went hot. "Customer. Singular. Just one." It wasn't like it was a trend. How did she know already, anyway? Then I remembered how close her sister's office was to Dan's. Trina. She must have overheard something somehow and already started spreading the word.

She shrugged. "Whatever. I hope you're okay. I can only imagine how you're feeling. You know why I can only imagine it? It's because I've never actually poisoned anyone here at the diner." She stared at me with her piggy little eyes in her unformed baby face, a near duplicate of her sister's. "Never. Not once."

I opened my mouth to respond, but she turned on her heel and hustled off. I was half out of my seat to follow her and give her a piece of my mind along with exactly what I thought about the last piece of pie she'd served me, but Garrett caught hold of my wrist. "Sit," he said. His voice was soft, but it didn't sound like he wanted to be argued with.

I glared at him. I'm not a big fan of being ordered around by anyone—except maybe Haley, and that was more force of habit than anything else.

"Please," he added, letting go of my arm.

That was more like it. I sank down onto the bench. I didn't really want to make a scene in the diner. Again. It didn't tend to show me in a good light.

"You're absolutely sure you don't recognize this Lloyd fellow?" he asked. "Not at all?"

"One hundred percent, but that doesn't mean he's never been in the shop. I'm not always out front." With Susanna and Dario serving customers, I could spend more time in my happy place: the kitchen. It's what I liked best about owning POPS. I liked the bubble and boil, the simmer and sauté, the chop and chiffonade of cooking and creating a lot more than I liked endless conversations about the likelihood of rain or the Grand Lake High Otters winning their next game.

Garrett nodded. "Okay. Let's relax, then, and let Dan do his job." He picked up his menu.

"I never intended on doing anything else!" I did not pick up mine.

Garrett set the menu back down and folded his arms over his chest and stared at me. "Sure you didn't."

"What's that supposed to mean?" I leaned toward him.

"You really have to ask that?" He matched my lean angle for angle.

"This is nothing like what happened to Coco or to Melanie. Nothing. I keep telling you all that. I've nothing at stake here. I'm more than happy to let Dan take care of it."

I really thought that I meant that when I said it. I really, really did.

I went to see Marta Hansen in the afternoon after having lunch with Garrett and picking up Sprocket from his office. I made a batch of my special hull-less popcorn to bring to her. Lots of older people had digestive problems with those little seeds. I made sure not to make it too spicy so it wouldn't upset anyone's stomach or too sticky so it wouldn't pull anyone's dentures out of their head or too salty so it wouldn't send anyone's blood pressure soaring or too sweet so it wouldn't send anyone into diabetic shock or too buttery so it wouldn't raise anyone's cholesterol. It was pretty much the most boring batch of popcorn I have ever made. Regardless, I packaged it up in one of my special POPS tins—they had to be good if even Trina liked them—and drove over to the Loving Arms.

It had been years since I'd been to the Loving Arms. The last time was when I'd had to do community service because of skipping school. It was that or picking up trash on the side of the highway. I'd figured that feeding Jell-O to someone's grandmother was probably preferable to needing a tetanus shot after cutting myself on a jagged beer can.

I'd been mainly right.

Most of the people living in the Loving Arms were pleasant and harmless, even if they were confused. There were a few who shouted a lot and cried, but most were happy to see a friendly face and be wheeled around the garden for a walk if the weather was nice.

Then there was Gracie.

Gracie roamed the halls, a crocheted cap covering her bald little head. She rarely spoke to anyone. She'd pointed at the book cart I'd wheeled in from the library and said, "You can't have that in here. It's against the rules."

"It's okay, Gracie," I'd said. "I have special permission."

She'd looked up at me, head cocked slightly to one side, and said, "Then I'll have to kill you."

When I pushed the cart past her, she'd rammed me with her wheelchair, taking me out at the knees. She was backing up, trying, I assume, to get some momentum for her next pass, but I was faster than she was. I leapt to my feet, abandoned my book cart, and raced for the nurses' station.

They were unable to help me due to being doubled over with laughter.

I'd started picking up trash on the side of Highway 10 the following Tuesday.

That had been close to twenty years ago. Surely Gracie couldn't still be around. Just in case, I brought Sprocket with me for protection. I stopped at the front desk to sign in. "I'm here to see Marta Hansen," I said, glancing up at the clock to note the time I'd walked in.

"Oh, wonderful. You brought the therapy dog," the older woman behind the desk said. She was one of those ladies whose faces looked like they'd been made from biscuit dough, all soft and pouchy with a fine dusting of powder over the top.

I froze. Sprocket was no more a therapy dog than I

was a circus performer, and I've been afraid of heights since I fell of a fence and broke my arm in fourth grade. I was about to explain that Sprocket was just a dog, when he sat up and begged, waving one paw at the woman.

"Oh, how cute!" she exclaimed. "The residents are going to love him!"

"Great," I said. Who was I to argue? For all I knew, Sprocket had a calling as a therapy dog that I didn't know about until now.

"What room is Marta in?" I asked.

The woman glanced up at the clock. "Oh, she won't be in her room right now. She'll be in the dayroom for music therapy."

She gave me directions, and Sprocket and I made our way into the building. We could hear the music therapy before we turned the corner. A very loud electric keyboard played "When the Saints Go Marching In," accompanied by what sounded like dozens of rattlesnakes but turned out to be little egg-shaped rattles. The quavery voices of a dozen seniors rose to belt out the chorus.

Sprocket sat down and howled. Some therapy dog.

The young man leading the song laughed. "Everybody's a critic!"

The group finished the song. I leaned over to the nursing assistant standing next to me and whispered, "Which one is Marta Hansen?"

He pointed to three women and one man grouped around a round table. "She's the one in the blue shirt."

"The one shaking her rattles with both hands?" I asked.

"Yep." He smiled. "She's got spunk."

I won't lie. There was something sweet about it. Everyone smiled, looking congratulatory for having finished the song with a rousing chorus. Their faces were pink from the exertion of it all. Sprocket and I made our way across the room to Marta's table. "Hi, Marta. My name is Rebecca Anderson. I was wondering if you could answer a few questions."

"After the music," she said, waving me to the side so she could see the keyboardist.

The man behind the piano started up "Those Were the Days." Marta started shaking her rattles. She gestured to the empty chair next to her with one of the purple egg-shaped items. I sat. And waited. I waited through "Those Were the Days" and "I Want to Hold Your Hand." I waited through "This Land Is Your Land" and "House of the Rising Sun." Finally we wrapped up with "This Little Light of Mine," which for some reason always makes me tear up. Sprocket whined and put a paw on my leg. He hates it when I cry.

Marta swiveled in her wheelchair and said, "So what can I do for you, young lady?"

I quickly blew my nose and said, "I was hoping to talk to you about the house you owned on Main Street."

"The house on Main Street? I sold that years ago to that nice young man. Allen something. Very handsome. Single, too. Are you single?" She peered at me as if you could discern my marital status from my face.

I shook my head. "Not really."

"I'm not sure what that means, but fine. You young people with all your crazy arrangements. Wouldn't have flown in my day. I can tell you that. A girl was single, going steady, engaged, and then married. There was an order to things." She coughed. "You shouldn't wait around too long. You're not getting any younger."

Ah, that was what she was seeing on my face. "Before you sold the house to Allen, did you live there?"

"Where, dear?" She looked perplexed.

I smiled to hide the fact that I was gritting my teeth. "In the house on Main Street?"

"Goodness, no! That house was a rental. It's always been a rental. Papa bought it and then he left it to me. He said a woman who owned property would always be a woman in control of her own destiny." She nodded for emphasis.

I was starting to like her papa.

"He was so right, too. Gave me a nice revenue stream for years. His one rule was no renting to Italians or Jews. They made too much trouble." She pronounced Italian as if it was spelled Eye-talian.

I no longer felt kindly to her papa.

"So would you happen to know who lived in the house during the 1950s?" I asked.

"The 1950s? Why would you want to know that?" A funny look came over her face, as if she was listening to something I couldn't hear. "Who did you say you were again?"

"My name is Rebecca Anderson. I have the shop that's in that house now," I explained.

"But that house belongs to that Allen fellow." Her look had gone from benign to suspicious.

"Yes. He rents it to me," I said.

"Oh." Again she seemed to be listening to something else.

Sprocket put his chin on her spindly little thigh.

"And who are you?" she asked, looking down at him.

"That's my dog, Sprocket." I bit my lip, hoping she actually liked dogs.

"Silly name, Sprocket, but you're a beautiful fellow." She patted his head. He leaned his head into her hands.

"The 1950s, Ms. Hansen. Do you remember who lived in that house in the 1950s?" I pressed.

She scratched behind Sprocket's ears. He looked up at her adoringly. "That's when Papa still rented to Italians and Jews. That's when there were problems."

My heart did a little skipping beat. Maybe my diary writer had had good reason to be frightened. "What kind of problems?"

She stopped petting Sprocket. "You know how those people are."

"No. No, I don't. Please tell me." I felt so uncomfortable. There didn't seem to be any reason to explain bigotry to her except that it would make me feel less slimy.

She waved her hand in the air. "It's all so long ago. Why would you possibly want to know?"

"I found an old diary. Something written by a young girl. I think she knew my grandmother." I decided to leave out the frightened part.

She snorted. "Likely so. Back then everyone in Grand Lake knew everyone else. Who was your grandmother?"

"Ella Conner."

"Bubbles? You're one of Bubbles's girls?"

I smiled. "One of her granddaughters."

"I heard one of them got a little wild. Are you the wild one?" She peered at me again as if my wildness might be written on my face along with my singleness.

I hesitated, then decided to err on the side of honesty.

After all, she'd probably forget whatever I said by the time I left. "Yep. That would be me."

"Good for you," she said. "Live your life."

Whew. "I'd really like to know more about her," I prompted.

"Who? Bubbles? Great swimmer. Heck of a gal." Marta smiled as if at a pleasant memory.

"What about the girl who lived in the house?" As nice as it was to hear about my grandmother, I still needed information.

Sprocket nudged her hand and she went back to scratching behind his ears. "Not much to know. That girl kept to herself. Then she was gone."

I froze for a second. "You knew her?"

She looked up at me. "Didn't I just say that everyone knew everyone else?"

"What was her name?" I asked, leaning forward. Finally, some information!

"Whose name?" Marta gave me a funny look.

"The name of the girl who lived in the house where my shop is," I prompted, anxious to hear the answer.

"What shop?" Marta patted Sprocket some more. "Who are you, handsome boy?"

"That's Sprocket. I have a popcorn shop. It's in a house that you used to own that you sold to Allen Thompson." I had a sinking feeling.

"Who?"

I put my face in my hands. We were playing the worst game of "Who's on First?" ever and I had a feeling there was no way for me to win.

Five

"So you didn't know the dead guy?" Cathy asked.

"Nope." I patted Emily on the back until she gave a little burp.

Cathy wrinkled her nose. "You didn't give him the poisoned popcorn?"

"Nope."

"You answered all of Dan's questions?"

"More than once."

Cathy got up from her bunk and began to pace her cell. "But somehow you're obstructing his justice?"

I shrugged. "According to Dan."

Cathy paused mid-pace and turned to look at me. "Just Dan?"

It hadn't been just Dan. I'd been betrayed by my boyfriend, too. "Well, Dan and Garrett."

"Just Dan and Garrett?"

I bit my lip, remembering what Cynthia had said about me being guilty. "I'm not sure."

She made a "keep on rolling" gesture with her hand. "Let's hear the rest of it."

I didn't have a chance, though. Dan came into the cell block. He stared at me through the bars. "What is my infant daughter doing in your cell?"

Cathy sauntered up to the bars. "Near as I can tell, eating, pooping, and playing peekaboo. Oh, and burping. Can't forget the burping."

He glared at her and then back at me. "Seriously, Rebecca, what is Emily doing in there with you?"

"Hanging out while Haley and Evan go to gymnastics." I picked up Emily and touched my forehead to hers. "Aren't you? Aren't you hanging out with your Auntie Rebecca?"

Emily gurgled and gave me a gummy smile. My heart melted into a tiny puddle of goo.

"Put her down and come put your wrists through the bars." His teeth were gritted so hard, I was surprised he could speak.

"No." If I put my wrists through the bars, he would cuff me. Then he would unlock the cell and take Emily. I wasn't having it. Emily had given me more joy in the past thirty minutes than I'd had in a while, and that included the changing of a poopy diaper.

"Damn it, Rebecca. Give me my baby."

"I don't think so. Haley asked me to babysit. I intend to do as she asked."

Dan turned and stalked back to the door, opened it, and yelled, "Vera, you are so fired."

Vera appeared in the doorway and pulled a piece of paper from her pants pocket. "Haley thought you might say that. She told me to give you this."

Dan unfolded the paper and read it, his face getting redder and redder as he did. He looked up at Vera. "Did you read this?"

She shook her head. "Haley asked me not to."

"Good," he said and walked out the door, his back stiff.

"Did you really not read it?" Cathy asked.

"What do you think?" Vera replied, a small smile playing across her lips. "Keep in mind that I totally want to make detective some day."

I slipped Emily onto my hip. "What'd it say?"

She shook her head. "I'm not telling. Well, I'm not telling the details. She did mention how early Evan goes to sleep on nights that he goes to gymnastics, though, and how much better she might feel with a little sleep. Also, your sister has quite the imagination on her. Dan's a lucky man."

She left and Cathy and I collapsed into a fit of giggles.

Cathy wiped her eyes. "So I'm still not understanding your obstruction-of-justice charge. Is Dan going to rearrest you for babysitting his kids? I mean, he looked like he wanted to today, but you didn't take Evan to a jail cell, did you?"

"I'm getting there," I said.

I'd left Loving Arms feeling like I'd made progress. I practically skipped back to POPS. "I've got a lead on a name," I told Carson.

"As near as I can tell, you've had a name your whole life." He handed me the end of a tape measure. "Hold this, will you?"

"A name for our diary girl, smart-ass." I took the tape measure end and watched as he walked backward across the kitchen.

He stopped. "Seriously? An actual name?"

"Yes! Someone Italian. Or possibly Jewish. Who lived there in the 1950s. At least, that's what it will be according to Marta Hansen." I adjusted to keep the tape as level as possible.

"Marta Hansen also occasionally thinks she's descended from British royalty." He marked down some numbers on his notepad.

"Who says she's not?" I asked.

He laughed. "Pretty much everyone."

"Oh." I turned in a circle around the kitchen. "Why are we measuring? I thought we'd already ordered everything."

"Doesn't hurt to double-check. I'm pretty sure you've heard that whole 'measure twice, cut once' saying. So assuming this person actually existed, how will you find out her actual name and where she is now?" He made some more notations.

"I'm not sure." I wasn't sure about my next step. Marta had said over and over again that everybody knew everybody else, but somehow nobody knew this girl. "Marta kept saying that everybody knew everybody else back then, but I wasn't exactly around in the 1950s. Neither were you or Dan or Haley."

"So maybe you should ask someone who was around in the 1950s?" Carson suggested. "How many Italian or

Jewish families could have lived here in Grand Lake back then? If everybody really did know everybody else, you'd have a shot. Know anybody?"

Of course I did.

I opened the door of Barbara's antique and collectables shop, Granny's Nooks and Crannies, and called out, "Hello! Anybody home?"

Barbara popped up from behind the counter near the back of the crowded shop so quickly it made Sprocket bark. "Rebecca, what can I do for you?"

I laughed. "What were you doing down there?"

"Trying to organize the invoices from the in-store purchases. It's a never-ending battle. I don't know why I even try." Barbara had started doing a pretty brisk trade on eBay. I was beginning to suspect she was only keeping the store open so she'd have some place to go during the day.

Not exactly being a big fan of paperwork myself, I understood what she meant about the invoices, though. I also knew my own reasons for getting things done. "Near as I can tell, the only reason to keep your files in order is so Annie won't yell at you when you don't know if you paid your quarterly taxes or not."

"It might not be the right motivation, but I guess it'll do." She shrugged.

I set the tin of popcorn I'd brought with me down. "I brought you a snack."

"Minus the poison, right?" She eyed the tin, but didn't touch it.

I glared.

"Oh, lighten up, girl. I know you didn't poison that popcorn. Everyone knows that. It's giving people something to fuss about and you know how people like to fuss." She opened the tin and ate a chunk of popcorn. "See? I trust you."

"Why can't they fuss over something besides me?" I sat down in a velvet Queen Anne chair with a thump, then sneezed from the dust that rose out of its cushion.

"Because you give them so much to fuss about. Try to be more boring. So did you stop by to whine or did you have other business?" Barbara asked.

"Other business." I traced my finger along the carved arm piece. "Do you remember who lived in the house where my shop is back in the 1950s?"

Barbara made a face. "Why on earth would you want to know that?"

"Carson and I found an old diary in the wall behind the stove. I'm trying to figure out whose diary it was." I leaned forward.

Barbara shook her head. "You are a Nosy Parker, aren't you?"

I sat back, causing another dust cloud to rise. Sprocket sneezed this time. "Why do you say that?"

"Because most people would find something like that, decide it was trash, and throw it out. They wouldn't spend time trying to figure out whose diary it was. Why do you even want to know?" Barbara wiped off her hands and came around the counter.

"At first I wanted to know because I think this person knew my grandmother. She talks about swimming with Bubbles and then going to her house for popcorn." Barbara had known my grandmother.

"This is how you become known as a Nosy Parker. You actually read it. You didn't pick it up and decide it was an icky mass of old paper probably coated with mouse droppings and throw it directly into the trash." Barbara pulled another side chair up next to the Queen Anne.

I sat back. "You really think someone would do that?"

"I think almost everyone would do that," Barbara said.

It seemed inconceivable to me. "Then everyone has no natural curiosity and no imagination."

"And you are cursed with too much of both. You said your grandmother was why you wanted to know more at first. What happened next that kept you from pitching it?" Barbara asked.

"I think something might have happened to this girl. The diary ends abruptly and the last entry says that she was frightened of something."

"Of what?"

This was the part that sounded crazy to me, so I could only imagine what it was going to sound like to Barbara. "She thought someone here in Grand Lake had been a guard at a Nazi concentration camp. I think she was going to expose somebody."

Barbara snorted. "A Nazi? Here in Grand Lake? You've got to be joking."

"My jokes are generally pretty funny and I don't see much humor in secret Nazis in my hometown." Nazis in general weren't funny. Pretty much only Mel Brooks could make Nazis funny.

"It's funny because this entire town was completely united in the war effort. You don't know what it was like here then." Barbara stabbed at her chair arm with her index finger.

Hard to argue that. World War II ended several decades before I was born. "So tell me. What was it like?"

"Everyone had victory gardens. We had scrap-metal drives every weekend. I started Knitting for Britain in kindergarten. First I knit squares to be stitched into shawls, but by second grade I was turning out a pair of socks a week. We were united in the war effort. Grand Lake would no more tolerate a Nazi in their midst than they would have tolerated a witch." Her eyes narrowed as if she might make out witches or Nazis in her shop at the moment.

"That's the point. No one knew he was a Nazi. He was a secret Nazi. Or I guess a secret ex-Nazi." Until CG started pointing fingers and getting slapped on Main Street.

"Who? Who was this hidden Nazi?"

"I don't know. My little diary writer uses a lot of initials and nicknames."

"Well, what's her nickname for this war criminal?"

"FW. Any idea who that could be?"

Barbara leaned on the counter on her elbows and drummed her fingers for a second. "Nope. Nothing's coming to mind. I can't think of anyone with the initials FW at all."

"It might not be initials. It might be kind of a code."

Barbara shook her head. "Still nothing."

"So do you remember who lived in that house back then? A girl? I'm guessing she would have been a little older than you if she was the same age as my grandmother."

Barbara squinched her eyes shut. "Nope. It's kind of fuzzy." She snapped her fingers. "I'll dig out my old yearbook and look through and see if that jogs my memory at all."

I sighed. "Thanks."

Barbara went to a shelf and plucked a slim volume out. "Got it right here."

"You keep your old yearbooks here at the store?" I was pretty sure I kept mine in a box at the back of my closet underneath a hair removal kit I bought from an infomercial during a fit of insomnia.

"You think I would keep an old dusty thing like this at my house?" She held up the book with the same look Dan got on his face holding up a dirty diaper.

Barbara's house was all sleek leather, chrome, and glass and was very, very minimalistic. Dusty yearbooks would really have no place there.

Barbara plunked the yearbook down on the counter, opened it up, and started turning pages. "There's your grandmother."

I came around the counter so I could look over her shoulder. It was one of those classic black-and-white photos of a girl with a helmet of hair, a sweater, and pearls. The caption read: "Bubbles Conner. Most Likely to Swim the English Channel." I ran my finger along the edge of her photo. "She looks nice."

Barbara nodded. "As nice as they come. Well, not nice enough on occasion to be fun. Too much niceness gets boring sometimes."

"If it helps you think about who might have lived here, Marta said something about Italians and Jews being trouble." I felt icky just saying the words out loud.

Barbara smacked her head. "You should have said! Of course! Esther Brancato!" She flipped through the pages and jabbed a black-and-white photo with her index finger "That's who lived in that house in the 1950s. Esther Brancato. She was two years ahead of me, class of 1954. Italian and Jewish."

I turned the book to look at the photo. It was a little hard to make out much detail. Dark hair. Dark eyes. Her face a pale oval, held at a slight angle. Glasses that would be hipster now, but were probably just embarrassing and unattractive then. I traced the outline of her cheek with my finger. "What was she like?"

"Smart. Quiet. A good girl, but not a Goody Two-shoes, you know?" She smiled.

"Kind of. Anything you can remember in particular?" The face looking back at me from the yearbook looked so calm and peaceful. It was hard to connect it with the angsty, troubled girl from the diary.

"Oh, yes. Probably almost anyone who was around back then would. She disappeared."

A chill ran down my spine. "Disappeared? When? How?"

"That part's harder for me to remember. There were lots of rumors. She met an older man who seduced her away. She was abducted by white slavers or maybe aliens. She ran away to New York to be a writer. I don't remember which one of them ended up being true."

"Do any of her relatives still live around here? Is there anyone I could ask?"

Barbara shook her head. "Not that I know of. I think they moved away."

"I wonder how I could find out."

"Well, you know who would have all the files on the investigation, don't you?"

Dan. Dan would have all the files. "I'm not sure he's much in the mood to help me out," I said.

She shrugged. "You could start with the newspaper, then. They covered it pretty extensively."

I pointed at her. "Good thinking."

"It's one of my specialties." She cocked her head. "If you leave the diary with me, I could look it over, see if I can pick out anyone else."

I started to agree, but then got a funny sensation. The same sensation I got when Antoine used to take bites of my meals without asking. I didn't want to share. On the other hand, Barbara would be what Sheri had called a primary source. Maybe she would recognize people or descriptions. "How about I make a copy and drop it off to you later."

"Sounds perfect."

This first call came in at ten on Thursday morning. Sprocket and I had just left the copy shop and I'd started getting ready for my big afternoon. Fridays were my busy day. I had special orders up the wazoo. It was one of the few ways I was keeping my head above water as the shop was fixed up. I counted on those orders. I needed them. I'd prepare most of them Thursday evening so they'd be ready for pick up on Friday.

"Oh, hi, Rebecca. I thought I'd get your voice mail." Wallace Thomas sounded weird.

Usually people were hoping to speak to real me when they called, but whatever. "Nope. You've got the actual me. What can I do for you?"

"I was, uh, calling to cancel my usual Friday order."

Wallace had ordered a dozen Kahlúa Caramel Balls and an order of Coco Pop Fudge every Friday for months. Every Friday. No exceptions.

"I hope everything's okay. You're not sick or anything, are you?" Wallace was a sweet guy.

"No. Nothing like that. Just doing something different this Friday." He laughed a weird high-pitched giggle.

Not good timing for me for him to suddenly be experimenting, but there wasn't much I could do about it, either. "Sure. I understand. I'll see you next Friday."

He made a funny noise in his throat and then said, "Uh, maybe not then, either."

"Wallace, what's going on?"

"Edna and me, we just thought that maybe it might be, you know, prudent if we didn't order your popcorn for a little while. Maybe just until this thing with Lloyd McLaughlin is cleared up."

"Lloyd?" I couldn't believe what I was hearing.

"Yes. You know. The guy you poisoned." He said it with a matter-of-factness that shocked me.

"I didn't poison him!" Unbelievable!

"Oh. Did we hear wrong? It wasn't your popcorn that was poisoned?" Now he sounded worried.

"Yes. I mean no. I mean, the poison was in my popcorn, but I did not put it there." Why on earth would I poison a man I didn't even know? Why would I do it in a way that would come back to me so quickly?

"So who did?" Wallace asked.

I paused. "How should I know?"

"Look, kid, you know we love your popcorn, but neither Edna nor I want to take any chances. We've got kids to raise, you know? We'll be back as soon as this is all resolved." He hung up before I could say another word.

Wallace was not the last. By two o'clock on Thursday afternoon every one of my usual special orders had canceled. Every one of them, and I knew why.

I knew why because I'd been told why. I'd taken Sprocket out for a walk. I'd run into Mr. Christensen near the intersection of Hyacinth and Rose. After a chat about whether the weather would turn cold or colder for the weekend, I said good-bye. We were nearly around the corner when he said, "You make sure that Carson cleans up that kitchen of yours real good."

I turned around slowly. "Excuse me?"

"I heard you had a little trouble. Some fellow that ate your popcorn died. You better make sure that kitchen is good and clean so nobody else gets sick." He shook his finger at me.

"Lloyd McLaughlin didn't die because of something that happened in my kitchen." My face got hot. It had to be beet-red by the way it felt. At least it was keeping me warm.

"Oh, my mistake, then. I'd heard he died from something in your popcorn." Mr. Christensen's face furrowed.

"He did, but it wasn't anything I put in there." I took a few steps toward him. "Where exactly did you hear this?"

"Over at the diner," he said, smiling big enough for me to see all of his dentures. "Megan was saying."

"Figures," I muttered. I looked him in the eye and said, "Lloyd was poisoned. Someone put poison in a batch of my popcorn after it left my shop. After."

He nodded. "So you say."

I did say. I had a whole lot more to say, too. I turned around and Sprocket and I marched to the diner. I flung open the door, making the little bell tinkle wildly. I pushed my way through to the kitchen.

Megan turned around as I pushed through the door, letting it bang shut behind me with a *whump*. The kitchen smelled great, which only infuriated me more. Megan must have been baking. I smelled butter and cinnamon and my mouth watered despite myself.

"What do you have against me? Why are you spreading rumors like that?" I demanded.

"Why are you always talking about how bad my food is?" Megan turned from the counter and assumed the power pose, feet spread, hands on hips. She must have been watching TED Talks in her spare time.

I wasn't posing. I had the power of truth on my side. "Because it is."

"It's been good enough for everyone in this town since you were five years old, missy. It'll be good enough when you decide you've had enough of Grand Lake and leave again." She picked up a rolling pin and tapped it against her leg.

"First of all, just because people don't know better doesn't mean you shouldn't strive to be your best. And second of all, I'm not leaving. I'm back for good." She could threaten me with three rolling pins. I didn't care.

She snorted. "Well, pardon me if I don't start a parade in your honor."

"I don't want a parade, but I don't want to be slandered." I took another step toward her.

She wasn't backing down, either. "Slandered? How

about what you tell everyone about my au jus? How about that? Or my chicken-with-rice soup?"

I pressed my lips together. I had not been complimentary about those two items. The soup was gloppy and I was pretty sure she made her au jus with a bouillon cube. "It's not slander if it's true, Megan."

"Not all of us got some fancy culinary school education. Some of us learned our trade at the grill, working our fannies off."

"Congratulations." It came out sounding snottier than I'd intended.

Megan shook her head and walked out to the dining room.

I watched her go. It was a shame, really. The diner had so much potential. I personally loved good diner food, but the emphasis had to be on good. Fresh ingredients. Simple cooking methods. It could be done.

But apparently not here.

Six

Cathy started doing sit-ups. I winced a little at what that concrete floor must feel like as she rolled and unrolled her spine up and down. Prison made you hard in more ways than one. "Now we're getting somewhere," she gasped. "This is where you got pissy, right? Megan was spreading rumors about your poisoned popcorn and hurting your business. It's always all about the Benjamins, isn't it?"

It was about the Benjamins, but it was about something more, too. I'd felt like I'd finally worked my way into the town's good graces. When I first came back, no one thought I was anything more than the wild child who'd raced out of here like Flo-Jo from the starting blocks as soon as she could. Everyone kept expecting me to screw up. The worst was when everyone suspected me of killing my beloved Coco. I'd really felt like I'd hit bottom then.

But then I proved I hadn't. I proved that I was better than they thought I was. They'd granted me a sort of grudging respect since then, but with each subsequent day, I'd felt like the grudging lessened and the respect got greater. To have it all ripped away hurt worse than accidentally dripping a dark chocolate roux on my wrist, and I had a permanent scar from that.

"It was about my reputation, too, Cathy," I said.

For a second, I didn't think she'd heard me. She didn't say anything. When she finally did speak, her throat sounded clogged. "Yeah, I get that, too. I know I did it to myself, but it hurts like hell to have people who used to look up to you act like you're dirt under their shoe. Geraldine Richards used to hang on my every word. The last time I saw her, she actually turned and walked away from me."

Cathy was right. She had done it to herself. That didn't mean she didn't deserve a little sympathy, though. I stuck my hand through the bars. She took it.

"I'm sorry," I said.

"Yeah," she said. "Me, too."

The door opened and Haley came in with Evan, followed by Vera. Evan was half asleep in Haley's arms, his left hand grasping a bit of her shirt. "Did Dan give you any trouble?" Haley asked.

"No. Well, he tried. Vera took care of him." I smiled at Vera and tucked Emily back into her car seat. I looked around to be sure I'd gotten everything back in the diaper bag and then thrust my hands through the bars so Vera could cuff me.

"Thanks, Vera," Haley said, taking Emily. "For everything."

After Vera relocked the cell and uncuffed me, I

reached through to pat Evan on the back. "How was gymnastics?"

"I did a flip into the cubes and Tiffany got a bloody nose," he reported.

I looked over at Haley. "Are those two things related?"

She shook her head.

"Why does Miss Vera keep putting those bracelets on you and then taking them off?" Evan asked.

"Because she doesn't trust me," I said. "Isn't that strange?"

Evan looked very serious. "Did you lie to her, Auntie Becca?"

"Nope." I shook my head.

"Did you cheat at a game?" he asked.

"Nope."

He pondered for a moment and then finally asked, "What did you do?"

"I tried to find out what happened to somebody so I wouldn't get blamed for it and now everyone's mad at me." It was the most accurate summary I could come up with on short notice.

Evan thought about that for a second. "That doesn't seem fair."

"Not to me, either. I think you should talk to your daddy about it tonight at dinner," I suggested.

"Rebecca," Haley said, loads of warning in her voice.

I shrugged. "Or not, Evan. Do what your conscience guides you to do."

"Rebecca," Haley repeated, her tone sharper.

I waved my hand at her. "Whatever. Evan, don't worry about it. I'll be fine and I'll be home soon." I said it with more confidence than I felt.

*   *   *

The night my special orders had been canceled, Garrett came over to my apartment. I'd been steamed and not quite sure what to do with my anger. Garrett pulled me down onto the couch next to him after I'd been pacing long enough to make Sprocket cover his eyes with his paws and whine. "You know you're not a serious suspect, right? You know Dan's only investigating your part in this because he has to. He knows you didn't poison Lloyd."

I had been trying to explain to him the depth of the disservice that had been perpetrated against me. He'd been trying to kiss me. I hated it when our goals weren't in sync.

"Yeah, well, you may know that. I may know that. The rest of the town doesn't know that, and with Megan telling everyone that my popcorn's poisonous, I might reopen POPS to find out I no longer have any customers." I leaned forward and put my head in my hands. I'd sunk everything I had and more into POPS. It wasn't like I wouldn't be able to reinvent myself again if I had to, but I certainly didn't want to. This reinvention had been painful enough. "Dan needs to focus on somebody else in his investigation and fast."

"You're not going to do this." Garrett rubbed my back. "Who am I kidding? Of course you're going to do this. Of course you're going to meddle in this situation. I really wish you wouldn't. Dan wishes you wouldn't. Haley wishes you wouldn't. The whole town wishes you wouldn't."

"The town is not giving me much of a choice, is it?"

How many times would I have to prove myself to the people of Grand Lake? Maybe it wouldn't take as much this time. Maybe I could scare up some other suspects for Dan so people would have something else to talk about. Then I'd totally peace out. I could probably get it done before Dan even realized what I was doing. "I'll try not to meddle."

Garrett's hand stopped rubbing my back. "Promise?"

I sat up so I could look him right in the eye. "Cross my heart. Hope to die."

"Let's hope it doesn't come to that this time."

Garrett stayed until I took Sprocket out for one last walk, then went back to his place. The sky had clouded over. No stars shone down on us. I could make out the hazy circle of the moon only as a bright spot behind the clouds. The air had a dampness to it. Rain was coming.

All those years in California had turned rain into a special event for me. It was kind of a pain. Sprocket didn't like to get his feet wet, so he wasn't excited about walking in it. In fact, he was downright recalcitrant. The humidity made my hair get huge and turned my bangs into unruly corkscrews. I still loved it, though. I loved waking up to the sound of it pattering down on the roof of my apartment. I loved the special scent that rose up from the ground when it first started falling. I loved making hot chocolate and feeling all cozy inside while it soaked the world outside. I especially loved what happened when the sun came out after a morning rain. The whole world looked washed clean with diamond sparkles on the puddles.

Plus I had bought super cute new rain boots and I was excited about getting to wear them.

I shooed Sprocket back up the steps to the apartment and got ready for bed. I cuddled into bed with the diary and started to read.

I talked to CG tonight. I waited until Mama and Papa went out for a walk after dinner. "I need to talk to you about FW," I told her.

"I thought your mama and papa told you to forget about what I said," she said.

"They did. I can't, though." I showed her the star and she started to cry.

I asked her how she could be so sure. The war was a long time ago now. It's been over for close to ten years. Maybe she wasn't remembering right.

She told me that if you go through something like she did, you never forgot anything. You prayed to forget. You begged to forget. You couldn't, though.

I asked her if maybe FW just looked like the same guy. She said no. She said she was sure. She looked so certain and so scared. I felt bad for her. I want to believe her just to make her feel better, but she also believed that if Mama sewed the hem of my skirt while I was still wearing it that the Angel of Death would think I was being sewn into my shroud and would take me during the night.

I reached over to scratch Sprocket behind his ears. "It sounds like Esther's starting to believe her cousin about FW, boy. What do you think?"

Sprocket thumped his leg.

"Good point. I should read more."
I went on to the next entry.

I don't ever think I've been so sick in my entire life. It was so humiliating. It started at school. In algebra class, no less! I felt so sick all of the sudden. Like my head was on fire and my stomach was being twisted into knots all at once. I remember standing up to ask Mr. Stevenson if I could be excused, and then nothing. Bubbles told me I made a funny noise and then crumpled to the ground like a balloon that someone let the air out of. Then I apparently barfed on Jimmy Allen's shoes. Total humiliation. My dad got sick, too. Dr. Halpern thinks it was food poisoning. I just know that I've never felt cramps anywhere that bad.

Could it have been someone deliberately trying to poison her? Two entries after that, I read something that chilled me even more:

I almost died today. Standing on Main Street waiting for the bus. It was almost to the stop when I felt hands at the small of my back, pushing! If HH hadn't been standing next to me, if he hadn't grabbed me by my book bag, I would have gone splat down in front of it. My heart is still racing. I turned to see who was behind us, but there were too many people. Then I saw FW walking away.

Maybe Esther had good reason to be frightened. I turned out the light and burrowed down into the covers.

Sprocket edged closer to me. I looped my arm around him and shut my eyes, but it was a long time until I slept.

Grand Lake boasts an actual Carnegie Library. Built in 1903 in the neoclassical style, it is a monument to grace and symmetry and geometrical harmony. At least, on the outside it is. Outside, the brick facade is studded with three Palladian windows on either side of a centered front door that is framed in granite and topped with a pediment. It speaks of solidity and congruence. It made something in my chest feel calmer and lighter by its mere presence.

On the inside, it is a busy public library with toddler story times and memoir classes for senior citizens and conversation groups for people wanting to learn foreign languages. It's all presided over by Juanita Arnold, a tiny little sprite of a woman with a temper the size of Cleveland and an electric wheelchair that she's been known to use as a battering ram.

To my surprise, Juanita had on a tutu and was carrying a wand when I walked in. She normally tended toward slacks and button-down shirts. She wheeled up to me.

"Nice getup," I said, gesturing to the tutu.

"Screw you, Rebecca." She stuck her tongue out at me, too, for good measure.

I smiled. I loved it when Juanita cussed at me. The tutu made it so much better. It was like having a tiny Latina Tinker Bell spouting obscenities. Really, does it get much better than that? "What's with the costume?"

"Freaking story time. It's going to be the death of me.

All those kids. All those germs. All that snot." She shuddered. "What is it you want from me?"

"I want to see the *Sentinel* from some time in the 1950s." I pulled Sprocket a little closer to my side as a small herd of kids ran past. He wasn't prone to chasing the small ones, but I wanted to be careful. I was pretty sure Juanita gave us some kind of special dispensation to even have him inside the library. I didn't want to abuse it.

"You know the 1950s are a whole decade, right?" Juanita tapped some information into a computer.

"It occurred to me."

She looked up from the computer. "And you know the *Sentinel*'s a daily newspaper, right?"

"I'm aware."

"So that's like three thousand, six hundred and fifty days of news. Want to narrow it down at all?" She pressed her hands together in a prayerful pose. "Try? For me?"

I whipped out the diary from my bag to look at the dates. I'd given Barbara the copy I'd made and kept the original for myself.

"What's that?" she said, suddenly straightening up.

"It's a diary I found in the wall of POPS during the renovations." I paged through the first few entries.

Her eyes were big and her breathing had gone funny. "Can I see it?"

I pushed it across the counter toward her.

She ran her hand over it, then held it to her face and sniffed it.

"Are you smelling my diary?" There really wasn't another explanation, but I was hoping.

"Nothing smells as good as a primary source. You

should definitely show this to Sheri. She's done some great historical workups of the town. This is right up her alley." She handed it back to me.

"Show me what?" Sheri was at my elbow, with two of her three kids.

I jumped. "How did you do that? Just materialize that way? Are you like Beetlejuice or something?"

Juanita rolled her eyes. "She's here for story time, Rebecca. That's why I suggested her. That and the fact that she's done some historical research on the town already."

Story time. That was something I could take Evan to. If Sheri was doing it, it must be good. I made a mental note to check dates and times and see how Haley would feel about it.

"Still trying to find out whose diary that is?" Sheri plopped a stack of storybooks onto the counter and dug in her purse for her library card.

"I think I have a pretty solid lead on that. Now I'm trying to figure out what happened to her." I resisted the urge to clutch the diary to my chest.

"What do you mean?" Sheri lined the books up so they all faced the same way.

"Barbara thinks it sounds like a girl named Esther Brancato. According to her, Esther disappeared some time toward the end of high school."

Juanita frowned. "Disappeared how?"

"In that one-day-here, next-day-gone kind of way." I wasn't sure there was another way unless it was in a puff of smoke. I was pretty sure Barbara would have mentioned a puff of smoke.

Juanita did a little head pop that I was pretty sure

would have dislocated something on me. "Don't take a tone with me, Rebecca."

"Sorry. I didn't mean to." It was true. I had a lot of tone whether or not I meant it. "I just meant that Barbara didn't really know. She couldn't remember if Esther had run away or if something else had happened. I figured it would have definitely been in the *Sentinel* one way or the other."

"Probably," Sheri said. "That's still a lot of microfiche to sort through if you don't have a date, though."

"I have a month and the year Esther Brancato disappeared. That should help." Unless, of course, my diary writer wasn't Esther, in which case I'd be back at the drawing board again.

"How do you know the month? Did Barbara remember it that specifically?" Sheri asked.

I flipped to the end of the diary. "That's her last entry. She says she's frightened and then nothing else."

"What's she frightened of?" Juanita paged through the diary.

"She thinks someone's following her. Then there were some weird little accidents." It sounded melodramatic as I said it. Coming from the mouth of a teenage girl, it would have been a million times more dramatic.

Sheri looked up. "Accidents?"

"Someone shoves her into the street in front of a bus." I took the diary back from Juanita and paged through to that section of the diary.

Sheri read it over my shoulder. "Who? Who would do that?"

"She wasn't sure. There was a crowd. Everyone there said she stumbled. She swears she felt hands on her back."

"Anything else?" Juanita asked.

I paged through to another entry. "Food poisoning. Or maybe just plain old poisoning." I tapped my finger against the entry where Esther, or whoever, described the painful cramping and illness.

"What kind of poisoning?" Sheri asked.

I shook my head. "She wasn't sure. Remember this was the 1950s, too. It wasn't exactly like an episode of *CSI*. Plus, her parents thought she was being dramatic, looking for attention."

Juanita snorted. "They always discount what we say."

Sheri shrugged. "Teenage girls can be a little dramatic."

"Whether she was being dramatic or not, she disappeared. I'd like to know more." Even broken clocks are right twice a day.

"What do you think you'll find in the newspaper?" Sheri asked.

"I'm not sure. I guess I'll know when I find it," I answered. "I'm hoping to see if anybody had any theories about where she might have gone."

Juanita asked, "How sure are you about the year?"

"Medium sure." I was sure about what year Esther Brancato was supposed to graduate; whether or not that was the year she actually disappeared or if it was even her diary was up for grabs.

Juanita looked at her watch. "Look, I've got the older kids' story time starting. Can you come back a little later and I'll step you through it all?"

"Sure."

I said good-bye to Sheri, who shepherded her girls into the stacks to look for books. I couldn't help but smile.

Their little chirping voices, excited about books they were going to read and videos they were going to watch, made me think of the little woodland creatures who danced around Disney princesses' feet.

When I came back, Juanita had changed clothes.

"No more tutu?" I asked. "It looked cute."

"The tulle totally crawled up my ass. I don't know how ballerinas stand it," she said as she led me to a back corner of the library.

"This is a little spooky." I looked around at the cracked linoleum and dim lighting.

"We haven't renovated back here yet. We might never. It's not exactly the sexy technology of the day." Juanita maneuvered her chair around a particularly big seam in the floor. "Here we go."

The here she referred to was a big metal filing cabinet and a giant machine that looked like an old prop from a 1950s science-fiction B movie next to rows and rows of old telephone books. It seemed appropriate.

She patted the cabinet. "Every issue of the *Sentinel* from its inaugural one to 2004 is here in this cabinet and every phone book since 1910 is on those shelves."

"What happened in 2004?" I asked, eyeing all five drawers of the monstrosity.

"They went digital, Rebecca. It's Grand Lake, but even we figured that one out." Juanita rolled her eyes.

"Right. So what do I do to read them?" I was pretty sure it was going to involve that machine. It looked intimidating.

Juanita pulled open a drawer. Inside were dozens and dozens of little cardboard boxes. "You said you thought you had a year to start with?"

"Yeah. 1954," I said.

"Right. Now look at the dates on the boxes and find that year." Juanita pointed at the drawer.

"Me?" I took a step back.

"Yeah. You. You're the one with the curiosity that needs to be satisfied." Juanita shot me a look.

"I'm pretty sure you're curious, too." I'd seen the way she'd sniffed my diary.

She shrugged. "I'm curious about a lot of things. You get to be the cat on this one." Then she froze for a second. "Although, given your track record, you might want to rethink all that."

I sighed. "It's a diary from the 1950s. So far Barbara's the only person I've stumbled across who seems to know anything about this girl at all."

She nodded. "Yeah. You're right. Who would be upset about something that happened that long ago?"

I looked through the boxes and found one that spanned 1953 to 1957. I pulled it out.

Juanita pointed over to the machine. "I'll show you how to thread it and then you're on your own, okay? I've got a preteen book club starting in fifteen minutes."

Operating the microfiche machine wasn't nearly as hard as I'd expected. It was all a matter of following instructions. Years of following recipes had primed me for jobs like this one. Start at Step One. Progress to Step Two. Don't question. Don't think too hard. Someone else has already done that hard thinking for you.

Which is why I was surprised when I couldn't seem to find the month and year I was looking for. I was pretty sure I'd progressed through all the steps just as I should. I hadn't skipped any steps. I hadn't added any, either. Yet for some reason May of 1954 wasn't there.

I started over and retraced my steps. Nope. It still wasn't there. Okay. It was a long time ago. Maybe something had gotten misfiled somehow. Who would ever have noticed? Who would be going back through these old papers? Maybe it was in another year.

I pulled out 1955 to see if it had gotten lumped into the wrong year. That month was missing. May of 1956 wasn't there, either. I looked down at Sprocket. "That's weird," I said.

He whined.

I pulled every year of the 1950s. The month of May was missing in every year from 1950 to 1959. It looked as if someone had burned that section out of every year.

I heard a familiar voice outside the cell block. "Stand back, you big oaf. Don't think you can intimidate me by looming over me like that." Ah, the dulcet tones of Faith. Faith was Barbara's niece. She'd started to help run Barbara's shop and had become a good friend.

"I'm not looming, Faith," Huerta said. "I'm holding the door open for you. It's heavy."

"Sure you are." Faith marched up to my cell.

I walked up to the bars. "Boy, are you a sight for sore eyes." I felt my own eyes start to well a bit. I hadn't realized how alone I'd felt until I saw a friendly face.

"This is totally unacceptable," Faith said, arms crossed

over her chest, looking over my cell. "Absolutely unacceptable."

I glanced back at the concrete-block walls and metal bars. "I haven't really had time to decorate."

She snorted. "That blanket looks too thin to keep a furnace warm."

She was right. It was pretty chilly here in the cell and the blanket didn't do much. "The floor doesn't help."

We both looked down at the gray concrete under our feet.

"And do they really expect you to use that?" She pointed at the metal toilet in the corner of my cell.

I nodded.

She sniffed. "We'll see about that."

"How?"

"Just wait." She snapped her fingers at Huerta. "Open up that door. I have work to do."

"Who was that?" Cathy asked after Faith had left.

"A friend." I smiled. "A good friend."

"That's lucky. That is not the kind of woman I'd want as an enemy," she said.

She didn't know the half of it.

"Must be nice to have visitors," she said.

"No one visits you? No one at all?" Cathy had been here for weeks. How was she holding it together? No wonder she was interested in my story.

Cathy shrugged. "My attorney, every now and then. Otherwise, no."

"Weren't you . . . married?" It seemed indelicate to ask, but we'd been pretty indelicate with each other for a while now.

"Yep." The pace of her sit-ups increased.

"Your husband doesn't visit you?"

"Nope." She lay back on the floor, arms stretched to the side. "That's not entirely true. He came once."

"Oh, that's good."

"It was to serve me with divorce papers." She started doing crunches again.

Ouch. "Sorry."

"Whatever. Now can we get back to how you ended up in here?" she asked. "I feel like your nephew got a better explanation than you're giving me."

The newspaper hadn't helped with my investigation into Esther Brancato, but it had listed a date and time for Lloyd McLaughlin's wake. I decided to attend. It didn't count as meddling. It was paying respects and perhaps gathering some information at the same time. If I happened to overhear word of someone who had had bad feelings toward Lloyd, it would be a bonus. I hadn't wanted to arrive at Lloyd's house empty-handed, but thought it would be tacky to show up with popcorn. Even if I wasn't the one who had poisoned him, it seemed callous. I made cookies instead. Chocolate chip with a little caramel surprise inside.

I didn't want to wear black. I hadn't known Lloyd and it seemed presumptuous to say I mourned him. Plus, I still only had the black chiffon party number I'd worn to Coco's funeral, and that had not gone down particularly well. I also didn't want to show up in my usual jeans, though. After a few minutes of staring into my closet, I chose a skirt and boots that said grown-up, but not stuffy. I put Sprocket in the yard with a peanut butter Kong, promised to be back before too long, and got into the Jeep.

Lloyd lived over off Highway 2. It was a nice neighborhood, newer than the one where I'd grown up. The kind of neighborhood where if you didn't know the exact address of the house, you'd be out of luck. There were no distinguishing features on the houses. Each one looked just like the next. Two stories. Shingled roofs. Attached garages. Round window on what was most likely the landing of the stairway. Each lawn looked just like the next. Rectangular patches of grass. Two trees. Flower bed by the front door. What distinguished Lloyd McLaughlin's house from his neighbors' was the thumping music coming from the house.

Everyone processes grief differently. I reminded myself of that as I walked up to the house and rang the doorbell. And then knocked because no one answered and I wasn't sure they'd heard me over the music. Then rang the doorbell again. That time, a woman answered the door.

I would have guessed her to be in her late forties or early fifties. There may have been a touch of gray roots showing in her otherwise dark hair, but only a touch. Her jawline was a little soft, but not jowly. What really distinguished her, however, was the open bottle of champagne in her hand, from which she was taking a healthy swig.

"And who might you be?" she asked. She enunciated each syllable like she was being careful to not slur her words.

"I, uh, just wanted to offer my condolences to Mr. McLaughlin's family." I held out my tray of chocolate chip cookies. It seemed prudent not to mention my name right out of the box. Even if I knew I hadn't poisoned Lloyd, his family might not know that yet.

She eyed the cookies. "Homemade?"

I nodded, hoping that wouldn't count against me.

She gestured with her head. "Come on in."

I followed her into the kitchen and set the cookies down on the table with platters of all kinds of food. It was such a Midwestern thing. Tragedy strikes and we tie on our aprons. After our parents died, Haley and I nearly drowned in casseroles. Good thing we had Coco to teach us what we could freeze and what we couldn't. We probably ate for six months off of what people brought us.

Nobody seemed to be deciding what to freeze here. In fact, the atmosphere was, well, like a party. Music was blasting. People were laughing. I'd heard of people having celebrations of life rather than memorial services, but this seemed to be taking it too far.

"Are you, uh, related to Mr. McLaughlin?" I asked my guide.

She smiled, her head bobbing to the beat of the music. "Not anymore. I got the papers to prove it, too."

"Excuse me."

"Ex-wife," she said, gesturing to her chest with the champagne bottle. "Been divorced from that tight-assed SOB for going on three years now. Best decision of my life to lose one hundred and ninety pounds of ugly fat." She threw her head back and laughed a big full-throated laugh.

"How, uh, nice." I'd felt a lot of relief when I'd divorced Antoine. It had been a wrenchingly hard decision to make. I'd weighed the pros and cons in my head and on pieces of paper for months before I finally made up my mind sitting in a hotel hallway in Minneapolis in January without even a clean pair of panties to change into. Once the decision was made, I'd experienced a nearly exhilarating sensation of a weight being lifted from my shoulders and the breaking of some sort of stranglehold on my heart.

I would never wish him dead, though. Never. I'd loved him once.

"Uh-huh," Mrs. No-Longer-McLaughlin said. "And get this. Lazy asshat never changed his will! This house he fought so hard to get during our divorce? It's mine." The noise she made next could only be described as a cackle.

"Congratulations?" I wasn't sure it was the right thing to say, but it was all I could come up with on short notice.

"Thanks." She hugged me, bonking the champagne bottle into my back as she did so. Then she stepped back. "Hey, wait a second. Who exactly are you?"

I didn't see any way to squirrel out of it this time. "My name is Rebecca Anderson."

Her face went blank for a second and I thought she might be one of those drunks with unpredictable mood swings. I took a step back in case the mood swing prompted her to take a swing at me with that champagne bottle. It might be only half full, but it would definitely leave a mark.

"The one who owns the popcorn shop?" she asked in as close as a drunk can get to a whisper.

I took a deep breath, ready to take whatever was coming at me. "Yes. The one who owns the popcorn shop."

"The popcorn shop where the poisoned popcorn came from?" she asked, eyes widening.

Her ability to get through that sentence was impressive. I wasn't sure I could do it stone-cold sober. "Yes."

She whooped and hurried into the living room. "Hey! Everybody! Guess who's here? The lady that poisoned Lloyd!"

I don't get a lot of applause. It's not a chef thing. Someone might clasp their hands together and hold them to their chest when I set their favorite dish in front of them. People made appreciative noises. Every once in a while there was a marriage proposal, but they were usually spoken in jest. Applause? Actual applause? People clapping their hands together in appreciation of me?

Almost never.

Lloyd McLaughlin's living room erupted in applause after Mrs. No-Longer-McLaughlin made her announcement.

I backed away some more. "No. You don't understand. I didn't poison him. I swear it."

"Well, ding-dong the witch is dead anyway," said a gray-haired man who looked like Fred Rogers's younger brother, right down to the cardigan sweater. "We're rid of that asshole regardless of how it happened."

"Sometimes the best things in life happen by accident," a young woman with a baby on her hip said.

I was getting the feeling that Lloyd McLaughlin was not universally loved.

By the time I left his wake, I had a list of potential suspects longer than the recipe for Gâteau Saint-Honoré.

Seven

Leaving Lloyd McLaughlin's wake had been trickier than I'd expected. It was a little difficult to say goodbye to the number of people who were hailing me a hero even though I kept trying to point out that I actually hadn't done the poisoning. It hadn't mattered. They'd toasted me. They'd toasted my store. They'd toasted the existence of popcorn. They'd toasted toast. They were totally toasted.

I stepped out onto the sidewalk surprised to find it was still light outside. I started toward the Jeep, but found my path seemed to be more meandering than I'd intended. I pulled out my cell phone.

Garrett answered on the second ring. "Hello, beautiful. What are you up to today?"

"I think I need a ride," I said.

There was a pause. I wondered if I'd slurred my words

too much to be comprehensible, but I didn't think I was that drunk.

"Where are you?" he asked.

I turned to look at the house and came close to losing my balance. "Thirty-seven twenty-eight Lone Oak Circle."

Another pause. "Where exactly is that?"

"Over on the southwest side of town. Those new developments."

"What are you doing there, Rebecca?"

"Paying my respects to the Widow McLaughlin. And bringing her cookies. The chocolate chip ones with the caramel inside." Garrett liked those. I'd held a few back for him.

"You're where?" Absolutely no pause that time. No pause at all.

"At Lloyd McLaughlin's house where his widow . . . Wait. Are you still a widow if you're divorced before your husband dies?" Was there some kind of technical term for that status? Ex-widow? No. That didn't sound right.

"Are you drunk?" Garrett asked.

"I'd describe myself more as festive. Little more than tipsy. Little less than drunk. Definitely not suitable to drive, though."

"I'm on my way. Don't move."

That seemed unnecessarily dramatic, but I parked my butt on the porch step and waited.

Garrett pulled up in his Subaru, but he didn't get out of his car. I stood up from the porch, gave myself a second to recover from the head rush, walked over to the car, and got in. "Thanks."

He kept staring straight ahead.

I buckled my seat belt and he put the car in drive. "I need to talk to Dan."

Garrett nodded. "That's one thing we can agree on."

"You should hear all the things I found out. Lloyd McLaughlin was a lying, cheating son of a bitch and a bad neighbor." I slumped down a little in the seat. Holding my head up was starting to feel like a bit of a chore.

Garrett turned left on Camellia. "Do tell."

"Get this. After Devin and Miriam Stevenson built their deck, the first time they had friends over, he called in a noise complaint. They were six sixty-year-olds sitting on a deck drinking wine and talking about their IRAs. The next time they had people over, he put 'Macarena' on repeat and blasted it over the fence." I wasn't even sure that song had words.

"Annoying."

"Totally. He would yell at people who parked in front of his house, but he couldn't do anything about it. Then cars parked in front of his place would be keyed. Nobody could prove it was him, but everyone knew it was. People stopped parking in front of his house because they didn't want their cars to get jacked up." Such a cowardly way of doing things. I hated that.

"Terrible."

"I know!" I settled farther down in the seat, feeling a little sleepy. "Maybe I should talk to Dan tomorrow. It's getting late."

"It's four thirty in the afternoon, Rebecca." He threw some side-eye my way.

"Really? It feels so much later. Must be because the sun's going down so much earlier." Would it be so bad to go to bed at five? Not every day. Just once in a while.

"The day drinking might have played a role, too, don't you think?" Garrett asked.

He had a point, although my day drinking had been done for a good cause. I shrugged. Fighting would take too much effort when I needed all my strength to keep my eyes open. Then again, why bother? It wasn't like I was driving. Closing them for a second wouldn't hurt anything. I'd just be resting them.

"We're here, sleepyhead."

I started awake. I must have fallen asleep despite my best efforts. I checked my chin for drool, then looked out the window. We were in front of City Hall. "I thought you were taking me home, that I'd talk to Dan tomorrow."

"I think you should talk to Dan today. I think you should talk to him right now." Garrett opened my car door.

I rubbed my eyes, then remembered I'd put on mascara that morning. I flipped down the vanity mirror to make sure I hadn't raccooned myself. I was a little smudgy, but still totally publicly presentable. Probably. "Fine. I'll do it now. You're right. Might as well get it over with so I can go back to worrying about POPS instead of Lloyd McLaughlin."

Garrett took my arm and guided me up the steps, which I thought was kind of unnecessary until somehow the toe of my boot caught on one of the risers. "They really should make those things a consistent height. Someone could hurt themselves."

"Mmm-hmm," he said, without looking at me.

Vera Bailey was at the desk when we walked in. "Hey, Rebecca. Hi, Garrett. Come on in. Dan's expecting you."

"He is?" I looked over at Garrett.

"I texted him from the car. I wanted to make sure he could see you now." He kept moving me forward.

"Oh." Garrett seemed to feel a lot more urgency about this conversation than I did at the moment.

"So when are you going to reopen POPS?" Vera asked.

"When Carson's finished redoing the kitchen." I followed her down the hall to Dan's office with Garrett still keeping that grip on my elbow.

"I'm totally missing it." She stopped, pulled the waistband of her uniform pants out to show that they were loose. "I lost five pounds since I stopped snacking on that Mexican chocolate popcorn you made. I don't want to gain 'em back, but those Snickers bars in the vending machine start calling my name around two thirty in the afternoon."

"I'll make you a special batch and drop it by." At least I'd still have one customer left when I reopened, despite Megan's smear campaign.

"Thanks, Rebecca. You're a pal." She knocked on Dan's open office door. "Rebecca and Garrett here to see you, sir."

Dan stood from behind his desk as we walked in.

"I have got so much to tell you!" I plopped down in one of the chairs in front of his desk.

"And you'll have plenty of time to do that," he said. He took my hands and then snapped handcuffs around my wrists. "Rebecca Anderson, you are under arrest for impeding a police investigation."

"Dan, you've gotta listen to me. That Lloyd guy was a jerk. Everybody hated him. Everybody. There are tons of people with motives to do him harm. I mean, maybe whoever it was didn't even really mean to kill him. Maybe that person just wanted to make him a little sick, you know? Payback? For all the trouble he caused around the neighborhood. Regardless, there are bunches of people who totally hated him and could have poisoned that popcorn." I sat back in my chair. "I can give you names if you want to make a list of people to investigate."

Dan tapped his pen against his notebook but didn't look like he was ready to take dictation. "Rebecca, what is it that you think I do here all day?"

It wasn't the question I'd been expecting. It took me a few seconds to make the transition. "You do sheriff-y things."

He took in a deep breath and blew it out. "What do you suppose sheriff-y things are?"

I shrugged. "I don't know for sure. You do the stuff that needs to be done to keep our town safe."

He smiled at me. "That's right. That's exactly what I do. Do you suppose that one of those things might be to investigate someone who had died under suspicious circumstances?"

"Of course. That's what I'm helping with." Finally, we were about to be on the same track. He could start investigating. I could go home.

"What makes you think I don't already know all about Lloyd McLaughlin and his neighbors?" His tone was pleasant, but his face was getting less smiley by the second.

"I, uh, don't know. I just knew that Megan was only talking about me poisoning Lloyd, not about anybody else poisoning him."

"And you think that Megan is the first person I go to when I discuss my ongoing investigations?"

"Well, no, of course not."

"So you think I'm bad at my job?"

"No! Absolutely not! Why would you say that?"

"Because you seem to think that it's beyond the scope of my capabilities to figure out that the victim was unpopular. You seem to think I don't know to check into the whereabouts of the people who hated him around the time he was murdered. You seem to think I don't know how to do my job." With each sentence he leaned closer and closer to me across the desk.

The truth of his words sunk into me. Oh, crap. I'd been a jerk. "Dan, I'm so sorry. I got so wrapped up in clearing my name that I didn't think to check what you were doing. I didn't know."

"Because you don't need to know. You're not a detective on a case. You're an ordinary citizen who needs to stay out of the way of my investigation." He had his cop face on. It was as if someone had wiped the expression clean off his face.

I'd thought he was joking. I'd been sure he was joking. I'd been absolutely flabbergasted to find out he wasn't joking.

Dan had arrested me. Thrown me in the hoosegow. Locked me up. Put me in the pokey. I couldn't believe it. Yet here I was, wearing orange scrubs with a pair of black plastic shower shoes. Vera told me I was lucky that Dan had let me keep my own bra and panties and that I probably shouldn't complain.

Shocked, however, didn't begin to describe how I felt about Garrett telling me that he was firing me as a client, though.

"I'm sorry, Rebecca, but you don't follow my advice and, frankly, representing you is a clear conflict of interest.

You're going to have to find another lawyer." He'd said it as if he'd been practicing the speech. Given the looks exchanged by Dan and Garrett, it was possible that he had.

"I am not going to be represented by Russ Meyer!" Russ was an okay guy if you needed to fill a plate at a dinner party, but trust him to get me out of jail? I didn't think so.

"Suit yourself, Rebecca. You can hire any lawyer you want except me." He rolled his shoulders like he was uncomfortable. "I'll go by your place and pick up some things for you, if you want." Then he left.

Vera had given me the scrubs, a pillow, some sheets and a very scratchy blanket and had led me to this cell.

After Faith left, Huerta came in to our cell block. "You want to take the beast for a walk?" he asked.

I jumped up. "You bet."

Huerta unlocked the cell door and both Sprocket and I practically ran through. I've always thought of myself as an indoor-type person, perfectly content in an interior space. Then I spent twenty-four hours in a cell. I could not wait to get outside, feel the sunshine on my face, the breeze on my skin. Huerta let us out of the cell and put a leash on Sprocket.

"Don't mind me," Cathy said, waving weakly from her bunk. "I'll be right here."

"You'll have your exercise time as soon as we get back," Huerta assured her.

She snorted. "Whatever."

We left the cell block and headed for the side door that

I knew led out onto the street. "Uh, where are we going?" I'd expected to go behind City Hall, not out onto the street.

"For that walk?" Huerta looked at me as if I'd suddenly become dim.

I pointed. "Out there? In front of everybody?"

"It's that or walk up and down the corridors. I thought you might want some fresh air." He held the door open.

I did. More than anything. Well, not more than anything. I didn't want it more than my self-respect, despite how good the fresh air smelled as it swirled in the door.

Sprocket whined and scratched on the doorpost with his paw. Then he looked up at me with his big brown melting eyes. I took a step toward the door. Apparently I wanted my dog to be happy more than I wanted self-respect. This was going to suck. The town gossips had already had enough of a field day with me. Now I was going to be strutting around downtown in my orange prison scrubs. There'd probably be video on YouTube before we even got back to my cell.

"It's Saturday, Rebecca," Huerta said as if reading my mind. "Downtown is half-deserted anyway."

"Whatever half is here will be on the phone with the other half before we get halfway down the block." I took a deep breath, blew it out, straightened my shoulders and said, "Let's go."

Huerta opened the door farther and I squinted into the sunlight. The air was crisp and the sky was that light blue you only see in the late fall and winter. I inhaled, sure I could smell the tang of the lake and taste it on my tongue. Sprocket danced down the steps as if the judges of Westminster were assessing his prance. My footsteps were almost as light. Who cared what people thought, anyway? Sticks and stones and all that.

A pickup truck slowed down as it went by us and honked.

I cringed. Oh, yeah. Apparently, I cared what people thought. My face got hot and I knew I was red to my curly brown roots.

Then Olive Hicks leaned out of the cab of the pickup and yelled, "Hang tough, Rebecca! You've got this!"

I looked over at Huerta. He shrugged. We kept walking. Sprocket stopped to sniff every other bush and tree.

A blue sedan with a dirty white top squealed over to the curb. Delia Woodingham hopped out and ran toward us, her arms wide. Huerta stepped in front of me and held up his hand. "No touching," he barked. "Stand down."

Delia stopped. She shot Huerta a look and then peered around him. "Don't let the turkeys get you down, Rebecca." Then she was gone.

"What's going on?" I asked Huerta.

He shrugged. "You remember how well Cynthia used the media when Antoine was in jail?"

I did. It had horrified me a little at the time. Dan had gotten caught in the crossfire at least once.

"Well, she's still good at it." Huerta smiled a little.

I stopped walking. I hadn't seen a newspaper or watched a television newscast since my unfortunate incarceration. "What did she do?"

Huerta stopped at the newspaper kiosk on the corner, popped in a quarter, pulled out a paper and handed it to me. The headline read: "Local Businesswoman Incarcerated." Underneath, a subhead read: "Sheriff Suspends Due Process." Underneath that was a big old photo of yours truly. I wasn't sure when the photo had been taken, but it looked like I was at least wearing lipstick.

"Crap." Poor Dan. No wonder he'd been so terse with me about Emily. He was probably ready to strangle me. Then another thought hit me. "You know that Antoine is going to see this, don't you?"

Huerta nodded.

"I'm surprised he's not already here." This was the kind of thing he'd use as an excuse to meddle. He'd want to rescue me, even though when I'd really needed rescuing he'd been useless.

Huerta shrugged. "Maybe he's finally given up."

"And maybe pigs fly." I didn't think Antoine even really wanted to get back together with me. I mean, don't get me wrong. I had been a good wife, but I hadn't been that good. It was more like he'd gotten into the habit of pursuing and didn't quite know how to stop it yet.

His presence always made everything more complicated, though. He irritated Dan and pissed off Garrett. On the other hand, I was pretty irritated at Dan and pissed off at Garrett at the moment. What did I care? In fact, maybe I should irritate them a little more.

A group of people were gathered on the stone steps in front of the courthouse. "What's going on over there?"

"I'm not sure. Some kind of announcement from one of the city council candidates." He checked the time.

We stopped to watch. Justin Cruz came out of the front door of the courthouse in a suit that fit him just right. No tie.

"Nice suit," Huerta observed. "He didn't get that here in Grand Lake. That's for sure."

I wasn't sure I'd seen Huerta in anything besides his

uniform since I'd moved back to Grand Lake. "I didn't know you were interested in clothes."

He shrugged. "You wear a uniform all day every day for work, you want to make sure what you wear in your off hours is worthwhile."

Justin cleared his throat and the crowd quieted. "I am coming forward because a blackmail threat has been made against me."

There was a little gasp from the crowd. This was juicy. Samantha Freeman snapped pictures as fast as her finger could click.

"I received a DVD with a recording of me letting myself into the back of the First Community Church on several occasions. The blackmailer assumed I was entering the church late at night for nefarious reasons and told me that the recording would be made public unless I dropped out of the city council race." He paused and looked around the crowd, making eye contact with several people. His gaze locked on me. He gave me a quizzical look and then nodded.

I nodded back, not sure if I'd just agreed to something or acknowledged something. I hoped nods weren't contractual.

"I decided to come forward myself. Yes. I have been letting myself into the church at least once a week late at night for the past year. I'll let Reverend Lee tell you what I've been doing." Justin stepped aside.

Reverend Lee stepped forward. "For the past six or seven months, I would come into the church to find minor repairs having been completed during the night. Sometimes it's been as simple as a squeaky hinge on a door, but there have also been plumbing repairs and some electrical issues resolved. I didn't know who was doing it. I mentioned it during a few of my sermons, but no one came forward to take credit." He clapped Justin on the shoulder. "I found out today that it was Justin who had taken the words of Matthew 6 very much to heart. He has been anonymously making repairs to keep the church running and safe."

Justin stepped up next to Reverend Lee again. "To the blackmailer out there, I will not be cowed. I want to serve the city of Grand Lake, and you will not stop me."

He walked down the steps with Reverend Lee. They walked across the street and got into Justin's sedan and drove away.

I couldn't wait to tell Cathy what I'd seen when I got back to the cell. Well, minus the parts about people running up to hug me and yell words of support. I didn't think she was getting much of that and I didn't want to lord it over her. I wanted to tell her about Justin.

"And at the end, he got into this car with Reverend Lee and took off like some kind of special God squad," I told her as I brushed out Sprocket's fur. He snorted.

So did Cathy. "That smarmy little son of a bitch. He lucked out on that one."

"What do you mean?" I hadn't thought being blackmailed represented any kind of luck at all, much less the good kind.

"Seriously, what are the odds of someone blackmailing you in a way that reveals a bunch of good deeds you're doing? I mean, I guess if they have proof that they aren't good deeds, they send anonymous notes to the *Sentinel* rather than DVDs to your doorstep. Still, though. He lucked out." She shook her head. "Some people really do have all the luck."

I stopped brushing. "You think Justin's up to something else?"

She stretched and yawned. "Actually, I don't. I tried like hell to dig something up on him since I knew he was planning to run and I couldn't find anything. He's squeaky-clean. Irritatingly so."

"Wait. You were digging around in Justin's life?" It sounded so sneaky, so underhanded, so like someone who had been embezzling from the city for years.

"Of course I was. It's called opposition research. It's how the game is played, my dear." Cathy rolled onto her side and did a few leg lifts. My hips creaked just watching her.

A thought occurred to me. "Do you think that's how someone found out about your scam? Someone did opposition research and figured out what you were up to and turned you in?"

"I prefer to call it my arrangement rather than scam. Scam sounds so . . . negative." She turned and did leg lifts on the other side.

I wasn't sure how you could put a positive spin on embezzlement, but that seemed like an argument for another time. "I mean, do you think that the person who sent the anonymous note to the *Sentinel* was one of the other city council candidates, someone who knew you were planning to run and wanted you out of their way?"

Cathy stopped leg-lifting and sat up, arms banded around her bent knees. "I suppose. I'm still not sure how any of them would have figured it out, though. Like I said, I was careful. Even my husband didn't know what I was up to. I don't think any of them are that smart."

"Well, someone was. Someone figured it out. You didn't turn yourself in." I finished brushing Sprocket and put away his brush.

"True enough," she said.

The door to the cell block opened and the three of us jumped to attention.

"Your buddy Faith stopped by with these," Vera said. At least, I was pretty sure it was Vera. She looked like a big stack of pillow and linens on top of two legs.

"What is all that?"

"Pillows, blankets, curtains, a throw rug." Vera set the stack down and unlocked my cell door. She slid the stack through with her foot and then clanged the door shut again. "She said it didn't look cozy in here."

She had a point, but I didn't think cozy was one of the concepts whoever had designed the holding cells had been going for. I went through the stack. There were enough pillows to turn the bottom bunk into a daybed arrangement. I knew what to do with most of it, but I wasn't sure what she'd thought I was going to do with the drapes. Vera saw me puzzling over them.

"She wanted us to bring in a frame so you could section off the, uh, bathroom area. She thought you might want a little more privacy."

She wasn't wrong about that. "And?" I asked.

Vera sighed. "I'll check with Dan. I couldn't figure out anything that you'd be allowed to have back here that would work." Vera pushed herself off the wall and left.

"Must be nice," Cathy said.

"Hmmm?" I wasn't sure what she was talking about

and I was trying to figure out how to use those drapes. Faith wasn't wrong about the privacy thing.

"To have friends bringing you things." Cathy gestured around her cell. "Nobody brought me any extra pillows."

"You want one? I'm pretty sure there are more than I can use here." I held one up.

Cathy eyed it. "I wouldn't say no."

It took both of us to get it through the bars from my cell to hers, me pushing and her pulling, but we did it. She set it on her bunk and lay down on it. "Ah," she said. "That's nice. My neck has been killing me since I got here. This will definitely help."

I sat down on my bunk. "Nobody has brought you anything? Nothing?"

She sighed. "Nope. I think everyone wanted to distance themselves from me as quickly and completely as possible."

"I'm sorry." I didn't know what else to say.

"It's amazing how happy everyone is to accept gifts without questioning where they came from and how fast they back away once they find out." She lay down on the floor and started doing sit-ups again. I was pretty sure her workout routine was fueled by anger.

"They're probably embarrassed," I said.

"My husband wasn't embarrassed to come on that trip to London with me. Geraldine wasn't embarrassed to ride in my Lexus. Neither of them were embarrassed to go on shopping trips to Chicago with me." The pace of the sit-ups picked up.

At this rate, she was going to look like Arnold Schwarzenegger in his glory days by the time she went to trial. "You're friends with Geraldine?"

"I thought I was. I'm not sure anymore." The sit-ups got even faster.

"She's one of the city council candidates."

"I know. She's using all the campaign ideas I was going to use." Cathy was starting to blur she was moving so fast.

"Why were you going to run?" She'd clearly had a pretty good thing going for her. London. Paris. Fancy cars.

"It was time to start moving up. That's the way these things work. You start out small. You make a few connections. You learn how the system works. People start to know your name. Next it's city council. After that, maybe mayor." Thank goodness the sit-ups were slowing down.

I made a noise in the back of my throat.

"I get your point," she said. "No one's going to be mayor of Grand Lake until Allen dies or decides to retire. So maybe state representative after that. Before too long, you're looking at senator and representative. Imagine the bank you can make on those positions."

"Bank?" Sometimes I felt like Cathy didn't even speak the same language I did.

"Sure. People need favors. They pay for them all kinds of ways. Sometimes it's actual cash, but a lot of times its trips and dinners and products. It's all good stuff." She collapsed onto her bunk. "Or it would have all been good stuff."

Sometimes it was hard to feel sorry for Cathy.

Eight

I was tired of playing Sudoku and reading. I'd counted the tiles on the ceiling of my cell. If I didn't find something to distract me soon, I was going to start exercising like Cathy. Instead, I decided to use Cathy to distract me.

"What were you going to do with all that money anyway?" I asked. She'd had a pretty nice life. A house. A car. A husband.

"What does anyone do with money? I was going to spend it. I did spend it." She turned on her side on her bunk so she could look at me through the bars.

"On what?" I knew some of the things I would spend a windfall on. It was always interesting to hear what other people's fantasies were.

She shrugged. "I always wanted to go to Italy. That's expensive. Don wanted a Jet Ski. I really like that one eye cream with the sea kelp. That stuff's crazy expensive."

"You wanted it bad enough to risk everything else?" It didn't sound like enough to me. I was as unhappy as the next woman about wrinkles, but I wasn't willing to break the law to fight them.

She said, "I didn't think I was risking it. I didn't think I'd get caught. I still can't believe I did. I was so careful."

I flipped over onto my stomach and kicked my feet up in the air. There really was no comfortable position on this bed, even with all the extra pillows. "How'd it happen? What was your big mistake?"

"I'm still not sure." She did a pull-up on the upper bunk. "Someone noticed, though. Someone did some digging."

Now that was interesting. Apparently there was someone else in town who couldn't resist digging into things that didn't make sense to them. "They haven't come forward?"

"Nope. Anonymous tip to the *Grand Lake Sentinel* and then they peaced out." She did another pull-up.

"What kind of tip? To look at your finances? Or into one of the companies?" I asked.

She plopped back down on her bunk. "What's it to you? Hasn't nosing around where you have no business gotten you in enough trouble?"

It had, but I was bored. "I can't see what more trouble I can get into now." I kicked the bars.

"You have a point. It was a tip to look into one of my companies. Hutchinson Paper Supply." She made a face.

Interesting. "So who would know to look into that?"

She sat up and stared at me. "Do you think I've thought about anything else since I got here? Do you think I wouldn't have found a way to bitch-slap whoever it was if I could figure it out?"

I'd sort of thought that she might be thinking about what she'd done and how she could make amends, but I might not have the full measure of Miss Cathy yet. "Did anyone know you had set up fake vendors? Anyone who might have had an inadvertent slip of the lip?"

She shook her head. "No. Not even my husband."

That didn't seem likely. "Where did he think all that extra money was coming from?"

She smiled. "My awesome investment skills."

I counted a few more tiles, and thought. "What about someone at one of the banks?"

She chewed her lip. "That's possible, but I really spread my business around. It would have taken one heck of a set of coincidences for someone at one of the banks to figure it out."

I stewed on that while I scratched behind Sprocket's ears. "What about someone who saw you at one of the other banks?"

"Nope. I did pretty much everything electronically."

"There has to be something. There has to be some way someone else found out."

"No shit, Sherlock," Cathy said and turned her back.

Annie showed up to my jail cell with an armload of flowers.

"I'm locked up for the weekend, not dying." Although the possibility that I might die of boredom had occurred to me.

"Faith told me what your cell looked like. I figured flowers brighten up everything. These were for an order that was canceled." Annie set the flowers down and pulled her long gray hair back and knotted it.

"They look like funeral flowers. Who cancels a funeral?" I asked. Lucky people, I supposed.

"Someone who didn't die. Well, the relatives of someone who didn't die." Annie moved a frond of fern into a different position and looked at it critically.

"Someone was sick enough that their relatives started ordering flowers and then got better instead?" Cathy asked.

Annie shrugged. "Pretty much. I think they might have actually been hoping to use them, but I'm not judging."

"Who?" That sounded like one callous group of relatives.

"Someone who's a tougher old broad than anybody realized." Annie sniffed a lily.

"Come on. Give. A little gossip might liven things up for us." Cathy leaned forward at her bars to try to sniff a bouquet.

"An old lady over at Loving Arms. Marta something." Annie rearranged some baby's breath.

I felt like my own heart might have just stopped. "Marta Hansen?" I asked.

She smiled and nodded. "Yeah. That's the name. Miraculous recovery. The doctors thought she was a goner. Apparently she's made of iron."

I sat down hard on my cot. "I don't believe it."

"I'm sorry," Annie said, setting down the flowers and walking over to the bars of my cell. "I didn't realize you were close with her."

"I'm not, but I just spoke to her. Only a few days ago.

She's the one who owned my shop before Allen did." She'd seemed frail, but not sickly.

"Oh." Annie bit her lip. "That's not good."

"People being at death's door is generally not good, no." It seemed like an obvious statement.

Annie cringed as she said, "Not just that. They think Marta was poisoned somehow."

"Poisoned?" I was up off my cot and over at the bars. "Like Lloyd was poisoned?"

Annie made a face. "Pretty much."

"And she got sick right after I visited her?" I pressed.

"Again. Pretty much." Annie took a step back from my cell.

"Crud." I started to pace.

"Did you bring her any popcorn?" Annie asked.

My heart sank. "Annie, I did."

"Don't panic. I'll leave the flowers and go see what else I can find out." Her face creased with concern.

I thought for a second. "See if someone else visited her. Maybe someone came after me and poisoned her."

"I'll see what I can find out." She looked over at Vera. "Could you open the cell door, please?"

"I don't think I can let her have those." Vera frowned at the flowers.

"Why not?" Annie asked.

She plucked one of the roses from a bouquet and poked her finger with the stem. "She might make a weapon out of them."

"Out of a Coral Beauty? What's she going to do, sharpen the stem into a shiv? And for Pete's sake, who's she going to stab? Sprocket?" Annie shooed her away from the arrangements. "And don't mess with the flowers. I spent hours on these.

"What about the vases?" Vera asked. "She could do something with them."

"No vases. These are actually cardboard. One hundred percent biodegradable, too." She smiled. "It's good to be green."

Vera sighed. "Well, okay, then."

"Thank you."

Vera cuffed me and opened the cell and Annie strode in and began arranging the flowers around the cell. She frowned at the toilet. "Too bad we can't use that as some kind of container."

"It's actually serving a purpose at the moment. I'd just as soon not stick flowers in it." It was already hard enough to keep Sprocket from using it as a water bowl.

"Suit yourself." She placed one last bouquet, plucked a pink pearl lily from it, came out of the cell and handed it to Vera. "I hope you have a lovely weekend."

Vera blushed. Apparently it had been a while since anyone had given her flowers. "Thank you."

Annie walked toward the door out of the cell block. "I'll see you tomorrow, Rebecca."

"Thanks, Annie."

The door clanged shut behind them. I went over and sniffed one of the bouquets, loving its delicate aroma and the steel underneath the soft exterior of my friend as she did whatever she could to help me. I swear those tears in my eyes had to be from allergies.

Cathy sauntered up to the bars between us. "So now you've poisoned two people?"

"Of course not!" I hadn't. I hadn't poisoned anyone. This was all a terrible mistake. I had to talk to Dan again. I had to make him realize what kind of mistake he was making. Someone was framing me. Someone was trying to ruin me and they were doing a damn good job.

Cynthia came by in the afternoon. She had some books and magazines and some puzzles and a lot of questions. Vera brought me down to the conference room to meet her. If I hadn't already felt shabby in my orange jumpsuit, I definitely did after seeing Cynthia. She had on the simplest outfit: black trousers with a white silk shirt and a string of pearls. She made it look like the essence of glamour and sophistication.

"How on earth did you manage to become a person of interest in yet another poisoning when you're safely tucked away here behind bars?" She thumped a file box onto the table. "And when will your brother-in-law enter the digital age?"

"I don't have an answer to either of those questions." I reached for the files.

"Uh-uh-uh," she said, giving my hand a whack. "No peeking at what they've got on you until I hear all about it. I don't want to taint your recollection."

I leaned back in the chair, nursing my smacked hand and trying to marshal my emotions. I knew I hadn't done anything wrong. I knew I hadn't poisoned Lloyd McLaughlin or Marta Hansen. I didn't know why I couldn't seem to convince anybody else of that. How many other people would get hurt in someone's attempt to bring me down? Cynthia was still my best way to clear my name, though. I needed to make sure she knew everything I knew. "You know everything about Lloyd already."

She nodded. "What about this Marta person? You knew her, didn't you?"

"Yes. Well, sort of. Not well. I visited her a few days ago."

"And you brought her popcorn," she prompted.

She made it sound like it was something I had to confess. "I didn't want to show up empty-handed."

She rolled her eyes. "You are so Midwestern."

"You're saying that like it's a bad thing." I'd come to appreciate a few things about my Midwestern roots over the years. Showing up with food was a good thing as far as I was concerned.

She held up her hand. "Whatever. Go ahead."

"That's it. I brought her the hull-less popcorn so it wouldn't upset her stomach." I wasn't sure what else to tell her about it.

Cynthia made a few notes on her tablet. "Considerate of you. Did you also lace it with some kind of poison?"

I shoved my chair back. "Of course not!"

"Easy there, champ," Cynthia said. "So if you barely know this woman, why did you visit her and bring her popcorn? Dan says you hate that place. Loving Arms Retirement Community, is it? Something about a bad experience in your teens."

"I've been trying to find out who owned the house my shop is in during the 1950s so I can figure out who might have written the diary that was hidden in the wall of my kitchen so I can figure out who the secret Nazi was and if something happened to the diary writer." I didn't see why it was relevant, but there was nothing to hide.

Cynthia blinked a few times before she responded. "Of course."

"Marta owned the house before Allen Thompson. She inherited it from her father, but they never lived there. They used it as a rental property. The Brancatos lived there, and their daughter, Esther, supposedly went missing right around the time she graduated from high school." I leaned forward. Maybe I could get Cynthia interested in Esther's case and she'd help me out. "Her diary makes it sound like someone was threatening her before she disappeared."

Cynthia tapped a few more notes into her tablet. "I still don't get why you would poison Marta Hansen."

I sat back. So much for getting Cynthia interested in a cold case. "Because I didn't. I wouldn't."

"But you did bring her popcorn." She made some notes on her tablet.

"Was it the popcorn that was poisoned? Are they sure about that?" I mean, the woman ate other stuff, didn't she?

Cynthia sighed. "Yes. They're sure it was the popcorn. Plus after she'd recovered, Marta told the doctor that she was sure that the person responsible was that meddling girl with the dog."

"Why? Why would she say that?" I cried.

Cynthia shrugged. "You tell me. Maybe you were the only person to visit her."

I nodded, feeling even more miserable than when we started. "Can I see the files now?"

She shoved the box over toward me. It was surprisingly full considering there didn't seem to have been much time to gather that much information. I pulled the first folder out. It held transcripts of a series of interviews Dan had done.

I felt the heat rising to my face as I read over them. He'd talked to every one of the people at Lloyd McLaughlin's wake who had a reason to hate Lloyd. Every one of them. I hadn't known. Of course, I suppose there was no reason for me to know. There might even have been a reason for me not to know. I guessed you weren't supposed to fill one of the suspects in a case in on what you were doing in your investigation. One thing was very clear. I owed Dan an apology. I'd acted like he wasn't doing his job when he was doing everything he could to solve the case and clear my name. Stupid Megan. It was all her fault. If she hadn't started all those rumors about me, I would have been content to just read my found diary and let Dan do his work.

I pulled the next folder out. It held photographs of various pieces of evidence. It included the tin Lloyd McLaughlin's poisoned popcorn had been in. I froze with it in my hand. It was one of the new tins. The ones that had just come in. The ones that I had only used to deliver popcorn to the city council members so far.

All that work Dan had done investigating who hated Lloyd McLaughlin had been for nothing. The only place he could have gotten that tin was from one of the city council candidates. It had never been meant for him. He wasn't the intended victim. "Cynthia," I said. "You need to talk to Dan."

"What about?"

"The popcorn that poisoned Lloyd was from the batch that I made for Allen to give to the city council candidates. It was never meant for Lloyd." A horrible thought occurred to me. "Cynthia, you've got to call Dan right now. Every person who's running for city council got a tin. They could all be poisoned."

"All?" Blood drained from her face. "You poisoned them all?"

"No! I didn't poison any of them. That's the point. I have no idea who put the poison in or when they did it or how many of those tins they could have poisoned. We have to get them back and we have to get them back now!"

Cynthia pounded on the door of the conference room. Huerta opened the door. He must have seen the look on her face and realized something was wrong because his eyes went from sleepy to alert in an instant. "What is it?" he asked.

"Get Dan. Get Vera. Get everyone. We have a potential mass poisoning on our hands," she said. "Lloyd McLaughlin might not be the only victim."

In minutes, everyone had mobilized. Phone calls were made. Officers were sent out to gather up tins of popcorn. I sat in the middle of it all feeling helpless. Finally, the hubbub died down.

"That's everyone," Dan said, looking at the list I'd given him. Every name was crossed off.

"Did anyone else eat it?" I asked.

He grimaced. "Pretty much everyone else ate it. Please, Rebecca, that stuff is like crack."

My stomach lurched. "But no one else got sick? No one else . . . died?"

"You think I wouldn't have mentioned it if someone else died, Rebecca?" He glowered at me.

Good point. "So only one tin was poisoned. That feels kind of Russian roulette-ish, doesn't it? Spin the popcorn tin and see which one blows up." Why would anyone only poison one of the tins? They weren't marked. There wouldn't be any way to know who was going to be poisoned.

"Kind of mixing your metaphors there, but yeah. It feels a little like that to me, too. Sort of hard to know who was going to get that tin. Anybody else get any of that special batch?" He rubbed his forehead.

Who else had gotten tins? It hadn't been just the city council candidates, had it? "Oh, no."

"Rebecca, what is it?" Dan asked.

"I gave some of that popcorn to Sally and Trina!" I leapt up from the table and ran out the open door, Sprocket at my heels. I ran down the hall, and burst into the city offices just as Trina raised a chunk of Bacon Pecan Popcorn out of the tin and to her lips.

I swatted it away from her and screamed, "Stop!"

She jumped back from the counter, stared at me for a second, then burst into tears.

Suddenly, I felt like I couldn't breathe. I bent over and rested my hands on my thighs like I'd seen Dario do when he took a break from running. It didn't help. I collapsed onto the ground and panted. Sprocket, always ready to be helpful, licked my face. When my breathing finally returned to something that sounded other than like a monster in a horror movie, I looked up to see Huerta looming over me.

He crouched down next to me. "You run pretty fast when you want to."

I couldn't help but notice that he wasn't breathing hard at all, although I thought I could see a little pink flush on his dark cheeks.

"Why?" Trina wailed from over behind the counter. "Why?"

"The popcorn." I struggled onto my knees and let Huerta help me the rest of the way to my feet. There still wasn't quite enough air going in and out of my lungs to make full sentences. "Might be poisoned."

Trina looked over at Huerta for more explanation. "Turns out the poisoned popcorn Lloyd McLaughlin ate was from the batch Rebecca made for the city council candidates. The same batch yours came from."

"Didn't want you to eat it if it was poisoned." I stumbled over to the counter and leaned against it.

"You cared enough about me to run? Everyone knows you don't run," Trina said wonderingly. She brushed away her tears with the back of her hand. "I'm touched, Rebecca. Really, I am."

"If you're so touched, why did you cry?" None of this was making any sense to me at all.

She blushed. Hard. Like almost to a brick color. "I've, uh, gained a few pounds recently. I thought you were saying I shouldn't eat it because I was fat."

"You're not fat," I said. It's a nearly automatic response. A woman says she's fat and the call and response of femininity requires a "You're not fat" in return.

"Easy for a string bean to say." That sour look she got when she pressed her lips together was back on her face.

I'm not going to lie. I have been blessed with a good metabolism and come from a line of thin people. It didn't seem the time to protest about my figure. "I know. I'm lucky. I still don't think you're fat."

She sighed. "Well, at least you weren't slapping snacks out of my hand as some kind of body-shaming ritual."

I cringed. "Why would you think I would do something like that?"

She shrugged. "Megan's always talking about how mean you are about her food. It didn't seem like too far a stretch to think your Mean Girl ways might extend to humiliating me at my workplace."

"Me? A Mean Girl?" Gobsmacked doesn't begin to describe how I felt. I had never been a Mean Girl. You had to be part of the "in" crowd to be a Mean Girl, and I'd been so far from in I wouldn't even know how to find the door to the outer lobby that led to in.

"Yeah. You know. With all your fancy education and your French husband . . ." Trina said.

"Ex-husband," I corrected almost as a reflex.

She shrugged. "Whatever."

Huerta tapped me on the shoulder. "Come on. Let's get you back to our side of the building before Dan adds attempting escape to the things he's planning to charge you with."

We gathered up Trina's tin of popcorn and went back to the conference room.

I practically danced my way back to my cell after we finished our conversation in the conference room.

"What's gotten into you?" Cathy asked.

"A big old helping of truth, that's what," I said as I stripped off the bed. No way was I leaving those sheets there. I'm not sure what the thread count was, but Faith definitely hadn't gone with the cheap stuff.

"Sounds like it was tasty." Cathy stood up and walked over to the bars to watch me. "What flavor of truth was it?"

"The flavor that says Lloyd McLaughlin was never the person who was supposed to get the poisoned popcorn.

So the way I see it, when I went to his wake and talked to the people there I wasn't obstructing justice because he wasn't the supposed to be the victim. If I wasn't obstructing justice, then I did nothing wrong and Dan has to let me out of here."

"Who was supposed to be the victim, then?"

"Still not one hundred percent sure. I just know it was one of the city council candidates. The poisoned popcorn came from the batch Allen commissioned me to make as their welcome-to-the-political-arena presents." I clapped my hands with the sheer joy of it.

"Well, okay, then." Cathy wandered back to her bunk, clearly unimpressed.

One thing still bothered me. Okay. More than one thing, but one thing most of all. "It's weird. Only one of their tins was poisoned. Everyone else actually ate theirs and was fine. What a relief, right? Although there was a bad moment when I thought maybe Trina and Sally were going to get poisoned, but they'd eaten half of theirs and weren't sick at all. Marta's popcorn came from her own special batch."

"Yes. A relief," Cathy said. She didn't sound relieved, though.

"There." I'd stacked everything up. It wasn't like I had a lot. "Vera," I yelled out the cell. "Huerta! I'm ready to go!"

I sat down to wait.

I waited a long time.

Nine

I sat across from Cynthia and put my head down on the table. I'd spent another night in jail. I'd had to remake my bed, which isn't easy with a bunk bed. I'd had to wash my hair with the icky shampoo that the jail provided and comb it with a comb that was not made for curly hair.

Cynthia had on trouser jeans with boots that made her legs look about three miles long. Over that she had on a white blouse and a cardigan. Somehow she made it look runway worthy. Her hair was smooth and her makeup was flawless.

My orange jumpsuit felt itchy.

"What do you mean Dan isn't dropping the charges?" I asked.

I'd assumed that if the popcorn hadn't been intended for Lloyd McLaughlin, I couldn't be charged for obstructing the investigation into his murder. He wasn't the intended victim. What could it possibly matter if I attended his wake, got a little tipsy, and bonded with all the people who hated him?

"I mean, he's not filling out the paperwork that would drop the charges. He's intending on going ahead with charging you." She held her hands up and shrugged. "He has a point. Lloyd is still the victim, whether he was intended to be or not. You still went to his wake and questioned people. You're still guilty."

"But it was the wrong investigation!" My protests were futile. I knew that. I sat up. Enough with the whining. I wiped my cheeks in case a few tears had leaked out due to frustration. They do that sometimes. "Okay. What's next?"

"Nothing's next. We wait for your day in court and get you out of here. At least, for the time being." Cynthia sat back in her chair, looking relaxed.

I was anything but relaxed. "Right. But shouldn't we be looking into who wanted to poison a city council member?"

She stared at me, her big hazel eyes unblinking. "Do you remember why you're here, Rebecca?"

"I'm here because I went to Lloyd McLauglin's wake and talked to people to find people for Dan to investigate instead of me." I was pretty clear on the concept.

"Right. You interfered in his investigation and he's locked you up. Now you seriously want to interfere with the next phase of his investigation?" She gave me the kind of smile that Ms. Renfrew used to give me when she thought she'd given me everything I needed to solve a geometry proof. One thing I knew for sure was that I never had everything I needed to solve a geometry proof.

"Hey! There wouldn't have been any next phase if it weren't for me. Dan would still be looking into who wanted to murder Lloyd. Now he can look into who wanted to murder . . . Wait a second. Who was supposed to be murdered? Which city council candidate was that tin destined for? Do we know that yet?" I sat back in my chair.

"I don't know and I don't care and neither should you." She pointed at me with her pen.

"It's still my popcorn that was poisoned. It's still blowing back on me until we figure out who really did this." Megan would not let go of this because the person who was poisoned wasn't the person who was supposed to be poisoned in the first place.

Cynthia leaned back and crossed her arms over her chest. "Not we, Rebecca. Dan. Dan needs to figure it out."

I thought about the file folders full of meticulous interview notes that I'd seen. Cynthia was right. Dan would figure it out. If he needed my help, he'd ask for it. "Fine. Did you find the diary? I could be thinking about that instead."

"No. I looked. Haley looked. Garrett looked. No one could find it in your apartment. Are you sure you left it there?" Cynthia packed her things away into her briefcase.

"I'm sure." I chewed my lower lip. Where could it have gone? "Hey! I know. I made a copy of it for Barbara. Do you think you could get it from her?"

"I'll give her a call and ask her to bring it by." She clicked the case shut and knocked for Huerta to come let her out.

"Thanks."

* * *

Cynthia must have been true to her word, because Barbara showed up a few hours later. Huerta came to retrieve me from my cell.

Huerta gestured for me to stick my hands through the slot in the bars so he could handcuff me.

"Is this strictly necessary?" Being handcuffed is surprisingly awkward. I'd already clunked myself on the cheekbone with the chain when I had an itch on my nose. I didn't want to accidentally break a tooth.

"It's a rule." Huerta unlocked the door after I'd withdrawn my hands.

"Haven't you ever heard that rules are meant to be broken?" I gave him what I hoped was a winning smile.

He shot me a look. "Only if you want to end up on your side of the bars instead of mine."

He had a point.

Then he grinned. "Although with you in here, at least Cynthia is coming around more."

"Have you two started going out?" I asked.

He shook his head. "I was, uh, hoping you would put in good word for me."

"Do you think you need one?" I was pretty sure the word for Huerta was going to be *yes*.

"I don't know. She's so sophisticated and elegant and I'm . . ." He gestured down at his uniform.

"Handsome? Strong? Smart?" I suggested.

"I'm a cop. I have an AA degree from the community college. She's a lawyer. She's so smart." He looked wistful.

I smiled. "Yes. She is. I think she's probably too smart to pass up a guy because he doesn't have an advanced degree."

"So you think I have a shot?" Huerta's face brightened.

I almost laughed. "Have you noticed how the temperature in the room goes up when you're both in it?"

"I thought maybe it was just me. I'm kind of hot-blooded." He must have seen the smile quirk at my lips, because he pointed at me and said, "Don't sing, Rebecca."

"Fine. I won't. But the two of you will be able to melt the snow off the roof of the courthouse just with your glances."

"It's that obvious?" He grinned again.

"Apparently to everyone but you. Ask her. Maybe just for a drink. It'll give her a chance to see you in something besides a uniform before she commits to dinner," I suggested.

"Great. I will. Next time she comes in." He let me into the conference room where Barbara was waiting.

"So what have you got for me?" I asked.

She pushed the copy of the diary toward me. "I think I figured out a few more people."

"Great! Which ones?"

"So Dentures McGee here? I'm pretty sure that's Saul Osborne. He had a way of sucking his teeth that was really unattractive. Also, Freckle Face has got to be Angelica Washington." She flipped open the yearbook and pointed at the picture. It was pretty obvious where the nickname had come from.

"Are any of these people still around?" I asked.

"No. At least not those two. Saul went away to college in Virginia and only came back to visit his parents. They passed away decades ago. He might not even still be alive." Barbara looked a little sad.

"What about the people who are just initials? Have you figured any of them out?" I asked.

"Maybe. I think HH might be Dominic Burns." She opened her copy of the diary to a page she'd marked with a colored Post-it. "See here? She talks about how he ran a five-minute mile. I think he was the only boy to do that when we were in high school."

"But HH aren't his initials." I wasn't following.

"I think it might still be a code. She really didn't want anyone to know what she was talking about if they found this."

"Why was she so secretive?"

Barbara blew out a sigh. "Parents were a lot stricter back then. I remember something about her parents finding out that she had gone to a meeting of the chess club and grounding her for a month. They didn't want her to join a club that had boys in it as well as girls. Her dad used to make her do this thing where she had to kneel in the kitchen until he said she could stand up. She had bruises on her knees all the time. All the time. She might not have wanted to risk them figuring out that she was talking about boys."

I shuddered. "That sounds like child abuse."

"It might be now, but back then it was just a father making sure his daughter didn't stray from the straight and narrow. It was a different time." Barbara made a face. "I'm not saying it was a better time, mind you, but people looked at things differently back then."

I thought about that for a moment. I'd chafed against every rule that had been made for me, including ones I'd known were only made to keep me safe. It was a teenager kind of thing. I couldn't wait to get away from Grand Lake, but I'd been willing to wait a little bit. Maybe Esther hadn't. "So different that she might have run away to get some freedom?"

"She wouldn't have been the first girl to do something like that," Barbara said. "It might have felt like the only way out."

Yes, but what would happen once she was out? Where would she go? What kind of job would she have been able to get? I'd had a place to run to. I'd had the Culinary Institute, thanks to Coco's guidance and help. Who had Esther had? A potentially crazy cousin who thought the world was infested with secret Nazis, that's who. "But before she graduated from high school?"

"That's the part that doesn't fit. She was a good student. Smart. Thorough. I would have thought she'd wait until she had that diploma safely in her hands before she took off." She paused. "She wasn't cruel, either. She may not have liked how strict her parents were, but she wouldn't have wanted to hurt them, either."

"What do you think happened, Barbara?" I asked.

She shook her head. "I don't know, Rebecca. None of it makes sense to me. I hate to think that someone could have killed that girl, someone that I most likely knew, but I don't see her running away, either."

I took a deep breath. "I'm going to talk to Dan about it."

"You think he'll listen?"

"I'm not sure, but I have to try."

When Barbara left, I asked Huerta to take me to see Dan before he took me back to my cell. He looked up from his computer when I walked into his office, and his shoulders slumped. "What now, Rebecca?" he asked.

I slipped into one of the chairs across from him. "There's another murder you need to solve."

He pushed back from his desk and laced his hand over his chest. "Who did you poison now?"

"What? Nobody! You know I didn't poison anyone." Part of me wanted to cry and part of me wanted to punch him in the nose. I wasn't sure either would get me what I wanted at the moment, but I was pretty sure both of them would feel really good.

Dan held up his hands before I could decide. "Everyone's a suspect until we figure out who was really responsible. Now whose murder am I supposed to be solving now?"

I plunked the copy of the diary down in front of him. "Esther Brancato's."

"Who?"

"Esther Brancato. The girl whose diary I found in the wall." I tapped the copy of the diary.

"What about her?" He made no move to pick up the pages.

"I think she was murdered. She had a bunch of freaky things happening to her. A weird case of food poisoning. Getting shoved into traffic. Someone put a Star of David in her locker. Then she disappeared. When I tried to read about it in the old copies of the newspaper, someone had burned out those sections of the microfiche." I sat back in the chair. I'd made my case.

"How on earth does that add up to her being murdered?" Dan looked at me the way he had when I'd explained how mayonnaise was made, like I had somehow stepped outside the bounds of logic.

I took a deep breath. Mayonnaise existed and I was pretty sure Esther had met with foul play. "I think it's a pattern, don't you?"

"No. I don't. I think someone pulled a prank on her at school and she tripped on a sidewalk and she got some kind of bug and then she ran away." He shoved the diary back at me.

"What about the microfiche?" I countered.

He shrugged. "Those bulbs burn hot. It'd be easy to accidentally mess up the film. It's a bunch of coincidences."

"A few too many, don't you think?" I leaned forward, trying to make my case.

He shook his head. "Not really."

"Dan!"

"Look. I have one murder and one attempted murder to solve. Even if Esther Brancato was murdered, it's not exactly high on my priority list at the moment. I'll get to it when I get to it." He sat back in his chair. "By the way, we found out how Lloyd got your popcorn."

I froze. "How?"

"One of the candidates told the messenger to keep the container of popcorn."

"Why?" I sat back offended. Why would someone not want my Bacon Pecan Popcorn? What was wrong with them? "Is the person a vegetarian?"

"No. The person is allergic to nuts."

Allen hadn't mentioned any food allergies to be concerned about, but I should have thought to ask. I blushed. "I could have easily made a nut-free batch if Allen had told me."

"Well, it's lucky for Justin Cruz that you didn't. Not so lucky for Lloyd, of course."

"It was Justin's batch?" I thought for a second. "But they were all the same. I didn't put names on them."

"So we still don't know who the poison was intended for. It was just random that it was almost Justin's." Dan didn't look any happier than I felt.

"It could have gone to any one of the candidates." That still bothered me. "Unless only Justin's was left when someone put the poison in. So when was it put in?"

Dan shrugged. "We haven't gone over the route yet."

"So Lloyd was delivering the popcorn?" He didn't seem like the messenger kind of guy, but then again I'd only really gotten to know him through the eyes of his ex-wife and ex-neighbors. Based on their observations, he was a sociopath.

"No. We're still trying to track down all the connections. Right now, all I know is that Justin is the only one who didn't still have his popcorn."

"So Lloyd could still be the intended victim? Someone could have put the poison in anywhere along that path." I slumped back in the chair. It felt like we kept taking two steps forward just to take three back.

"I suppose. It seems less likely, though."

"Nightmare," I said, leaning my head down on the desk.

"But not your nightmare, right?" He tapped me on the shoulder.

I lifted my head up to look at him. "Definitely still my nightmare. Until you find out and prove who poisoned that popcorn, my reputation is on the line."

He sighed. "Then leave me alone and let me figure it out."

"How about you tell Megan to leave me alone?" No one seemed to understand that I was a victim here, too.

"If she was doing something illegal, I would. While I'd be one hundred percent behind making gossip a punishable crime, I don't think we have enough jail cells to put that into practice," Dan said.

"So who hates the city council?" I asked Dan.

He snorted. "Nobody hates the city council."

"Now," Huerta chimed in. "No one hates them now."

"What does that mean?" I turned to look at him.

"You weren't here for the big showdowns," he said.

That so didn't sound like Grand Lake. "There were big showdowns in the city council?"

Dan shot a look at Huerta. "It's ancient history, Huerta. It doesn't have anything to do with what's going on here."

"Are you sure?" Huerta asked.

"Yes. I'm sure. You know who it was that caused all those problems, and you know he's gone now," Dan said firmly.

"Gone like dead gone?" I asked.

"No, Rebecca. Gone like off the city council and moved away." He leaned down to retie his shoelace. "Not everybody in Grand Lake gets murdered."

"I know that. *Gone* seemed ambiguous. And if whoever it was happened to be a troublemaker . . ." I shrugged.

"And what a troublemaker!" Huerta said. "Didn't matter where he went, there was trouble."

"Who exactly are we talking about?" I asked.

"Reston McGinn," they said in unison and then stared at each other wide-eyed like they might have done something wrong.

"If you say his name two more times, does it conjure him?" I asked.

"I hope not." Dan shook his head. Dan was a calm kind of guy. He wanted to sail through life with smooth water all around him. This McGinn guy didn't sound like a smooth-water person at all. "I'd probably have to get him a personal protective detail."

"That bad?" Wow.

"Yes and no. Reston's heart was in the right place," Dan said.

Huerta snorted.

"It was, Huerta. Really. He wanted protections in place for city workers. He wanted the city to invest in our infrastructure. He wanted good stuff for Grand Lake."

"Those all sound really good to me." Who doesn't want protection and solid infrastructure?

"And he went about getting them in the most obnoxious way possible. People who would have normally been on his side went the other way just so they wouldn't have to vote with him," Huerta pointed out.

"So what happened?" I asked.

"He got voted out."

"Who took his place?"

"Hector Goodwin."

"What happened to him?"

"He, uh, died."

"It sounds like that spot on the council is kind of cursed." One person voted out. One person dead.

"Don't be ridiculous. It's just a coincidence." Dan waved his hand at me like he was shooing a fly.

"If you say so." I shrugged.

"I do." Dan looked at me through narrowed eyes.

"Except that now someone's blackmailing people running for office and trying to poison them." Sounded a little cursed to me.

Dan put his head down on the table. "There is that."

Less than an hour later, Huerta was back at our cells.

"You have a visitor," Huerta said.

"I have lots of visitors." I gestured around my cell, which was looking less intimidating and feeling less uncomfortable practically by the hour.

"I know." He looked uncomfortable.

I looked up from the notes I was making. "Cynthia's back? Did you ask her out?" Maybe he didn't like people seeing them make googly-eyes at each other.

He shook his head.

"Annie?"

More head shaking.

"Faith? Haley? Who?"

He grimaced. "How about you come and see?"

I did like surprises. I wasn't sure being surprised in jail sounded as good as maybe people jumping up from behind the couch and yelling "happy birthday," but I was willing to go with it.

"You know, this would be a lot easier if we didn't have to do this dance with the cuffs every time I had a visitor," I said, rattling at my chains.

"Trust me, it's under discussion," Huerta said. He didn't sound happy about it.

"It is?" I'd mainly been intending on being a smart-ass. I hadn't realized I'd hit on something.

"In the few days you have been in this jail, you have

had more visitors than any other visitor ever. Even prisoners who have had to wait here for weeks before going before a judge or being transferred elsewhere. You also have had more rules broken for you than any other inmate. What's one more? Besides, no one here thinks you're going to make a break for it. Where would you go? No one thinks you're going to get violent, either." He looked down at Sprocket. "After you're done with your visitor, do you want to walk Sprocket?"

"That would be great. Thanks." I gave him what I hoped was a winning smile. "Sorry I've been such a pain."

Huerta shrugged. "It is what it is."

Sprocket and I followed him out of the cell and down the hallway. Sprocket began to growl low in his throat when we were only a few steps in. I patted him as best I could with my cuffed hands. "It's okay, boy. We'll get through this."

Then we went into the interview room, where we found Antoine, my ex-husband. Who didn't live here. Who had no business here. Who could not seem to leave me alone. Sprocket barked.

He leapt to his feet as I came in. "Rebecca, *mon Dieu*! They have you in chains! Shame! Shame on all of them. It is a travesty, a mockery of the system of justice. It shall not stand, Rebecca."

"What are you doing here?" I gave Sprocket a look and he quieted. I should have known when he'd started growling in the hallway. There were only a few people who seemed to raise his hackles just by being in the same space as him, and one of them was Antoine.

"I saw the news of your arrest and, of course, the subsequent outcry against this tyranny. I came to lend my assistance." He made a little bow.

"I have Cynthia. I have all the assistance I need." I took a step away from him.

Antoine made a noise in his throat that he usually reserved for a sauce that had separated. "Clearly not if you are still in here."

"Cynthia will get me out of here as soon as possible. You know how good she is. There's no need for you to be here. No assistance I need. Go back to California." Antoine's presence always complicated things. Always. Never in a good way.

"At least sit down and let us catch up a bit." He gestured to the chair.

One of the things I hadn't really expected about jail—not that I'd ever in a million years expected to be locked up in one—was the boredom. As many times in the year or so since I'd opened POPS that I'd dreamed of a day with nothing to do stretching in front of me, I hadn't known what that would really feel like.

It didn't feel good.

At least Antoine was never boring. I sat.

"How is the kitchen renovation coming?" he asked.

I shrugged. "Behind schedule and over budget. Pretty much what you would expect."

"Did you decide to replace your range with the same model, or are you taking the moment to upgrade?" His bright blue eyes bored into me. When you were the focus of Antoine's attention, you were absolutely the focus.

I bristled. "What was wrong with my range?"

Antoine laughed. "You know what was wrong with it. You are probably the last person I would need to explain that to."

He was right. I did know. I just didn't like to be judged. "I upgraded. Just a little. It seemed silly not to."

"I agree. What about the refrigerator?" he asked.

I shook my head. "The insurance would only cover so much."

"You should let me help." He reached his hand out toward me.

I didn't take his hand and I shook my head harder. "I appreciate the offer, but no." I didn't actually appreciate the offer. The offer made my skin crawl. If POPS was anything, it was my independence from Antoine. Borrowing money from him? Letting him invest in it? Any scenario that had him getting any of his sneaky little Antoine hooks into it would simply not do. I changed the topic. "So how are you?"

"Fine." He inspected his fingernails. "A little bored."

"I can relate. Boredom sucks."

"Indeed." He crossed his legs. "I was thinking about starting something new."

That was good news. Antoine had laser focus. Whatever he was working on, whoever he was with, had his absolute attention. A new venture would take that laser focus off me, where it had been pretty much since I'd left him. "That's great. What's the new project? A new product line? Maybe a line of kitchen gadgets?"

"That last suggestion has merit, but no." He uncrossed his legs and leaned forward on the table. "I am thinking of starting a small dining establishment. Sort of a L'Oiseau Gris East."

"Where?" I asked, a very bad feeling creeping into my chest.

He opened his arms wide as if to embrace the entire room. "Here, of course."

I choked. "You mean here? In Grand Lake?"

"Where else?" He asked as if there weren't a whole lot of real estate in the United States outside of Grand Lake, Ohio.

Maybe if I could appeal to the businessman in him . . . "There's hardly the kind of clientele here that you get in Napa."

"So maybe I will take it . . . How do you say? Down market? Something more homey. Less demanding on the palate." His smile was sly.

I really did not like where this was going, not one little bit. "That's not really your style, is it?"

He shrugged. "The comfort food is a big trend these days. You know me. I can cook anything."

That was true. He really could. Antoine married both the art and science of cooking in his approach. There simply wasn't a cuisine that could withstand his combination of intellectual rigor and flair. "But won't it be difficult to have two places? It won't be easy to split your attention like that."

He shrugged. "L'Oiseau Gris practically runs itself these days. Besides, I'm here all the time it seems anyway. I might as well have something productive to do."

If he had a restaurant here, he really would be here all the time. I could not imagine the kind of chaos that would make of my life. I was going to have to put a stop to this, but not by openly opposing him. Standing directly in Antoine's way only guaranteed that you would be run over. "Where are you thinking about opening your place?"

He checked his fingernails, which were of course immaculate. "Coco's shop still stands empty."

Coco's shop. The shop next to mine. Hollering distance from my kitchen to its. I walked over to the door and knocked. "Huerta, come get me. This conversation is finished."

Ten

It was finally my day in court. Vera led me in through
the back entrance. The courtroom was packed. I was a
little embarrassed being led in still wearing my orange
jumpsuit. At the sight of me, a pained noise went up from
the crowd. I took my seat next to Cynthia. "I think you
should have brought me some street clothes," I whispered.

"No. I shouldn't have. Trust me on this one. You want
to look as pathetic as possible." Cynthia smoothed the
skirt of her own immaculate suit.

I'd spent most of life trying to avoid looking pathetic.
"Why?"

"Public sympathy. It's totally working in your favor."
She pulled up a photo on her phone and pushed it across
to me. People holding signs. Signs that read "Free Rebecca" and "Let Rebecca Go." The last time people held

up signs with my name and face on them in front of the courthouse, it had been the Belanger Bunnies calling for my head on a platter.

"Who's organizing that?" I pushed the phone back to Cynthia.

She shrugged. "No idea. I'm not sure anyone is. It's kind of a grassroots thing. Grew up all on its own."

"Wow." I felt tears pricking at the back of my eyelids. "Can I see it again?"

"Sure." She returned the phone to me.

I enlarged the photo and scanned the crowd. Annie and Faith were front and center, but that didn't surprise me. Jasper was there, bless his heart. So was Janet with her double stroller. Dario and Eric were there. Lloyd Mc-Laughlin's widow was there. Olive Hicks from the Lighthouse League was there, too.

"You okay?" Cynthia asked.

I nodded, not trusting myself to speak.

"Didn't know you had so many friends and supporters, did you?" Cynthia smiled. She turned to the district attorney. "Did you see all of Rebecca's supporters out front, Phillip?"

"O. J. had a lot of public support, too, Cynthia," he said.

"And he was acquitted, wasn't he?" she purred back.

"I sent you some motions last night, by the way." He made it sound dirty, somehow.

"I saw them. Not a lot of notice there, Phillip. I'm not sure how the judge will feel about that." Cynthia's tone was equally as flirtatious. I glanced around for Huerta, but didn't see him. Lucky for Phillip. Huerta could totally take him.

"I did more than I had to, Cynthia. I could have

dropped them on you right here and now. I gave you the advance notice out of the goodness of my heart." He touched his hand to his chest.

She sat up straight. "Really? I didn't realize you had a heart."

Phillip was saved from answering by the entrance of Judge Romero. I had a soft spot for the Honorable Judge Romero. He'd pretty much sided with me on every case that had come before him. While I knew he was a bit of a foodie, I felt that he was also fair. He hadn't sided with me to get free food. In fact, he'd turned down a box of fudge I'd brought him. "As much as it pains me, Rebecca, I must both be above the law and appear to be above the law," he'd said with such a sad look on his face that I'd wanted to cry. No man should have to say no to food if he really wanted it, in my opinion.

I'd given the box of fudge to his secretary and hoped he got to sneak a few pieces that way.

After we did the requisite up-down of standing for the judge and sitting when he did, he banged his gavel and we were off.

"Ms. Anderson, you've been charged with obstructing justice. How do you plead?" Judge Romero sounded a little bored.

Cynthia jumped in. "My client pleads not guilty, Your Honor."

I shot her a look. Hadn't she said I was guilty?

She narrowed her eyes at me and I kept my mouth shut. Cynthia knew what she was doing and after having seen her subdue a man with her bare hands once before, I didn't want to piss her off. Come to think of it, she and Huerta would make an amazing crime-fighting team.

She scribbled a quick note to me: *Just because you are guilty doesn't mean you should plead guilty.*

I nodded. "That's right, Your Honor. Not Guilty."

Romero stared at me for a moment. I couldn't read his expression. He then turned to Phillip. "I see you're charging Ms. Anderson with a felony rather than a misdemeanor."

"I am, Your Honor. This is not Ms. Anderson's first flirtation with this kind of offense," he replied.

Romero sighed. "I'm aware."

That didn't sound good.

"Bail?" he asked.

"We are asking that Ms. Anderson be held without bail, Your Honor," Phillip said.

"You have got to be kidding me," Cynthia shot back. "First of all, this should be a misdemeanor if it should be anything at all. And no bail? Do you seriously think Rebecca is going to flee the country over this?"

Phillip shrugged. "Her ex-husband is in town. He has international ties and plenty of money."

"The operative word being *ex-husband*. Why should the international ties of someone not even related to Ms. Anderson have anything to do with whether or not she gets bail?" Cynthia threw her hands in the air as if completely exasperated.

"Antoine is here?" Judge Romero asked, sitting up a little straighter.

"*Oui*, Your Honor. I am here."

I turned. Antoine stood at the back of the courtroom.

"Welcome back to Grand Lake, Monsieur Belanger," Judge Romero said. I couldn't decide if this was going to be good for me or bad for me. Romero loved Antoine.

Well, maybe not Antoine himself, but Antoine's television show and products.

"Thank you so much, Judge Romero. I am happy to be back. I only wish that the constabulary of this fine town would stop wrongfully imprisoning me and people I care about." Antoine looked like he might cry over the injustice of it all.

Romero cocked his head to one side. "You feel Ms. Anderson has been charged unjustly?"

Antoine shrugged. "I am not an expert in legal matters, but it appears to be curious to me."

Romero stroked his beard. "Ms. Harlen? Anything to say?"

"Your Honor, I move the charge be dropped to a misdemeanor and my client be released on her own recognizance. Anything else is simply ridiculous. She has strong ties to the community. She's a business owner and an upstanding citizen."

"She's in my courtroom an awful lot for someone who's upstanding." Romero leaned back and crossed his fingers across the expanse of his stomach.

"Through no fault of her own," Cynthia replied.

"Whose fault would it be?" Romero asked, head cocked to the other side.

"Each situation has been unique, Your Honor," Cynthia said.

Romero sighed. "As is your client, Ms. Harlen."

I couldn't decide if that was a compliment or not. Based on the tone, I was leaning toward not.

"Your Honor," Phillip cut in. "We are talking about Ms. Anderson deliberately getting in the way of a possible homicide investigation. This is not the first time she's done so. The other times have ended with violence and property destruction. It is for her own safety and the safety of the entire community that I recommend her being held without bail."

"Tell me more about your concerns for the safety of the community," Judge Romero said.

Yeah. How on earth did I endanger the community?

"The last two times Ms. Anderson meddled in an ongoing investigation there was, respectively, a shooting and a fire. We all know the dangers of gunplay in public places, Your Honor. Imagine how terribly wrong things could have gone if not for the quick actions of citizen and fellow attorney Garrett Mills." Phillip looked around and nodded. "Mr. Mills is present and available to testify if Your Honor so desires."

I twisted around in my seat. Sure enough, Garrett was leaning against the wall in the back of the courtroom. I gave him what I hoped was a withering glare. "The traitor," I whispered to Cynthia.

She patted my hand. "Not to worry. We'll make him pay."

"Is that all?" Judge Romero asked.

"I feel it should be sufficient, but no, Your Honor, there's more." Phillip shuffled some papers and brought out a stack of photographs. "If I may, Your Honor?"

Romero gestured for Phillip to bring the photographs to the bench.

"These are photos of Ms. Anderson's shop after the recent fire there. The fire was set by the person who had murdered Ms. Anderson's ex-husband's assistant. She did it to get rid of Ms. Anderson because of Ms. Anderson's interference in the investigation into that death."

Romero winced looking at the photos. "Terrible. Just terrible."

Cynthia got to her feet. "Your Honor, if I may?"

Romero laced his fingers and rested his hands on the desk. "Of course, Ms. Harlen."

"This is all immaterial. It has nothing to do with the case before us and only has to do with other people's actions against my client. She's not responsible for any of these things." Cynthia stood straight and tall.

"But she is responsible for her own behavior, and that's what led these people to do what they did," Phillip said.

"It's ridiculous to blame the victim," Cynthia fired back.

"Her presence is like screaming *fire* in a crowded theater," Phillip said.

Romero held up his hand. "Enough."

Everyone quieted.

"My job, first and foremost, is to apply the rule of law to the matters brought before me. It seems clear to me that Ms. Anderson did indeed insert herself into an investigation where she did not belong and that she did so deliberately."

I hung my head. Cynthia patted my hand and whispered, "Told you that you were guilty. It's not over yet, though."

"My second responsibility is to protect this community." He turned toward me. "Ms. Anderson, you did not deliberately bring about any of these happenings, did you? You did not mean to set off a chain of events that led to public gunplay or arson?"

"No, Your Honor. Absolutely not." There. Someone understood! It wasn't my fault.

He steepled his fingers. "Yet these things occurred anyway. I can only find that your unsupervised presence in the community at this time could endanger yourself and others. You will remain in the Grand Lake jail until the time of your trial, which will be . . ." Judge Romero turned toward his chief of staff.

"In three weeks," she said.

I turned to Cynthia. "What did he say?"

She was already on her feet. "Your Honor, this is a travesty! My client is no more a threat to this community than her dog is."

Romero pointed his gavel at her. "Careful there, Ms. Harlen. Don't push me."

She took a deep breath and shut her eyes for a second. I could almost hear her mental count of ten. She opened her eyes and said, "Your Honor, my client did not shoot a gun or light a fire. She was the victim of those crimes, not the perpetrator."

"And yet trouble seems to follow her. Why don't we keep her and everyone else safe until Sheriff Cooper figures out what's been going on? Or until her trial date. Whichever comes first."

"I strongly protest, Your Honor." Cynthia squared her shoulders and glared.

"Yeah. I got that." Romero winked.

"What if she was supervised?" Garrett stepped up to the railing between the observers and the lawyers.

Romero paused, gavel in air. "Excuse me?"

"You said her unsupervised presence was a danger to the community. What if she was supervised by an officer of the court?" Garrett asked.

"What officer of the court would be taking that responsibility, Mr. Mills?" Romero asked.

"I would." He took another step forward.

I whirled. "Supervise me? Like you're my boss or something?"

"No. Not your boss. Just someone deeply invested in keeping you safe," Garrett said to me.

I still didn't like it.

"That's a big responsibility," Romero pointed out.

"I'm aware," Garrett said.

"What if I don't like it?" I asked.

"Would you rather stay in jail?" Romero asked. "That can be arranged."

I thought for a second. "What kind of supervision would it be? Would we have to be together all the time?"

Romero stroked his beard. "That seems draconian. He should be aware of your whereabouts at all times, but you don't have to be physically in his presence."

I stood. "Judge Romero, may I speak frankly?"

"Are you sure that's wise?" he asked.

"No," I answered. "I'm not sure, but I'm not going to keep quiet any longer."

"Rebecca," Cynthia hissed at me. "Sit down. Let me handle this. We're going to get you out today if you keep quiet."

"No, Cynthia. I will not keep quiet. I am sick of keeping quiet." I turned back to the judge. "Judge Romero, do you understand why I'm in this predicament in the first place?"

"I believe it was well laid out by the attorneys in the matter. You have, in the past, inserted yourself into

investigations and as a result have ended up putting yourself and others in danger."

"Your Honor, you may call it inserting myself into an
investigation as these other men might. I call it searching
for the truth. I never had any intention in any of these
cases of getting in the way of any official investigation.
I simply wanted the truth."

"Okay," he said, sounding unsure. "Where exactly are
you going with this, Ms. Anderson?"

"I'm going right here, Your Honor. I would not be the
first woman who sought the truth and who sought it on
her own terms to be brought down by the patriarchy."

"What?" Cynthia squawked. "What are you doing?"

"I'm just pointing this out. These men here," I said,
pointing at Dan and Garrett, "had me locked away for
trying to clear my own name. Now you're saying you'll
only release me if one of them volunteers to supervise
me? What year is this, Judge Romero? Are we back in
the 1950s, when I would need my husband's permission
to open a bank account? Or get a job?"

"Of course not," Judge Romero spluttered. "I assure
you, Ms. Anderson, I was in no way intending for this
ruling to be sexist."

"It might not be your intention, but it's what's happening, Your Honor." I stopped and took a deep breath. "Ask
yourself, which side of history do you want to be on? The
side that sought equality for women or the side that kept
them down?"

The courtroom was more silent than I'd ever heard it
be. I wasn't sure if anyone was even breathing.

"Your argument is interesting, Ms. Anderson, but in
the end I'm more interested in the safety of this town than

I am in the philosophical underpinnings of this decision," Romero said. "Ms. Anderson will be released into the custody of Mr. Mills until her trial, which will be on . . ." He looked over at his chief of staff again who gave us a date.

Romero banged his gavel and everybody stood up.

Garrett said, "Rebecca, can we talk?"

I glared at him and then turned my back. "Tell him I'm not speaking to him," I told Cynthia.

"I'm sorry, Rebecca," he said. "We're trying to protect you for your own good."

I whirled around. "What kind of patronizing crap is that?"

He took a step back. "I'm trying to keep you safe."

"I'm not a vase to be put on a high shelf out of the way. I'm a person, Garrett." The adrenaline high that had propelled me to my feet was fading away and I was nearly shaking.

"I know that. You're a person who's very dear to me. You're a person that I . . . that I love." He flushed to the roots of his dark hair.

I threw my hands in the air. "Really? This is where you're going to do that? That's how you're going to tell me you love me for the first time? In a courtroom?"

"It'll make a great story to tell our kids," he offered.

"Our what?" What on earth was he talking about?

"Our kids. You want kids, right? I want kids," he said, taking a step toward me.

It was like he was speaking in riddles. "What are you saying?"

Cynthia was leaning back against the table, long legs stretched in front of her. "I think he might be proposing."

I turned to her. "Seriously? You think that's what he's doing?"

"He's not doing it well, but I think it's what he's doing." She shrugged and started packing up her files.

"Did he ever propose to you?" I asked.

She shook her head. "No. He didn't. There were a few times I thought he might be warming up to it, but he never managed to get down on one knee."

I looked up at him standing on the other side of the rail. "He's still not. He doesn't have a ring, either." I turned back to him. "Do you? Do you have a ring?"

"Not yet." Impressively, his cheeks got even pinker.

"Then as far as I'm concerned it's not a proposal, and I'm still not speaking to you." I leaned back. "Huerta, I'd like to return to my cell and gather my belongings now."

"Yes, Your Majesty," he said. "Anything I can do for you, Ms. Harlen?"

To describe the look that passed between Cynthia and Huerta as *smoldering* would be disrespectful to fires everywhere. I needed to fan myself because of the heat coming off the two of them.

"I'm fine," Cynthia said. "Thank you, Officer Huerta."

"You certainly are," Huerta said under his breath as he took my elbow to escort me away.

"Did you ask her out?" I asked, watching Huerta watch Cynthia walk away.

"Not yet. I'm waiting for the right moment." He opened the railing for me to walk out of the courtroom.

"Bwak bwak bwak bwakahhhhh!" I clucked at him.

He clenched his jaw. "I'm not chicken."

"Sure you're not," I said. "Not chicken at all."

* * *

Huerta let me into my cell and didn't close the door after me. "Go ahead," he said. "Pack up."

Once again, I stripped the sheets off the bunk beds and folded them up.

"It's for real this time?" Cathy asked. Her voice sounded so small.

I stopped what I was doing and walked over to the bars between our cells. "Yeah. Well, sort of." I explained the arrangement to her.

She laughed. "You're kidding."

"Nope. Not one little bit." I still wasn't happy about it, but on the other hand, I was pretty excited about going home.

"I swear, Rebecca, nothing ever goes the normal way with you, does it?" She gave me a smile and I felt relief course through me.

"Do you want any of this stuff?" I gestured at the piles of my belongings. "Maybe the sheets? I don't have a twin-sized mattress back at my place. They'll only go into the linen closet and sit there."

She hesitated. "Sure. Maybe one of those pillows, too."

"You bet." Once again, I felt tears prick at the back of eyes. "I'm going to miss you, Cathy."

She waved her hand at me. "Yeah, sure you will. You'll get out there in the world and forget all about me."

"I swear I won't, Cathy. You . . . you really helped me get through this. I'm not sure how I would have survived all this without you. I'm not going to forget that and I'm not going to forget you."

She dropped to the floor and starting doing push-ups.

"Cathy," I said. "Stop for a second. Look at me."

She lowered herself gently to the floor, then took her time sitting up. "What, Rebecca? What more do you want?"

"I'm not going to forget. I don't know how much more plainly to say it than that." I didn't always understand Cathy, but I knew how much she'd helped me through the last few days.

She got up and walked over to the bars so we were nose to nose. "Well, you should forget. You should forget you ever knew me. Want to know why?"

"Why?"

"Because I'm guilty. I did everything they've accused me of doing and a few other things they haven't found yet, although I figure that's just a matter of time." She brushed her hair back from her face. "Want to know something else? The only thing I regret is getting caught."

"That's it? That's the only thing?" I couldn't believe that was true.

"Yes. I'd like to know who the asshat that turned me in is and curse them to their grave." She looked like she was going to spit on the ground for emphasis and then thought better of it.

I took a deep breath. "Fine, then. I'll find out who turned you in."

"Rebecca . . ."

I cut her off with a held-up hand. "I'm leaving. Stay strong, sister. Be fierce. I'll be back."

Cynthia, Sprocket and I walked down the steps of City Hall together. "Thanks for putting together this outfit for me."

She had been waiting for me with some clean clothes for me to wear. I would never have chosen this blouse with these slacks or topped it off with this scarf. All the pieces were mine, but I'd never assembled them in this particular way and, frankly, they looked great on me.

She smiled. "I always loved playing with Barbies when I was a little girl. Usually nobody lets you dress them up to suit your own whims. It's one more perk of being a defense attorney!"

"Treating your clients like dress-up toys is a perk?" It sounded like a hideous chore to me.

She looked over the top of her sunglasses at me. "Spending time alone in a kitchen is a perk to you?"

I nodded. "I'm taking it's not your cup of tea."

"Nope. So *vive la différence*?" She put her sunglasses back up and kept walking.

"Absolutely." I followed her.

Garrett met us at the bottom of the steps. "You look nice," he said, and leaned in to kiss me on the cheek. I pulled back. He turned to Cynthia. "When does she need to be back?"

"I'll contact her and let her know. That's kind of my job." She cocked one hip.

"Well, it's my job to keep her safe and keep the town safe around her. It would help if I knew where she had to be when."

Cynthia leaned in close to Garrett. "It is not my job to help you do yours. You'll have to figure that out on your own. I'll get the charge against her dropped."

Garrett did not back down. "What good will that do if she's been shot or burned or whatever else might happen around her?"

"You both know I'm right here, right?" I asked.

Garrett ran his hand over his face. "Yes. I know. Come on. I'll take you home." He took my arm.

I shook him off. "I don't know if I'm even speaking to you, much less letting you anywhere near my house."

"Rebecca," he said, a note of pleading in his voice.

It was going to take a lot more pleading before I decided to let him off the hook. Sprocket and I would be fine walking home. Before we could take more than three steps down the stairs, however, Antoine pulled up in a cherry-red Mustang. "Rebecca, get in. I'll give you and the *chien* a ride."

I hesitated. My better angels told me to thank Antoine and keep on walking. They also said to be careful not to do something that couldn't be undone. Then my less-better angels punched them in the nose and told me to get in the convertible.

So I did. "See you at the apartment," I called as we drove off.

Eleven

I regretted my decision almost immediately. Antoine shifted into gear and then let his hand slide over onto my thigh. Of course he'd rented a manual transmission. He was such a control freak. He couldn't even let a car change gears automatically. I picked up his hand and put it back on the gearshift and gave him a pointed look. He shrugged, but grinned at me. In addition to being a control freak, he also had no sense of shame.

One thing I'd prided myself on during our divorce was not sending mixed signals to Antoine. I'd been clear since I'd left. Our marriage was over. Our relationship was over. The grand adventure that had been Antoine and Rebecca was over over over. Now I'd left my boyfriend on the sidewalk with his ex-girlfriend and jumped into a car with Antoine. Not smart.

"Where to, darling?" he asked.

"To my apartment," I said.

"Excellent."

"To the driveway in front of my apartment," I amended. "You're not coming in."

"No?" His face fell. "Not even for a few moments? I could whip us up something to eat."

"That's okay," I said. "I'll figure something out on my own."

"But you must be exhausted after your ordeal! You should be waited on hand and foot." His hand went to his heart as if the idea of me making my own meal actually hurt him.

I honestly wasn't exhausted. There wasn't that much to do in jail unless you went with the Cathy Exercise Program and spent all your hours doing calisthenics. I probably hadn't slept this much since before I moved back to Grand Lake.

We pulled into the driveway. Garrett's car was already there, as was Garrett, standing with his arms crossed over his chest and his foot tapping. I rolled down my window.

"Not funny, Rebecca," he said.

"It wasn't intended to be." I waited while Antoine came around to open my door, as I'd known he would, and stepped out. Then I tipped the seat forward to let Sprocket out. Sprocket danced over to Garrett and sat next to him. I could have been mistaken, but he seemed to be glaring at me, too. He might even have been tapping his paw.

"Yes, well, that's good, because if Judge Romero had seen that, you'd be back behind bars before nightfall." Garrett reached down to pet Sprocket, who responded by licking his hand. "That would have been a laugh riot."

Antoine pulled my bags out of his backseat and started toward the stairway to my apartment. Sprocket leapt over to the steps, planted himself on the bottom stair and growled.

"Sprocket," I called. "Come here right now."

Sprocket ignored me.

Garrett walked over to Antoine and took the bags. "I'll handle it from here." Sprocket moved out of the way, and Garrett marched up the steps, took the key I hid under the watering can and let himself into the apartment.

I sighed and turned to Antoine. "Thanks for the ride."

"I'm here to help whenever you need it, Rebecca. However you need and whenever you need. Do not ever forget it." He took my hand, kissed it, returned to his car and drove away.

Garrett and Sprocket stood in the middle of my apartment, both glaring at me. "Is that how this is going to be?" Garrett asked. "Are you going to be acting like a sulky teenager until this matter is resolved?"

A series of answers went through my head, ranging from "yes" to "maybe" back to "damn straight" and over to "hell no." I settled on the last one.

"You can't blame me for being mad, though," I said. "This whole situation is ridiculous."

"I don't see anything remotely funny about it." Garrett stomped over to the couch and sat down. Now who was acting like a sulky teenager?

I went to my bedside table, where I was certain I'd left Esther's diary. It wasn't there. I opened the top drawers to see if someone had slid it into one of them. No diary.

Maybe I'd left it on the kitchen counter. Nope. It was diary-free.

"What are you looking for?" Garrett asked.

"The diary."

"Oh, for Pete's sake. Let the diary drop. If something happened to that girl, it happened more than sixty years ago. No one cares." He loosened his tie and leaned back on the sofa.

"I care." I sat down next to him. "I think someone else must care, too, Garrett. Someone cared enough to mess up the microfiche at the library and to steal the diary from my apartment. If I hadn't made a copy, it would be gone. I think someone doesn't want me to figure out what happened to Esther Brancato."

Before our argument could progress further, there was a knock on the door. It was Faith, Annie and Allen. They all came by to celebrate my freedom. Barbara volunteered to babysit for Faith's daughters so she could have a night out.

"I swear," Faith said as she came in through the door with two bags of groceries. "I've had more nights out as a single mother than I did when I was married. I seriously am questioning whether or not men and women were meant to live together at all."

Annie and Allen were right behind her. The bags they were carrying clinked. Bottles. Nice. There were many things you could count on Allen for: a sailboat ride on a sunny summer day, a patronizing explanation of how business works and a really good martini. It was too late for the ride, but I'd happily put up with the patronizing explanation to get my hands on a martini at the moment.

Faith stopped dead in her tracks and stared at Garrett. "Are we speaking to him?"

"Oh, come on!" he said. "How am I the bad guy here?"

Faith came the rest of the way into the apartment and started setting up a series of truly delicious-looking snacks on the breakfast bar in the kitchen. I saw good cheese and bread, olives, dark chocolate. I couldn't help it. I clapped my hands like a baby looking at her first birthday cake.

"How are you the bad guy?" Faith asked as she unpacked. "Well, let's see. You colluded with the sheriff to get her arrested, made sure she'd have to spend four days in jail before she even got to go before a judge, refused to represent her and didn't even take care of her dog while she was locked up."

"I totally planned to take care of Sprocket while she was in jail. He wouldn't stop howling," Garrett protested. "People were complaining."

"Well, Counselor, I'm not sure motive matters. Actions do." She gestured to Allen and a cleared-off place on the bar.

Allen looked tired, which was so not an Allen thing. Allen looked tan and healthy all year. When most of the rest of the town turned pasty white in February, he still looked golden and glowing. It was part of why I'd always been suspicious of him.

"What's wrong?" I asked, putting ice in an ice bucket.

He took the gin, the vodka and the Lillet Blanc out of the bag. "Well, a lot less in a minute or so." Ah, he was going to make my favorite martini: the Vesper. It was the original James Bond martini and packed a punch that could hit you harder than Sugar Ray. It was also seriously delicious.

"Just a long day?" I asked. I'd been about to pull my cocktail shaker out of the cabinet, but then noticed that Allen had brought his own. My respect for him rose another notch. I'd been horrified when he and Annie had first gotten together—in part because I thought he might have murdered someone—but since then he'd done nothing but make me like him more and more.

"A little more than that. I'm worried about what's happening with the city council race." He filled the shaker with ice and added shots of gin and vodka.

I picked up the lemon he'd brought and started shaving off twists. "Why?"

"First there was the popcorn, then someone tried to blackmail Justin out of the race. It's intimidating." He put the top on the shaker and mixed.

"Somebody made sure Cathy didn't run, either." I lined up martini glasses for him.

"Cathy? Embezzler Cathy?" he asked, pausing mid-pour.

"Yeah. She was considering running, but then someone gave that tip about what she was doing to the *Sentinel*." I gestured for him to keep pouring.

Allen shrugged and complied. "Good thing they did. She is not the kind of person I want to see running our city. Can you imagine?"

I knew what he meant, despite the recent soft spot I'd developed for her. "Yeah, but don't you think that's strange? First she gets knocked out of the race by being exposed for embezzling, then someone tries to poison one of the city council candidates, then someone tries to blackmail Justin. Sounds fishy to me." I took a sip of my martini. "Good drink, Allen." I didn't spend a lot of time behind the bar, but mixology had a lot in common with baking. Good ingredients mixed in the right proportions at the right temperatures yielded superior results. I respected the person who knew that, too.

He acknowledged the compliment with a head nod and started handing out the rest of the drinks.

"It feels fishy to me, too. But who?" Allen asked.

Faith took her drink and asked, "Who's left in the race?"

"Geraldine, Sheri, Chris, Taylor and Justin," Annie said.

"And someone already tried to poison and blackmail Justin." The fact that whoever it was had tried to poison him with my popcorn made me extra upset and worried about the whole situation. "Who's next?"

"I hope it's not Sheri. You know it's because of Sheri that the elementary school garden has gone completely organic," Faith said, sipping her drink. "She came up with a whole slew of natural ways to cut down on the insect problems in the school garden."

"Very admirable." Allen raised his glass in a toast.

"She also started the recycling program at the schools," Faith said. "And she started a meditation group to help kids deal with stress."

"I see we know which way you're voting," Annie said.

Faith blushed. "I know she'll represent the ideas that are important to me. She's all about keeping the kids safe and making the planet a better place."

"That does sound pretty good." I took a sip of my martini, a small one.

Annie nodded. "Those are all good things, but she doesn't always have a way to pay for all those pretty plans. The high school had to petition the school board for two thousand extra dollars to pay for that recycling plan. That money could have gone to buy books or subsidize kids who can't afford to go on field trips. Plus, some local businesses suffered. Didn't Justin's landscape company have the contract for the schools before she got everyone to go organic?"

"He still does," Allen said. "It's just costing him a lot more to fulfill the contract than he expected. They had quite a fight about it."

"So everybody else loves her?" I asked.

Faith made a face. "Of course not. Nobody is universally loved. All the right-minded people love her."

"And by *right-minded people* you mean . . . ?" I asked.

Faith smiled. "People like me."

I handed over a cracker with Brie. "We really need to work on your self-esteem. You're not confident enough in your own convictions."

"I'll start saying an affirmation about it." She popped the cracker and cheese in her mouth.

"Are you mocking my affirmations?" Annie asked.

Faith swallowed. "I'm not sure. Are we still saying 'The tulip crop will be amazing' every morning three times while looking deeply into our own eyes in the mirror?"

Annie shot me a look. "Of course not. That was last year's affirmation. This year we're saying 'Seasonal flowers will stay in style.' But back to Sheri. Who doesn't like her?"

I tossed a towel at her. "You are such a gossip!"

She shrugged. "Honestly, it's like a business thing for me. If I know who's fighting or who's getting lovey-dovey or who's not feeling well, I know what kind of flowers to stock."

"Justify it however you want. It's still gossip." I drank a little more of my martini.

Faith took an even bigger sip of hers. "Cheryl Watson hates her."

"Why?" Annie asked.

Faith waved her hand. "It's ridiculous."

Annie licked her fingers. "I love ridiculous."

Faith looked back and forth as if she were checking for spies. "It was a birthday-treat issue."

"You've got to be kidding." Annie rolled her eyes.

"I am not kidding. Sheri wanted the parents to pledge not to put peanuts in the birthday treats they brought into school."

"Was someone in the class allergic to peanuts?" Peanut allergies aren't funny. People die.

"No." Faith shook her head.

Now I was confused. "Then why bother?"

"Someone could be and not know it yet. She just wanted to err on the side of caution. She said that it takes a village to raise a child and that if any one child in the village was allergic to peanuts, she wanted to be as vigilant in keeping that child safe as if she had given birth to him or her herself. Cheryl thought it was too much caution and since her son's favorite dessert is a rocky-road fudge with peanuts in it, she brought it anyway. Sheri threw it out."

"Threw out fudge?" Inconceivable!

Faith nodded. "Every last square."

"I might hate her a little, too. Who are you voting for?" I asked Annie.

"I haven't made up my mind yet. I'm still weighing the possibilities." She twisted a lock of hair around her finger.

"Okay. Who are you voting for, Allen?" I asked.

He made a face.

Annie laughed. "He won't tell. He takes this political stuff very seriously. He doesn't mess around."

"How many people are on the council?"

"Four members plus me."

"Are any of the people already on it?"

Allen gave me the look that Chef Emanuel, the pastry teacher at the Culinary Institute, used to give me when I didn't take the time to let my eggs and butter come to room temperature before I started baking. Disappointment. It cut. "You don't know your city council members, Rebecca?"

"No. I guess I never paid that much attention."

"You should. Your city council steers the town. The decisions they make affect everyone in all facets of their life."

I snorted. "All facets, Allen? Really?"

"Yes. Really. We make zoning decisions. That means we impact what kind of business is next to yours or next to your house and how fast the city grows, which might impact the worth of your house. We make decisions about your trash pickup, equipment for law enforcement, signage." With each subject he pounded on the table. "We are everywhere."

"Now I'm a little frightened. I'm making Sprocket look under the bed before I go to sleep."

"Don't be a smart-ass, Rebecca."

"She doesn't know how to be anything else," Annie said. "You might as well ask her not to breathe."

I shrugged. She had a point. "Okay. The council is important and I should know their names. Educate me."

Dana Nelson, Sophia Estrada and Isaac Turner have been serving on the council for the last two years and each have a year left in their terms. Hector Goodwin passed away last month, leaving an open seat."

"How did Hector die?" I'd always kind of liked Hector. He was a bit of a lush, but he was a lovey lush. He was more likely to tell you that he'd always admired and respected you than to try to pick a fight. I liked that in a man.

"Hit by a train." Allen shook his head.

I winced. "How? Did his car stall on the tracks or something?"

"No. He'd been at the tavern all night and decided to take a shortcut. Best we can guess, he stopped to, uh, relieve himself on the tracks and got tangled up in his pants and couldn't get out of the way of the train." Allen looked uncomfortable just talking about it.

I stifled a laugh. "What an entirely undignified way to go."

"The poor conductor has had a very hard time. He refuses to work on any night with a full moon." Annie slipped off her shoes and put her feet in Allen's lap.

"Okay. So you've got one open seat and five people running for it? That's some pretty stiff competition." Odds were not in anyone's favor.

"Lots of good civic-minded people here in Grand Lake. It's one of the things that makes us so special." Allen rubbed Annie's feet. She moaned a little.

"We've also got lots of people with their own agendas in Grand Lake. That makes us a different kind of special," Annie said.

"What do you mean?" I sank down onto the floor with my martini.

"Well, each of the people running is doing it for reasons that aren't entirely altruistic." Annie sipped her drink.

"What can you get for being on the city council?"

"Did you not hear what Allen was saying? The city council controls how this town runs. A little shift here or a little shift there can make a big difference. Sheri has a whole organic agenda, which, granted, isn't going to line her pockets, but it's important to her. Justin is going to stand in her way because having to go organic is hard for his landscaping business. Geraldine is very pro-business. She's going to do everything she can for business owners in town."

"What about Chris and Taylor?" I asked.

Annie looked over at Allen, who shrugged. "I'm not sure what their agendas are yet, but rest assured, they have them."

"What do you say to that, Allen?" It seemed to contradict his thoughts on altruism.

"I say the bears get some. The bulls get some. But the pigs get nothing." He set his drink down with a thump.

Garrett had insisted on spending the night, but I was still mad, so he'd ended up on the couch. He woke up about the time that my coffee started brewing.

"That smells good," he said, rubbing his eyes. Then

he cringed and rubbed at his neck. My apartment is small. So is my couch. My boyfriend? Not so much. The couch was about six inches shorter than Garrett. Watching him try to work out the crick in his neck almost made up for the nights I'd spent on the crappy plastic mattress in the jail before Faith had brought me that memory-foam topper for it. Almost.

"I'm making the coffee to take over to Haley," I said.

"You can't spare a single mug?" he asked, looking forlorn.

"I don't know. Are you certain it won't endanger you somehow? I might be a poisoner. I need constant supervision, and you were asleep while I made this." I peeked in my fridge. Everything was old. With any luck, Haley would have cream and sugar at her place.

I put on my thickest cardigan, picked up my French press and headed toward the door with Sprocket at my heels.

"Hold on for two seconds," Garrett grumbled, shoving his feet into his shoes. "I'm coming."

Outside, the frosted grass crunched under our feet. Garrett picked up a tennis ball from the box of Sprocket's toys at the bottom of the stairs and tossed it. Sprocket leapt and caught it midair. I couldn't help but smile. There was a crisp perfection to the air, and the way his apricot fur looked against the background of the grass and trees made a picture that gladdened my heart.

Sprocket dropped the ball at Garrett's feet and Garrett threw it again. Grudgingly I said, "I suppose there's enough coffee for you to have some, too." It's hard to stay mad at someone who's nice to your dog.

We all trotted up the stairs. I knocked lightly even though I was pretty sure everyone was up.

The door flew open, but instead of my sister, it was Dan.

"Oh. You're still here, then," I said, shouldering past him.

"I live here," he said, following me into the kitchen.

"Sister!" Haley jumped up from her chair and gave me a hug.

Evan wrapped himself around my knees and crowed, "Auntie Becca!"

For a second I couldn't move. The feelings rushing through me were too strong and they were all mixed up. Relief. Love. Frustration. Anger. Hurt. Pride. I set the coffee down and wiped at my eye. "Hi, champ," I said, kneeling down to give Evan a hug.

I sat down, pointedly keeping my back to Dan and Garrett.

Haley stayed standing. She looked from me, over my shoulder, to them. Then shook her head. "This won't do. We need to sit down and talk this out."

"What's there to talk about?" I asked, pouring myself a mug of coffee and helping myself to the cream that sat on the table. "They and the rest of this town are a bunch of Big Brother asshats who think women should stay in their place in the kitchen."

"But you love being in the kitchen," Garrett protested.

"Beside the point." I waved a hand at him to dismiss him.

Haley said, "Dan, I think you should start. You're the most at fault here."

That surprised me enough to make me turn and look at him. Dan is not the chatty sort. When he does want to chat, he usually meets me on the porch with a beer. Of course, it was getting a little cold for that and the fact that he'd kept me locked up in a cell downtown for the better part of a week made that trickier than usual. Desperate times, I supposed.

Garrett and Dan both walked around so they were in front of me, backs to the refrigerator. They stood in that weird fig-leaf position that some men stand in, as if they thought I was going to kick them in a sensitive spot. They shouldn't do that. It gave me ideas.

My eyes narrowed. Were they going to say something that would make me want to kick them in a sensitive spot? Pretty much everything out of their mouths for the past week or two had made me want to do exactly that.

Dan cleared his throat. "Rebecca, Garrett and I would like to apologize."

I set my coffee cup down with a soft thump and leaned back in my chair. "You do? What brings this on?"

Dan spun one of the kitchen chairs around and straddled it. "Don't do this, Bec. Don't break my balls over this."

"Excuse me? You keep me locked up in a cell without even decent toothpaste or a wide-toothed comb for my hair and then I'm not supposed to break your balls when you go all googly-eyed and meek? What the actual heck, Dan?" I turned to Garrett. "And you? Are you sorry, too?"

"I am." Garrett sat down, chair facing forward like a normal person. "I really am."

"You need to tell her why," Haley prompted. "You need to explain it to her or nothing's going to change."

Dan nodded. "Here's the thing, Rebecca. I don't want you to keep your nose fully out of it. Your nose has proven to be too good. What I want is to be able to consult you, to talk things over with you, to bounce ideas off you. If you hadn't seen that popcorn tin, I would have still thought someone had been trying to kill Lloyd McLaughlin. I needed your input to get on the right track. You see things that I don't. You hear things I don't. I need us to communicate."

I had never done anything to keep him from talking to me. Never. "Of course you can talk to me. We've been talking to each other since we were seven. You're the one who went all silent about stuff. Not me."

He dropped his head for a moment, but then looked up again, fixing me with those bright blue eyes of his. "I want to be able to talk to you and know that you're not going to go running off and putting yourself in danger."

He had a point about that. There was a reason that Phillip had such a compelling argument about the safety of the community when we were in court. I still had bad dreams about Sprocket getting shot, and the smell of smoke made my heart race faster, which isn't a great thing for someone who works in a kitchen. "I don't like being in danger any more than you like me being in it."

Garrett shoved back from the table and started to pace the kitchen. "Then why do you do what you do? Why do you confront people in lighthouses? Why do you go to the wake of someone who ate the popcorn people think you poisoned?"

I sat back in my chair. I wasn't sure I had a good answer to those questions. I thought through what had brought me to those particular places in the past. "I think when they handed out fight-or-flight reflexes, I got an extra helping of fight."

Dan snorted. "I've known that since you punched me in the nose for putting a worm in your chocolate milk in second grade."

"It's part of who I am. If I feel attacked, I push back." I studied my hands for a moment.

"Rebecca," Haley said. "Do you have anything to say?"

Did I? I thought about the file on Lloyd McLaughlin. All the interviews Dan had done with the very people I thought I was so smart to point out as suspects. All the evidence he'd sifted through. All the work he'd quietly and efficiently done. "I'm sorry."

Dan straightened in his chair. "For what?"

"For not giving you the credit you deserve." I felt too bad about it to actually look him in the eye as I said it. I turned my coffee mug in slow circles on the table. "You're good at your job and you deserve my respect."

Dan asked, "Are you playing me?"

I looked up at that. "Playing you? When have I ever played you?"

He made a face at me. "Well, there was the time you convinced me you knew how to drive and we nearly rolled a station wagon into the lake. Then there was the time you got me to break into the junior high by telling me that you thought the janitor was hiding gold bars in the supply closet."

I held up my hands. "Point taken. No. I'm not playing you. I'm being one hundred percent sincere."

"What brought about this change of heart?" Dan asked.

"Seeing the files you'd compiled on all this already. I . . . I wasn't giving you the credit you deserve. You're good at your job. You're smart and efficient and loyal and kind and . . ." Damn it. Something was making my eyes sting.

"Okay. That's enough," Haley said. "Enough with all the lovey-dovey stuff. Are we all on the same page, then?"

"If it's the page where I make everyone cinnamon rolls, then absolutely." I stood up and started getting out mixing bowls.

Twelve

I slid the plate of cinnamon rolls away from Dan. "Leave at least one that we can drop off at Garrett's office." He couldn't wait for the time it took for the rolls to rise, so he'd left. Apparently leaving me in the custody of the sheriff was good enough to satisfy the terms he'd agreed to. He'd looked really sad, though. I wasn't sure if it was because he wasn't getting cinnamon rolls or if it was because I wouldn't kiss him good-bye. I wasn't one hundred percent ready to forgive him.

Dan licked icing off his fingers. "Does that mean you're going to say yes?"

"To what?" I cleared off the rest of the table.

"Are you serious?" He went over to the sink to wash his hands. "Have you forgotten that he proposed to you?"

I hadn't. Not really. I'd been purposefully not thinking

about it. "He didn't really. He didn't have a ring. He didn't get down on one knee. There was no champagne or flowers, and let's not forget, he didn't actually even ask. I don't think it counts without those things."

"Did Antoine have all those things when he proposed?" Dan dried his hands on the dishcloth and then leaned back against the counter.

He had. He'd had dozens of bouquets delivered to the soufflé class I was taking at the Culinary Institute. Then as class ended, a string quartet started playing in the hallway. Antoine had strode in, gotten down on one knee, and in front of my entire class, he'd professed his undying love and told me that I would make him the happiest man on earth if I would agree to be his wife. The room had gone wild when I'd said yes. I looked over at Dan and nodded.

"How'd that turn out?" he asked.

"Not fair, Dan." Sometimes it was a drag when people knew you too well.

"Whoever said life was fair?" He held up his hand to stop me from answering. "Fine. We can start small, with you giving Garrett a cinnamon roll. After that, though, we need to figure out where along the delivery route your popcorn got poisoned. You free today?"

"Unless you lock me up again, I'm all yours." I gave him a sickly sweet smile.

He ignored the dig. "Excellent. We need to trace the route the popcorn tins took. I know the general outlines, but we have to dig down more," Dan said, sitting down and taking out his notepad. "Start at the beginning."

I sat down across from him. "I loaded them up in Haley's fold-up wagon to take to City Hall."

He made a note. "Where were they before that?"

"In my apartment. I made them and boxed them up the day before. They didn't leave until I left."

"Were you out at all that night?"

I thought for a moment. What had I done that night? "No. Garrett came over for dinner."

He looked up. "So they were never out of your sight?"

I started to reply in the affirmative, but then thought I should be specific. "Well, technically they weren't in my sight when I was asleep. My eyes were closed."

Dan tapped his pen against the table. "How deep do you sleep?"

"I don't know. Like a normal person."

"Do you think you would have woken up if someone had let themselves into your apartment?"

That didn't seem possible. "How would they do that? I locked the door after Garrett left."

"Yes. I'm sure you did. Still, everyone knows you leave a key in the watering can by the front door." He frowned.

"How do they know that?" I asked.

He laughed. "There really isn't another reason for the watering can to be there. You don't garden."

"It's decorative." I could garden if I wanted to. I just didn't have time.

"And handy for hiding keys."

So maybe it wasn't exactly high security. "Fine. Someone could have let themselves in with the key. I suppose there's a minute possibility I wouldn't have woken up, but Sprocket definitely would have."

"What if he knew the person?" Dan tapped his pen again.

I paused. Sprocket was notoriously friendly. The only person he growled at was Antoine, and he'd even stopped doing that if Antoine had cheese with him. Sprocket will do nearly anything for cheese. "I don't know. I think he would make some kind of noise. At least enough to wake me up. Even Garrett gets a yip or something when he walks in, and Sprocket loves him."

A smile quirked at Dan's lips. "Yeah. Sprocket does. I'm sure he's the only one, too."

I ignored him. "So let's say that the popcorn was safe when it left my apartment."

Dan shook his head. "I'm not sure it would hold up in court, but it should be okay for our purposes at the moment. It seems highly unlikely that anyone snuck into your apartment and poisoned one tin of popcorn. Where did you go next?"

"After your house?" I asked.

"Yes. After my house. I'm pretty much crossing Haley, Evan and Emily off my suspect list." Dan shot me a look.

I tsked. "Nepotism rears its ugly head."

"Rebecca, this is serious."

"I know. Sorry." I thought for a moment. "Sprocket and I walked over to the lake to go by the lighthouse. We saw Dario. He was out running."

"Did he touch the popcorn?" Dan made more notes.

"No. He was all sweaty from running. Plus, why on earth would he be carrying poison out on a run?" Wasn't running poisonous enough on its own?

"Maybe it wasn't random that he ran into you," Dan suggested.

I stared at him. "Dan, we're talking about Dario here."

"That's the problem, Rebecca. There's really not anyone involved in this situation that we don't know. Everyone is someone we think we understand. Everyone is someone we would never suspect." He rubbed his face, a sure sign that he was frustrated or tired.

He had a point. "Dario didn't touch the popcorn."

"Good. Then?" he asked.

"Then directly to Allen's office, where I turned the tins over to Otis. Well, except for the ones I took to Trina and Sally." I'd taken those over right away, though.

"Good. Then our first stop is Otis."

"Our first stop?"

"Yes, Rebecca. Our first stop."

Sprocket growled, then there was a knock at the door. I looked at Dan. "Are you expecting anyone?"

He shook his head. "You?"

Sprocket growled again and the pit of my stomach tightened. Then a very French accented voice called out, "Hello, is anybody at home?"

I ducked down so I wouldn't be visible from the kitchen window. "It's Antoine," I whispered.

"I got that. What are you doing down there?" Dan crouched down to talk to me.

"Hiding." I made a shooing gesture. "Go get rid of him."

"My pleasure." Antoine had never been Dan's favorite person, and since I came home and he had made it his calling to win me back, he hadn't risen in Dan's estimation one bit. He'd probably been waiting for a while to have permission to get rid of Antoine.

"What do you want, Antoine?" Dan said from the front door.

"I am looking for Rebecca. She did not answer the door at her apartment and I smell from here the scent of cinnamon rolls. It is one of her specialties. She makes them when she is happy. I think she is here," Antoine said.

I pulled Sprocket toward me and held my fingers to my lips to shush him. He still growled, but very quietly. Then he licked my nose.

"Sorry. No. She's not," Dan said. "Not here at all."

"May I ask where she might be? It is imperative that I speak to her." Antoine used the tone he used to order camera people around. Under the best of circumstances, it wasn't the right way to approach Dan.

"Nope. No idea," Dan said, his voice bland.

"*Vraiment?* I would have thought you would be keeping track, what with her recent release from incarceration." There was a sly tone to Antoine's voice.

"Not my job." Dan's voice didn't sound sly at all.

"I see." There was a pause. "Please tell her that I am looking for her when you see her."

"I'll try to remember."

I heard the door shut with a bit more of a bang than Dan usually caused. It wasn't quite a slam, but I think the message came across.

Dan came back into the kitchen. "He's gone."

"I didn't hear his car leave," I said from my spot on the kitchen floor.

Dan looked out the window, then made the "I'm watching you" gesture with two fingers pointed to his eyes and then out the window. A car engine started.

"So is this the very mature way you're going to be dealing with your ex from now on?" Dan slid down and sat next to me on the floor.

"Maybe." I leaned my head on his shoulder.

"I can support that. Now go finish getting ready so we can figure out who the hell poisoned your damn popcorn." He gave me a little shove. The kind of shove that he used to give me back when we were best friends.

Both Sprocket and I had a spring in our step as we walked out of the house into the crisp morning.

"You don't have an appointment." Otis didn't even look up from his computer when we walked into the mayor's office in City Hall.

"We don't need one." Dan tapped his badge.

"You always need one. Mayor Thompson is simply too busy to talk to anyone who walks in off the street." Otis kept typing.

"What makes you think we want to talk to Allen?" Dan impressively did not mention that he wasn't just anyone off the street.

Otis stopped typing and looked up. "Then what do you want?"

Dan smiled. "We want to talk to you about the day Rebecca dropped off the popcorn tins to be delivered."

"Sure. I remember that." Otis nodded.

"Were the tins ever out of your sight from the time Rebecca dropped them off to the time the messenger service picked them up?"

"Nope." Otis finally turned away from his computer to face us.

"You're sure?" Dan asked.

Otis nodded emphatically. "Yep."

"Care to elaborate?" Dan pulled a chair over from the

waiting area and sat down. I followed suit. My phone buzzed. I took it out and checked the caller ID. Antoine. I put the phone back in my pocket.

Otis made a face. I didn't think he loved the idea of us rearranging the furniture. "Not really."

Dan sighed. "Humor me."

"I had already notified the messenger service. The messenger arrived less than ten minutes after Rebecca dropped off the tins. She took them away. I was here the whole time." Otis crossed his arms over his chest, clearly resigned to the questioning.

"You didn't leave to go to the bathroom?" Dan asked.

"No."

"You didn't walk away to get a cup of coffee?" I asked.

"No."

Dan turned to me. "Then it happened after it was here."

I had a thought. "Otis, did you mark which tins were supposed to go to which candidate?"

Otis kept casting sidelong glances at his computer. Whatever he'd been working on, he wanted to get back to it. "No. Why would I? They were all the same, weren't they?"

They had been when I'd dropped them off, but that had changed eventually. Eventually one of them had been laced with poison.

Otis had used pretty much the only messenger service in Grand Lake. In a town that was barely five miles across, not too many people had need of one, but when they did they called Janine at XTra Speedee Deliveries.

Janine had pretty much had a need for speed from the moment she left the womb. Maybe even before. Her mother claimed that she'd almost had Janine in the backseat of her husband's Subaru because Janine had been in such an all-fired hurry to get out.

When Janine wasn't biking or snowmobiling items around and across Grand Lake, she was training. She'd completed two Ironman Triathlons in the past year and was getting ready for number three. We'd clearly interrupted a workout. She answered the door wearing way more spandex than anyone should wear anywhere, even in the privacy of her own home, her face dewy with sweat and a towel over her shoulder.

"Sheriff Dan! Rebecca! What can I help you with?" She even spoke fast. Everything came out staccato. Nor did she waste any time with small talk.

"We want to talk about the deliveries you made for Mayor Thompson last week," Dan said, not wasting any time himself.

She motioned us into the house, ponytail swinging. "Oh, the poisoned popcorn deliveries."

I cringed.

"Sorry, Rebecca. I guess it's a sore spot for you." Janine plopped down on the floor into a hurdler's stretch.

I waved it away and sat down on the couch. "Whatever."

Janine stretched her arms up over her head and then slowly lowered her nose down to her knee. "So what is it that you want to know?" she asked the carpet.

"Were the tins ever out of your sight?" Dan asked.

Janine straightened up and shrugged. "Probably. I didn't know at the time there would be a whole chain-of-custody thing."

Neither had I. Someone had, though, and I wanted to know who.

"Do you remember when? Where?" Dan asked.

She switched legs and stretched again. I wondered what it would feel like to be able to do that. "Why?"

"We're trying to figure out who might have put the poison in it," I said. "Knowing where someone would have that opportunity might help us figure out who did it."

"Wouldn't that someone be you?" Janine looked confused.

My face went hot. "No. Of course not. I would never poison anyone."

"Well, not intentionally, I'm sure, but . . ." Janine had that look on her face that said exactly what she thought I might do by accident.

"No, Janine. Someone else put the poison in the popcorn. I swear it. I need to figure out who it was for just this reason. If everyone thinks I'm a poisoner, especially an accidental poisoner, I might as well never even reopen POPS. My business would be a failure. Just imagine how you would feel if XTra Speedee went out of business because everyone thought you'd done something you hadn't done." Darn it. Why did my throat feel all clogged up like that?

Janine pulled her legs into the tailor position and leaned forward, back straight as a rolling pin. "Yeah. I see your point. So what is it you want to know?"

"We want to know exactly what order you delivered the tins in, where you might have left them unattended and who might have been around when you did," Dan said.

"Let me get my logbook." Janine bounced up from the

floor as if her legs had springs in them. She came back into the room a few minutes later with a small bound book. "Okay. Ready?"

Dan nodded, pen poised over his notepad. I felt my phone vibrate in my pocket. I ignored it.

"I picked up the tins from Otis at City Hall. It was dry out that day, so I was on my bike. I loaded the tins into my panniers. It took two trips. While I was getting the second set, someone could have messed with the ones I'd already put in the panniers."

"They don't lock?" I asked.

"They do," she said. "But I didn't think anybody would be stealing popcorn from my bike in the time it took me to go back and forth from the mayor's office, especially with the sheriff's office in the same building."

"How long did it take?"

Janine looked in the air and thought for a moment. "More than two minutes. Less than four."

Dan arched a brow. "That's pretty accurate."

She shrugged. "I spend a lot of time trying to shave a few seconds off how long it takes me to bike, run or swim a mile. I've got a pretty good sense of seconds passing these days."

It wasn't scientific and it might not hold up in court, but it would do for what we needed here today. "So if someone was going to put the poison in there, they would have had to have it ready and be watching. It would have taken some pretty split-second timing," I said.

"Where was the bike parked?" Dan asked.

"At the racks by the east door," Janine said.

"Excellent. We have some cameras there. It's possible we can check the film and be certain if someone messed with the popcorn then. All right. What did you do next?" Dan tapped his pen on his pad.

"Next was Geraldine's tin." Janine tapped at her logbook in return. "Her place was the farthest from my place. I figured I would start there and work my way back in."

It made sense. "So Geraldine's. Did you bike straight there?"

"I did. I went along Magnolia and then out to Greenhaven and cut over to Alderwood," Janine said.

"You have that written there?" I asked.

She nodded. "I like to keep track of my mileage. Just a personal thing. Geraldine was home. She answered the door when I rang the bell. My bike was with me the whole time. Did you know she wears pantyhose and heels when she's at home for the day?"

I hadn't, but I wasn't terribly surprised, either. You didn't look as put together as Geraldine did on a regular basis without practice.

Janine continued. "After I went there, I went to Taylor's office, over on Spruce Street. She wasn't there. I left the tin with her secretary. My bike was outside unattended for the five minutes or so it took to go in, drop off the tin and get a signature, but I locked the panniers that time since I didn't know how long I'd be gone."

"How secure is the lock?" Dan asked.

Janine thought for a moment. "It probably wouldn't be that hard for someone to break it, but I'd know if they had."

"Where next?" Dan asked.

"Sheri's house." She smiled. "Are her kids cute or what?"

"Very cute," I said, remembering how Ada had shared her crackers with Evan. "Very sweet."

"Great kids. They wanted to know all about my bike and what it was like to be a messenger and how long it took me to swim a mile." She paused. "That Ada could totally be a great runner. Have you seen how long her legs are?"

"And then?" Dan asked.

"Then I went over to Brixton Accounting."

"Which of the candidates was there?" I asked.

"None of them. I'd gotten a call on my cell phone about another delivery. It wasn't a rush, so I figured I could work it in. Their office was only a little bit out of the way, so I detoured a little."

"Okay. Was the popcorn out of your sight at all then?" Dan asked.

She grimaced. "You know, it was. I left my bike in the lobby. They have a security guard. He was there when I went in, but when I came back down he wasn't. I was a little pissed. I mean, that bike is expensive. Was it so much to ask for him to watch it while I went up two flights of stairs and back down?"

No. I didn't think so. "Why do they have a security guard?"

"They were having some vandalism problems. Some folks aren't crazy about their work for the banks," Dan said. "Did you lock your panniers there?"

Janine shook her head. "Nope. I thought the security guard would be watching so I didn't bother. I was gone longer that time. At least five minutes. Maybe seven."

"After that?"

"Next was Chris. I didn't actually make it into his office. He was in his car in the parking lot, so I gave him the tin right there." She paused. "Taylor was with him."

"Taylor?"

She nodded. "They both got out of his car and she walked over to hers and drove away while Chris talked to me."

Hmmm. Was there a little collusion going on between the council candidates? Interesting. My phone buzzed. Again. Dan gave me a quizzical look. I shook my head.

"Okay. After that, then?" he asked.

"Justin. Except he wouldn't take his." Janine tapped the logbook.

"Why not?" Dan asked, although he already knew.

"He said he's allergic to nuts."

That still really steamed me. All Allen would have had to do was let me know about someone's dietary restrictions and I would have been happy to work around them. Nut allergies are no joke. People die. Actually, now that I thought about it, why the hell hadn't Justin ever mentioned it?

"He wanted me to take it, but no way was that happening. Even without poison being added that stuff is poison. I mean, seriously, Rebecca, how much butter is in that stuff?" Janine shook her head.

"Enough." If by *enough* you mean *a lot.*

"You mean enough to clog a few dozen arteries, right? And the sugar? There's got to be a lot of that, too. And don't even get me started on the bacon! Nitrates. Fat. Sodium. I don't understand why anyone would want to put that stuff in their body!" Janine shuddered.

"Because it tastes good?" I offered.

"Nothing tastes as sweet as a five-minute mile, in my humble opinion, and there's no way I'm going to keep

that up eating your Bacon Pecan Popcorn." She wagged
a finger at me.

"So what did you do with it?" Dan asked.

"I was going to throw it out."

I resisted the urge to hit her with something. Throw it
out? Who threw out perfectly good food? This was like
Sheri with the rocky-road fudge. What was wrong with
people?

"What stopped you?" Dan asked.

"I had that one last delivery to make, the documents
to drop off at Campos Realty. Carolyn saw it in my bas-
ket and asked what it was. I told her and she told me to
put it in the break room."

My face paled. Poisoned popcorn had been put in a
break room where anyone might have eaten it. Anyone.
How many people might have gotten sick or died?

"How did it get from the break room at Campos Realty
to Lloyd's house?" I asked.

Janine shrugged. "Hell if I know." She glanced down
at her watch. "Are we done here? I need to get going if
I'm going to get my run in before it gets dark."

"By all means. Thank you for your time." Dan stood
up and motioned for me to follow him out of the house.

We walked down Janine's sidewalk back to Dan's
cruiser. "What do you think?" I asked.

"I think I'm going back to the office to check the security camera footage of the bike rack and to see if Brixton Accounting has video footage, too. Can I drop you
off somewhere?" he asked.

"You don't want help reviewing the footage?" I asked.

He paused. "That video footage could end up being actual evidence that gets used in a trial. I don't want to take any chances on a defense attorney getting it thrown out." He opened the front door for me and the back door for Sprocket.

"Do you think that would happen?" I slid into the car and waited until Dan came around and got in on his side.

"I bet Cynthia could make a case for it." He looked over at me before he started the vehicle. "I promise that I will tell you everything that's on the tape. Everything. I might even make a copy and bring it home for you to watch tonight. I just don't want you in the station as I get it."

"Good enough." I thought about what my next move should be. "Could you drop me at the diner?"

"The diner here in Grand Lake?" he asked.

"Do you know another one?" I folded my hands in my lap.

"Rebecca, I know you're angry with Megan. Please don't make trouble. Not for you and not for me. We don't have time for your feud." He put the car in gear.

"I promise. I'm not making trouble for you, Megan or me." I did, however, want to make trouble for someone, and I had a plan to make it work.

"Well, as long as you promise," he said with a sarcastic note in his voice.

It was a slow point in the afternoon, around three. Too late for lunch. Too early for dinner. The pie crowd wasn't there yet. The diner was nearly empty. I plunked myself down at the counter, an area reserved exclusively for Megan's favorites. She narrowed her eyes at me and squinted. "I heard you were out."

"You heard correctly." Would Megan and I ever talk in a way that didn't feel like the precursor to a gun battle? I doubted it. "We need to talk." I turned over the coffee cup at my place setting to indicate that I wanted a pour.

Megan and I said "okay" in unison, as if we both needed someone to keep an eye on us.

Her lips tightened. If she squinched anything else up, she was likely to implode. "What could we possibly have to talk about?" She poured the coffee.

I cringed at its color. Barely tan. "My ex-husband is talking about starting a restaurant here in Grand Lake."

She shrugged. "So? Whatever kind of high-end, hoity-toity, snobby, nose-in-the-air place he'd run wouldn't have anything to do with me. That's not who eats here."

I dropped my bombshell. "He's talking about serving comfort food."

She sat down heavily on the stool next to me. "You're joking, aren't you?"

I shook my head. "Nope. It's not a joking matter, Megan. Not one little bit."

"I don't suppose *comfort food* is some fancy phrase from your snobby culinary school that means something different from what the rest of the world means when they say it?" She poured herself a cup of coffee.

My back went up instantly. It was like Megan's superpower. "That's about the twenty-seventh time you've brought up culinary school, Megan. You got a problem with education?"

Her face flushed. "No. I don't. I just seem to know that

not everyone has those kinds of opportunities and that you seem to take that opportunity for granted."

Now my face flushed. She had a point. If it hadn't been for Coco, I probably never would have applied to culinary school and I definitely wouldn't have been able to afford it. I gritted my teeth and said, "You're right. I do take it for granted that I got to go to culinary school. Don't sell what you've learned here in the kitchen short, though."

Megan swiveled on her stool to look at me. "What?"

"Nothing I learned in the classroom really sank in until I did it in an actual kitchen. Until I put it into practice, it was all a bunch of ideas and thoughts. What counts is what ends up on the plate."

"Truth," Megan said.

I knew what really bugged me about the diner. Well, I did if I was actually being honest with myself, which is one of my least favorite things to do. I owed it to Megan, though. "Here's why I'm so hard on your food. It could be really excellent. A few tweaks. Use fewer things from cans or the freezer. Shorten the menu a little. This place would be off-the-charts amazing. People's tongues would be slapping their brains out, the food would be so good."

"Tweaks? That's it? Tweaks?" She made a face at me. "You've been busting my balls over tweaks?"

"Yeah. Tweaks." I reached my hand out across the counter and put it on her forearm, praying she wouldn't pick up a steak knife and stab me with it. "I could show you."

The eyes narrowed again. "Why would you do that?"

I shrugged. "For grins. To show I could."

"Aren't you afraid we'll steal business back from

POPS?" Her chin went up as if she was expecting a blow to it.

I shrugged. "POPS will be fine, but I'm hoping we fill the niche that Antoine's looking to settle himself into before he gets a chance. Plus, I want credit."

"What kind of credit?" she asked.

"I don't know. Something that says I had a hand in it. Something that tells everyone that we're working on it together." An idea percolated in my head. "Megan, have you ever heard of popcorn soup?"

Thirteen

Megan and I talked for quite a while. "Do you think you can do it?" I asked.

"I think so," she said. "Shall we go over the menu one more time?"

"Absolutely." She pushed the pad across the counter to me. "So we're starting with the popcorn soup? What supplies do I need to buy and when do we intend to launch this thing?"

"I say sooner rather than later." I gestured toward the kitchen with my chin. "Do we have enough help back there?"

She shrugged. "We could maybe use one more set of hands."

I dialed a familiar number and a lovely deep voice answered. "This is Dario."

"Do you want to work a little?"

"Sure. You got too many special orders to handle on your own?"

"I wish. No. This is something entirely different. Megan and I are talking about collaborating."

"I'm sorry. I thought you said you were collaborating with Megan. I clearly need to get my hearing checked."

"You heard right." I glanced over at her, wondering if she could hear. Based on her facial expression, she could.

"Your sworn enemy? Your nemesis?" Dario asked.

I blushed. "Megan's not my nemesis."

"Well, she's not your friend." He chuckled.

"We're trying to change that."

"Interesting. How many hours per week?"

"Fifteen. Twenty at the most."

"Front counter or kitchen?" he asked.

"Probably a little of both."

"Count me in."

I hung up and turned to Megan. "We've got that extra set of hands. Now, what else do we need?" I looked down at my coffee mug. "A decent coffeemaker, for one."

"Some people like my coffee," Megan said, arms crossed over her pink bosom.

"Which people?"

"Freddie Stokes, Christopher Mitchell and Clifton McBrike all like my coffee. They come here every morning for eggs, toast, hash browns and coffee." She sat up a little taller.

I knew those men. Those men had worn the same brand of blue jeans and bought the same color of plaid flannel shirts for decades. Their trucks were always Fords and they took baths on Saturday nights whether they needed them or not. "The comfort of ritual doesn't mean they actually like it."

"Yours is too strong. I've heard people say it's a little bitter." She pressed her lips together, which made her face look even more featureless than usual.

I resisted the urge to say it was because I liked my coffee like I liked my men. "We can have both. They can choose."

"Will we keep a tally?" She waited with her pen poised over her notes.

"A what?"

"A tally of who orders what."

"Why on earth would we do that?"

"To see who wins." She shrugged.

I let my head loll back on my shoulders. "Megan, the whole point of this situation is for both of us to be winners. The only loser we want around here is Antoine."

"So you do want me around here?" A deeply accented voice said.

I whipped around. Of course. Antoine. He'd been stalking me all day and now he'd caught up with me. "How much have you heard?"

"Only that you want me around here." He smiled.

I shook my head. "You're taking me out of context."

He slipped onto the stool next to mine. "I will take wherever and however I can, *ma chérie*."

Megan looked like she was going to swoon.

So, of course, that was the exact moment Garrett showed up to pick me up.

The door banged behind him in the empty diner. Antoine twirled on his stool to face him.

"You," Garrett said.

"*Oui,*" Antoine replied. "*C'est moi.*"

"Gentlemen," I said.

Garrett turned to me. "What is he doing here?"

"It is a free country," Antoine said. "At least, that is what I hear."

"Well, you're free to leave. Anytime." Garrett held the door open.

Antoine glanced at me. I shook my head. He sighed and got up and sauntered—very slowly—out the door.

"How did you know I was here?" I asked Garrett. "Did you LoJack my phone?" Haley had done that when she was expecting Emily so she would always know where I was. Garrett didn't have any excuse like that.

"No. Dan told me where to find you. He, at least, is sensitive to the fact that I made a promise to the court." He sat down next to me at the counter.

"Coffee?" Megan offered.

He shook his head. "No. We should be going."

"Going where?" I asked.

"My office. I still have work to do." He motioned for me to follow him.

I grabbed my jacket and waved good-bye to Megan. "And what am I supposed to do there?"

"Do what everyone else on the planet does. Go on Facebook. Play a game on your phone." He opened the door for me. A swoosh of cold air swirled in. Outside an eddy of autumn leaves scurried in the street. Clouds lowered in the sky. It looked like a storm was coming in.

I shot him a look and stopped in my tracks.

He'd already gone a few steps ahead before he realized I wasn't walking with him. He stopped, turned and sighed. "What would you like to do?"

I thought about it. "I'd like to go over the diary again. Barbara thought she recognized some more of the people in it. I think I might be on the verge of breaking Esther's code."

"Great. How much trouble can you get in looking at an old diary?" he said, as we started walking again.

"Virtually none. Except . . ." My words trailed off because what I was about to say seemed so far-fetched.

"Except what?" Garrett's tone got sharp.

"Except someone stole the diary from my apartment while I was in jail."

"It's probably just tucked away in a drawer or something. You'll find it."

"It's not tucked away in a drawer. You know how small my place is. There are only so many drawers and I've looked in all of them." Twice. Plus under my bed and in the closet and in the couch cushions.

"Why would anyone steal an old diary?" he asked, holding the door to his office open for me.

Why indeed?

"So what were you and Megan talking about? You looked like you were hatching plans for a bank job." He sounded suspicious.

"Better than a bank job." I couldn't keep myself from smiling.

"Hopefully more legal as well."

"Absolutely." I hesitated. Megan had been the only person I'd really talked to about our plan, but we were going to be going public really soon. It was time to let people know. "Megan and I are going to have a joint venture."

Pearl snorted. "You and Megan? You've got to be kidding me. What brought this on?"

I glanced over at Garrett, hoping I'd get through the

explanation before he got mad. "Antoine visited me in jail."

Garrett's jaw clenched a bit. "I'm aware."

"When he was there, he told me he was considering opening a new restaurant, a sort of L'Oiseau Gris East. He thought Grand Lake would be a great place for it. He thought Coco's old shop would be the perfect spot. He wants to serve comfort food cooked in a gourmet style."

Garrett sank down into one of the armchairs. "No," was all he said.

"Yes," I said. "That's exactly what I thought. No no no. It would give him a reason to be here in Grand Lake all the time if it took off. So I thought I would see what I could do to make sure it didn't take off. I figured Megan would be invested in making sure he didn't open a place that would so directly compete with her diner, too. I asked her if we could collaborate. We're going to try out a new menu and see how it goes."

Pearl's eyes glistened. "Does anyone know about this yet?" Pearl was pretty much Stop Number One on the Gossip Train of Grand Lake, but it was a spot that she had to regularly defend. A scoop like this would be just the thing to keep her on top for a while. It wasn't a mistake that I told Garrett about my venture with Megan in front of her.

"We haven't announced it yet, but we need to get the word out." I smiled at her.

"Consider it done."

Pearl found a table and a chair for me to set up in the corner of Garrett's office and got me a pad of paper and

some pens. I started making lists of the nicknames that
Esther had used and who Barbara thought went with each
one, working from the copy that Barbara had made for
me. A lot of them were straight-up nicknames, like my
grandmother being Bubbles. Twinkletoes was probably
Lola Buchanan, who had been taking ballet since she was
three and apparently had a brief career as a Rockette later
on. Barbara was pretty sure Dixie was Glenda Sanders
who had moved to Grand Lake from Alabama.

Then there were the initials. Once I'd lined them up
on the pad of paper, it didn't take a rocket scientist to
figure it out.

ET = Dana Sharp
CX = Bertha Warren
FB = Eugene Allison

My cell phone buzzed on the table next to me. I
checked the caller ID. It was Dan. Safe to answer.

"Hey," I said. "I think I figured out some of the diary
code."

"Congratulations. Who do you think your secret Nazi
is?" he asked.

"I'm not sure, but I think his initials are going to be
EV." I knew it didn't sound like much, but it was a step
in the right direction. I was nearly sure.

"Doesn't exactly narrow it down," he observed.

"That's where you're wrong. I'm going over to the
library. They have phone books for Grand Lake going
back to the 1910s." I'd seen them when Juanita had taken
me to the microfiche. "I'll look through the Vs and see
how many Es are there, too."

"Very clever. How will you narrow it down from there?"

I wasn't sure about that. It would depend on a lot of factors. How many EVs there were. How many of them could be eliminated in one way or another. "I'll cross that bridge when I come to it."

"Well, before you cross that bridge, I think we have another one to cross. Two more city council candidates have dropped out of the race."

I sat back in my chair. "Who?"

"Chris and Taylor. Want to go chat with them to see if it's part of the rest of this fiasco?" I could hear the smile in his voice.

"Really? You want me to come with you?" I could barely contain my glee.

"Absolutely. You might see something I miss. Will you help me?"

"You bet. I'm at Garrett's office. I can be at City Hall in five minutes."

"Sit tight. I'll pick you up."

Ten minutes later, I was back in Dan's cruiser with Sprocket in the back. "Did you get a chance to look at those videotapes?" I asked.

"I watched the one from City Hall. You can just see Janine's bike. No one goes near it. Security at the Fairview Building didn't want to release their tapes without a court order. Something about protecting the privacy of their tenants. I had to get a subpoena from Judge Romero."

"How long will that take?"

"I'll have it tomorrow, if not sooner. Huerta's walking it through for me. That should expedite the process." He put the car in drive and we headed out.

We went to Taylor's office first. Her secretary's eyes

got big when Dan showed her his badge. "Is Taylor expecting you?"

"No." Dan didn't explain further.

"I'll just see if she's available." She picked up the phone. Dan put his hand over hers and hung the phone back up.

"She's available for this." He turned and went through the door into Taylor's office.

"So commanding," I whispered behind him.

"Make sure to tell your sister about it," he murmured back.

Taylor was at her desk, but it didn't look as if she'd been working. It looked like she'd been crying. Her eyes were red and puffy and a pyramid of crumpled tissues had been constructed on her desk, laced with wrappers from the tiny candy bars that had undoubtedly come from the open bag at her elbow. They were piled like a shrine in front of a photo of Taylor with her husband and their three-year-old son. Her hair, however, looked fantastic. Blond and smooth and shiny. "What do you want?" She sniffled.

Dan slowed his steps. He sat down across the desk from Taylor and leaned forward. "Are you okay?" he asked, his voice soft and low.

Dan was a caring sort of guy, but this was impressive. He'd gone from take-charge, barge-into-the-office to sensitive-guy-who-just-wants-to-help in two steps. My respect for his abilities went up a notch or two.

Taylor shook her head. "No. I'm not really okay."

"Is there anything we can do?" Dan asked, motioning for me to sit down next to him in the other chair.

I slipped in quietly, but Sprocket made his way around

the desk directly to Taylor. He put one paw up on her leg and looked up at her. I knew that look. I knew those big melting brown eyes that made it feel like he was looking right into your soul. I knew how much solace it could bring.

Taylor burst into tears and buried her face in Sprocket's fur.

Dan and I waited until the storm passed. Taylor finally hiccupped herself back into some form of self-control. "Uh, why are you here?" she asked.

"We need to ask you some questions," Dan said. "Why did you drop out of the city council race?"

Taylor's head shot up, blond hair bouncing like a shampoo commercial. "Why do you need to know?"

"We're concerned that someone's been targeting the candidates for the open city council seat. We wanted to know if someone has threatened you or made you feel like you needed to drop out of the race for your own safety."

Two bright circles of pink formed below Taylor's freckles. "Nothing like that. No. It was just taking so much more time than I thought it would. I felt like it would be better to drop out than get in any more over my head."

Dan didn't respond. He sat there. He didn't tap his foot or drum his fingers or jiggle his knee. He sat.

The pink circles spread across Taylor's cheekbones. "You know, I already have a full-time job and a family. It didn't seem like the whole city council thing was going to work for me. Plus, there were other people running who would do a good job."

Dan still didn't say anything.

Taylor turned to me. "You understand, don't you?"

I glanced over at Dan, who gave an ever so impercep-
tible nod of his head. I was on. "You know, Taylor, we
think the poisoned popcorn might be part of this effort
to attack the candidates. Someone died here. Maybe it
wasn't the person who was supposed to die and maybe it
wasn't someone that anyone liked very much, but Lloyd
McLaughlin was a human being. If whatever made you
decide to get out of the race is related to what happened
to Lloyd, you may have information that could lead to
his killer."

Taylor squeaked and put her hand up to her mouth.

"You also might be in danger," I pressed on. "If the
killer thinks you might know something incriminating,
that person might decide to get rid of you. They've killed
before. They could kill again."

Tears began to well up in Taylor's eyes. "I told Chris
we should have told the police. I told him so."

"Told us what?" Dan asked, his voice a little sharper
than it had been before.

"I can't." The tears started to spill down her cheeks.
"Not without him. Let me call him."

Dan's eyes narrowed for a moment and then he nodded
his assent. Taylor pulled out her cell and pushed a button.
Chris was apparently on her speed dial list.

"Sheriff Cooper and Rebecca Anderson are here
talking to me about why I dropped out of the city council race," she said, and then waited a moment.

"No," she answered. "I said I couldn't without you
here."

She waited again and then looked over at the two of
us. "I think they've probably guessed most of it already."

I certainly had.

She hung up and said, "He'll be here in ten minutes."

He was there in five.

Chris's tie was askew when he ran into the office. He glanced at Dan and me, but went around the desk to stand directly next to Taylor. "What did you tell them?" he asked, his voice low and terse.

Taylor shook her head. "Nothing. Nothing yet. But, Chris, they think it's related to the poisoning. They think we might be in danger."

"Or they're telling you that so you'll talk." Chris turned to glare at Dan. Dan did not budge.

"You have to admit," I said. "It does seem like someone's out to get anyone who's running. Whoever it is has already killed once. How many other people might get hurt? If you have information that might help Dan stop whoever it is before they harm another person, can you live with yourself if you don't give it to him?"

Chris paced the room. "Can this stay between us?"

"I can't guarantee that," Dan said. "I'll do my best to be discreet, but what you tell us could end up being evidence in a murder trial."

"You're serious about that?" Chris stopped. He shoved his hands through his hair.

"Serious as a heart attack," Dan said, then winced at his own words. "We can get a subpoena if we need to, but that's one more way that word could get out."

"Yeah. I get that." Chris looked over at Taylor. "It's not like what we were doing was illegal. We won't go to jail for it. Go ahead. Tell them."

Taylor took a deep breath. "The only reason we were running in the first place is that it gave us both excuses to be out of our houses and with each other. Away from our spouses. Neither of us really cared about winning. We just . . . we just wanted to be together."

Chris came over and put his hand on her shoulder, his wedding ring on show. She put her hand over his.

"So how did whoever did this convince you to drop out of the race?" Dan asked.

Taylor reached into her desk, unlocked a drawer, lifted out some books and pulled out an envelope. "By sending us these."

Chris put his head in his hands. "You kept them? What were you thinking? Someone else could have found them."

Taylor shrugged. "There was that one where I looked really good. I thought maybe I could crop it and use it as my profile picture."

He stared at her. "You have got to be kidding."

"No. I'm not kidding. It was a good pic." She smiled up at him.

Dan opened the envelope and slid out a stack of photos. Taylor got up and reached over his shoulder and plucked out one of them. "See? If I crop you out from behind me there and make sure I don't show anything below my shoulders, I look really good."

"You can't use a blackmail photo as your profile shot on social media!" Chris exploded.

"Says who? I don't see any rules about that anywhere."

Chris opened his mouth to argue, but Dan held up his hand. "I'm glad you kept them, Taylor. These could help us track down a killer."

Chris flung himself down on the couch. "Do you think they'll help me track down a good divorce lawyer? Because I'm going to need one if those photos get out."

As I buckled myself into the cruiser, I said, "Taylor might not have been a bad city council person. You know, the fact that she wouldn't tell us without Chris's permission speaks to a certain amount of integrity."

"Yep. Tons of integrity. Except for that part where she was cheating on her husband." Dan made a face. He'd always hated cheaters. He got suspended in junior high for punching Roland Blair in the nose for cheating at dodgeball. He still thought it was worth it.

I won't lie. I didn't mind one bit that a person who hated cheaters was married to my sister. It gave me a certain amount of confidence in their relationship. I turned the photos over so I wouldn't have to see everything there was to see of Chris and Taylor, and the pictures showed pretty much everything there was to know about the two of them. There was a date and a time stamp on the back of the photo.

"Dan, did you see this?" I held up the photo so he could see the back.

He nodded. "I did. That'll be the date and time the photos were printed."

"If we can figure out where, we might be able to figure out who printed them out." I sat up, excited.

"That's why we're on the way to Costco right now. We'll ask them to pull up a record of people who had photos printed around that time. There should be some kind of record." Dan turned onto the highway.

"How do you know it's Costco?" I asked.

"We've gotten photos printed there. I recognize the printing. I could be wrong, but it's a place to start."

"We're going right now?" Talk about being a man of action.

"You got somewhere else to be?" he asked. "Besides, I bet your chances of running into Antoine at Costco are somewhere between slim and nil. That should be a plus, considering how you've been dodging him."

I cringed. "Was it that obvious?"

Dan thumped his chest. "I am a trained investigator, in case you haven't noticed."

"Oh, I've noticed, all right." I thought for a moment. "What if whoever it was paid cash?"

"Won't matter. You have to give them your membership card when you pay." He leaned back in his seat. I wasn't sure how long it had been since I'd seen him look so relaxed.

I hadn't thought of that. "Won't you need a warrant or something to get that information from them?"

"Possibly. Sometimes flashing the badge is enough. You'd be surprised how many people want to cooperate. If they don't want to, then we'll go through the hassle of a warrant."

Dan was right. He flashed his badge and people were falling over themselves to help out, especially the manager, who also was nearly falling over because she was fluttering her eyelashes so fast at Dan I was worried she might give herself a seizure. I think all he would have had to do was flash his smile and she would have dropped everything for him, panties included.

"Hey, Dan," I said. "Maybe we should pick up dinner

while we're here. You know, so your wife who's home with your two small children won't have to cook? I could text her right now."

The manager's eyelashes slowed to a more stately speed. "I'll be right back. I should be able to pull up the information you need pretty quickly."

Dan looked over at me after she left the room. "Was that really necessary?"

"Uh, yeah. I think it was." If there was one thing I had in life, it was my sister's back.

"You really think I'd step out on Haley with someone to get a list of people who printed photos on a specific day at the local warehouse store?" He fixed me with those bright blue eyes of his.

"No. That was for her. Better not to get her hopes up." I did know better. Dan was about as likely to cheat on Haley as he was to grow wings and fly. It was good for Little Miss "Anything for You, Sheriff" to know that, too.

"Oh. And yes, we should pick up dinner. Text Haley and see what she wants." He took out his phone to check something.

By the time Warehouse Supervisor Barbie returned with the list in the form of a computer printout, we'd settled on a dinner of roasted chicken, salad, rolls and pie for dessert.

She handed the list to Dan. "I hope this helps."

By the expression on Dan's face as he glanced over the list, it had.

"Can I see?" I asked.

"Later," was all he said. He thanked Supervisor Barbie, got a cart and picked up dinner, paid and then went back to the car. The only questions he would answer during that time were about what kind of salad dressing he preferred (vinaigrette, as if I didn't know) and what kind of pie he wanted (he surprised me by not wanting pecan). Oh, we also picked up diapers. Lots and lots of diapers.

Finally, we were back in the cruiser. Dan started the car, then reached into his pocket and pulled out the list and handed it to me.

I scanned it quickly. One name jumped out at me instantly.

"Justin Cruz? Justin? He printed out the photos of Chris and Taylor doing the desktop tango and sent them to them? He's the one who's blackmailing people?"

"We don't have any proof of that yet, Rebecca. What we know now is that he printed out some photos at about the same time that someone printed out photos of them." Dan stared straight ahead.

"But, Dan, that makes no sense. If he's the one who's going after city council members, who blackmailed him? And why would he nearly poison himself?" My head was spinning.

"He didn't poison himself. He poisoned Lloyd McLaughlin," Dan pointed out.

I thought back on the long list of city council candidates who had been in trouble. "Do you think he's the one who sent the information about Cathy to the *Sentinel*, too?"

"It's a stretch, but I think we ought to consider it." Dan pulled back onto the highway to head home.

"But wait. If Justin's the blackmailer, who blackmailed him?" Now my head was definitely spinning. "We should investigate the blackmail attempt on Justin. Just because it backfired on the blackmailer doesn't mean it's not part of this overall attack on all the council candidates."

"It was kind of a dead end."

"You already investigated it?"

Dan sighed. "Rebecca, what is my job?"

I sank down in my chair. "Oh, yeah. You investigate crimes."

"That's right. Blackmail is a crime. I went to see Justin after his press conference. He gave me the DVD the blackmailer sent him. The envelope it came in, too."

I hung my head. "I'm sorry, Dan."

He sighed. "I know. I just wish you'd give me a little credit."

"I do! I give you tons of credit!"

He shook his head. "Whatever. It didn't come to much anyway. There were no fingerprints on the DVD or the envelope except Justin's. Whoever sent it must have worn gloves. There weren't any labels on it or anything that would help us figure out who sent it."

"How did it get to Justin?"

"He said it showed up in his mailbox. There wasn't a stamp, though. Whoever was blackmailing him must have slipped it into the mailbox him- or herself."

"Have you seen it? The DVD?" I asked.

"I watched it. It was just Justin walking in and out of the back door of the church. There wasn't much to see."

I chewed on my lip. I'd been around Antoine's set enough to know that there was a lot more that went into taping something than what was happening in front of the camera. "Any shadows that you couldn't explain? Any sounds that might give a hint as to who was taping it?

What about where the camera was positioned? Could that maybe tell us something?"

Dan's eyebrows went up. "Maybe. I didn't think of that. I'm not sure I would know what to look for. You would, though, wouldn't you? Want to take a look at it?"

"I thought you'd never ask."

"First thing tomorrow, then."

"First thing."

I'd texted Garrett from the car, so he was waiting for us when we got back to the house. "I need to walk Sprocket," I told him.

"Let's go, then."

"Don't be too long," Dan said. "Dinner will get cold."

"You'd be amazed at what I can do with a cold Costco chicken." I snapped Sprocket's leash on.

"Nope. I wouldn't. I'd expect miracles and you would meet expectations and then some." He went inside, and Garrett and I headed off for the lighthouse.

"So what's your plan for tomorrow?" he asked. "It'd be nice to have a sense of where you're going to be."

"I'll be at the diner with Megan." I pulled the collar of my coat up against the growing chill in the air.

We'd walked a few blocks in silence when he said, "So am I forgiven yet?"

I thought about it. I didn't actually like being mad at him. "I'm thinking about it."

"Are you thinking about anything else?" he asked. "Like maybe what we talked about in the courtroom?"

"You mean your non-proposal?" I pulled my collar up tighter. "It's crossed my mind."

"Can you give me an indication of which way you're leaning?" He took my arm as we stepped down off a curb.

I turned to face him, grabbed him by the lapels of his coat and laid a big, fat, sloppy kiss on him. By the time I was done, I wasn't cold anymore. I was pretty sure he wasn't, either.

"I'll take that as a yes," he said, sounding slightly out of breath and pulling me even closer to him.

"Don't," I said. "I didn't say yes. I just let you know which way I was leaning."

Fourteen

It was eight thirty in the morning and we were huddled around Dan's computer. I'd spent the day before at the diner prepping and doing some publicity work. Everything was in place or as in place as it could be until this afternoon when the last-minute preparations would need to be made. So we were going to make some headway on the investigation. By *we*, I mean Dan, Vera, Glenn, Garrett, Sprocket and me. "What are we looking for?" Glenn asked.

"I'm not sure yet. There might not be anything, but I think it's worth looking. If you see anything that might give a hint as to who's behind the camera, say something," Dan said.

"What kind of hint?" Vera asked.

"Anything would help at this point. Maybe we could

figure out how tall the person taping was." Dan looked doubtful.

Huerta thought for a second. "Unless they were using a tripod."

"Ooh! Good point. If the tape is really steady, they were likely using a tripod or something else to steady the camera. It's ridiculously hard to keep a handheld video camera steady," I said. I'd learned that from hanging around the set of Antoine's television show.

Dan hit play. First we saw the empty parking lot behind the church, then a car pulled in. Justin Cruz got out of the car and looked around as if he was checking to see if anyone was watching. He then walked quickly across the parking lot to the back door of the church and after once again glancing around, let himself into the building.

The scene played out again, but with a different date and time stamp on it. Then it played out a third time. Dan hit pause. "Anything? Anybody?"

"It was definitely being steadied on something," I said. "What about the angle? It's like whoever it was knew exactly where to position the camera to get a clear shot of Justin's face as he got out of the car and right before he let himself into the church."

Huerta shook his head. "I'm trying to visualize the parking lot. I can't quite figure that out."

Dan stood up. "Field trip!"

It took a while to gather up everything we thought we might need. A laptop to watch the video on. A camera to see if we could duplicate the shot. A tripod. String. I'd given Vera a funny look as she put that last item in the box. "Haven't you ever seen that on TV? How they take string to show how bullets would go, or blood spatter?"

I shrugged. It wasn't like it would hurt.

We all piled into our vehicles and drove to the church. "Huerta, go let Reverend Lee know we're here and what we're up to."

Huerta nodded and knocked on the back entrance. No one answered. He turned back and shrugged. "I don't think he's here."

"Let's get set up, then," Dan said. "Garrett, you're about the same height as Justin. Go stand by the door."

Garrett did as he was told. Then with Vera holding up a laptop with the blackmail video playing, Huerta started moving around the edge of the parking lot in the trees to see if he could get the same angle on the video camera.

"You're too far away," Vera said. "Maybe it was zoomed in."

"It can't have been zoomed in. If it was, you wouldn't be able to get the car in the frame, too." I looked over her shoulder.

Vera shook her head. "Okay, then you have to take a few steps forward."

"That doesn't make any sense, either. Back here in the trees is the only place to hide," Huerta said.

"Figure out how to match the view and then let's figure out what makes sense, okay?" Dan said. "Our job is to collect evidence."

Huerta took a few more steps forward with the video camera and stopped. Vera stood next to him and the two looked back and forth. "This is it," Vera said. "We have the exact same view."

Dan looked over their shoulders. "Okay. Now try zooming out and moving back toward the trees."

Huerta did and then shook his head. "Doesn't work."

Dan took off his hat and scratched his forehead. "No. It doesn't."

For the next twenty minutes, the three of them moved around the parking lot two to three steps at a time, shook their heads and then came back to basically the center of the lot.

"It doesn't make sense," Vera insisted. "If the camera was set up here, there's absolutely no way that Justin wouldn't have seen it."

"Which can only mean one thing," Dan said.

"Justin knew the video was being shot," I said.

"Which would only make sense," Dan continued.

"If Justin was planning on being blackmailed," I finished.

"Or if he blackmailed himself," Dan said.

We exchanged a look. It reminded of when we were in high school and could have an entire conversation with a few glances.

"Why on earth would anyone blackmail themselves?" Garrett came over to look back and forth between the computer and the video camera. "That makes absolutely no sense."

"It's like the worst humblebrag in the history of humblebrags." Vera sounded disgusted.

"What the hell is a humblebrag?" Garrett looked over at me, his brow furrowed.

"Does he live under a bridge or something?" Vera asked.

"No. I honestly think he might be so good and pure

he doesn't even hear about things like humblebrags." I turned to Garrett. "A humblebrag is when you point out something about yourself as if it's bad so that people notice something good about you."

"I don't get it."

"Let's say Dan says something about how it's so hard for him to buy decent shirts because his shoulders are too broad for regular dress shirts. He makes it sound like it's something bad: He can't buy decent shirts. But in the process he points out how broad his shoulders are."

Garrett nodded. "Oh. Now I get it. So Justin gets up and makes this big brave announcement about being blackmailed so he can show everybody how he was trying to do good deeds at the church without taking credit, thus making sure that everyone knows he should get the credit."

"Yes! I knew you'd get it!" I clapped.

"So he actually blackmailed himself to do that." He shook his head. "That's really pretty funny."

"You know what might be funnier?" Dan asked.

"What?"

"Poisoning the popcorn that was supposed to be yours and then sending it off to someone else so it would look like someone was trying to kill you."

No one laughed.

I started to feel really cold. "That's too crazy, Dan. No one would do that."

"I'll admit, it's crazier than setting up an elaborate fake blackmailing scheme to out yourself as a Good Samaritan, which is crazier than blackmailing two of your opponents for a seat on the city council to get them out of the way, but how much crazier is it?" Dan looked grim.

I took a few steps backward as if I could distance myself from the thought. "A lot crazier, Dan. A man died. Anything you do deliberately that causes the death of another human being is basically at the very top of the craycray pyramid."

"What if he didn't intend for anyone else to die?" Vera asked. "The coroner said that Lloyd wouldn't have died from eating that popcorn if he hadn't had a bad heart or if someone else had been around when he got sick. He would have gotten the medical attention he needed and he would have been fine."

"What do we do?" I asked, feeling sick all over again at the thought of someone dying because they ate my popcorn, even if it wasn't my fault.

Dan straightened his shoulders. "We arrest him for blackmail and then we sweat him."

"Sweat him? We're taking him for a shvitz?" I asked.

Dan rolled his eyes. "We'll interrogate him."

"Oh. That makes more sense than wanting to make sure his pores were clear." I glanced at my watch. "Can you take me over to the diner now?"

"Tonight's the night?" Dan asked.

"Yep." Butterflies took up residence in my stomach. "Tonight's the night Megan and I show Grand Lake how it's done."

I'd convinced Megan to close for the afternoon. She did a fairly brisk trade in coffee and pie around three thirty, but I assured her it would be worth it. It would give us some time to goose up the décor along with the food. Some white tablecloths. Some simple votive candles. It didn't take much to completely change the atmosphere. Again, it was a matter of tweaks. Just like it was in the kitchen. Fresh mushrooms instead of canned. Homemade stock instead of stuff from a box. Fresh herbs instead of dried from a jar. Suddenly the diner went from being meh to swell!

Dario was already there when I arrived, chopping mountains of onions and mushrooms and snipping up fresh herbs. I walked in, gave Sprocket a treat and tied on my apron. It wasn't long before we had a rhythm going for our prep. Megan, Dario and me. Who would have thought? Dario turned on the radio. Our rhythm picked up.

It was like a dance, but not just with our bodies. We danced with our sense of smell and our sense of taste. We moved to the beat of scent and sound. We bowed before the steam and pirouetted around our saucepans.

It was so good to be back in a kitchen again. I hadn't realized how very much I'd missed it. I hadn't noticed how heavy my heart had become until it lifted. Cooking wasn't just my job, it was my joy. Cooking never let me down.

All of which left me extra dismayed when we unlocked the doors at five thirty and there was no one outside to barge in.

"Where is everybody?" I asked, turning to look at Megan.

Megan looked distinctly as if she'd bitten into a lemon. "Yeah. Where are they?"

I didn't understand. I'd gotten people to tweet about it and the *Sentinel* to run a piece and put up flyers. There should be a line out the door, down the street, around the corner and halfway to Toledo. Instead there wasn't anybody.

"Maybe it's too early." I bit my lip.

Megan gave me a look. "Do you know how many farmers eat here? Five thirty is late for dinner for them."

"You have regulars, right?" Dario asked, leaning out the door to look down the sidewalk.

She glared at me. "Of course I have regulars. Who doesn't have regulars?"

"Regulars you could call and ask if they're coming? Maybe offer them a free dessert to entice them?" Dario suggested.

She sighed. "I could maybe do that." She headed back toward the office.

I stayed at the front door and chewed my lip harder.

My phone dinged. It was a text from Haley: **Save us a table.**

I texted back: **No problem.**

Then I contemplated going to the bathroom to cry.

In the end, Megan and Dario and I had five people at our grand opening. Six if you count baby Emily, although she didn't actually order so it seemed like a stretch to count her as a customer. Haley, Dan, Garrett and Evan were at one table. Antoine was at the other.

"Why are you here?" I asked Antoine after seating him. He had on a shirt and shoes, so he was going to get service.

He smiled up at me. "I would never miss an opportunity to eat your cooking, *chérie*. Surely you know that by now."

He'd missed plenty of opportunities when we'd been married, but it seemed smarter to let that vichyssoise run under that particular bridge at the moment.

He opened the newly printed menu and asked, "What do you suggest?"

I hesitated. I knew I should probably tell him I didn't care what he ordered, but he had such a good and educated palate. It wouldn't hurt to get his opinion on a couple of things. "Try either the popcorn soup or the beer cheese soup with the popcorn garnish."

"Any particular reason?" he asked.

"I'm trying to figure out if we've put too much emphasis on the fennel instead of the basil. I can't decide and Megan thinks I'm crazy."

"Done. One popcorn soup. What else?"

"The wedge salad and then for dessert the vanilla ice cream with the caramel and chocolate popcorn garnish," I said in a rush. "Are we overdoing the Green Goddess dressing with the salad and are we putting enough popcorn on the ice cream?"

"I cannot wait. It sounds lovely." He handed me the menu. "As are you."

I didn't feel very lovely. Not lovely at all. I felt dejected and sad and frustrated, but we'd already cooked the food. It seemed a shame not to serve at least some of it.

After we closed the diner, Garrett and I walked home. It was cold but not windy, and I needed to clear my head. What had gone wrong? Why hadn't anyone come? Even if it had been a few of Megan's regulars, they could have tasted the food and told other people. My heart was heavy and my head was spinning. The cold air helped, but only a little.

"You sure spent a lot of time at Antoine's table," Garrett observed.

"I wanted to know if there was too much fennel in the popcorn soup." I kicked at a pebble on the sidewalk.

"You didn't ask me if I thought there was too much fennel in the popcorn soup. I have a mouth. I have taste buds. I have opinions." He jammed his hands into the pockets of his jacket.

"No. I didn't ask you about that. I also don't ask Antoine about legal matters. You know the law. He knows food." It seemed perfectly obvious to me.

"I know food." He seemed to be very interested in his feet at the moment, not meeting my gaze at all.

How on earth was I going to explain this? "No. You don't. You eat food. You're lovely to cook for. You're the most appreciative audience, but you're just an eater."

Garrett stopped walking. "Just an eater? That's how you see me? As an eater?"

I stopped, too. "Of course I see you as more than an eater. I see you as a smart, handsome, kind, lovely man who I love to spend time with. But in the kitchen, you're an eater. I don't see you as a fellow chef."

He stared up at the branches of the elm trees that sheltered the street. "I suppose that's fair. I don't like it, but I guess it's fair."

I slid my arms around his waist and rested my head against his chest. "It would be nice if something tonight were fair."

The next morning, I'd been up for close to an hour by the time Garrett got out of bed and through the shower. "What's that heavenly smell?" he asked.

"It's a frittata." I slid the pan out of the oven. The

frittata had begun to brown on top, but was still fluffy beneath. I set it on the counter and set a timer for five minutes to let it cool so it could set up before slicing but would still be hot.

Garrett looked at it with longing. "Is it for your sister?" he asked.

I shook my head and took a step closer to him. He smelled like shampoo and shaving cream and toothpaste. His dark hair was still wet.

He smiled. "Is it for me?" he asked.

I nodded and took another step. There wasn't any space left between us anymore.

"Okay if I say I love you again?" he asked.

It was nice to hear it when it was just the two of us alone. No courtroom. No audience. No pressure. Just truth. I nodded harder and then kissed him. Hard. With feeling. Frittatas are good cold, too, after all.

A little later, I propped myself up on one elbow in bed. "You know what I think I should investigate today?" I said.

"No." Garrett pulled me back down to rest my head on his chest.

"Do you want to know?" I asked.

For a second it seemed like he was going to make some kind of smart-ass remark. Then instead, he said, "Very much so."

I pulled back for a second, ever so slightly stunned. "I think we should investigate the second poisoning. It's got to be related, but I don't quite see how. I can't see the connection."

Garrett sat up. "Well, the obvious answer is you. You

and your popcorn are the connection between Lloyd Mc-
Laughlin and Marta Hansen being poisoned."

"Yes, but we both know that I didn't poison anybody.
That means there has to be another common denomina-
tor." Why on earth would Justin want to poison Marta
Hansen? It made no sense. She had nothing to do with
the city council race.

He stretched and yawned. "You're right. How do you
want to start?"

"Let's look at who visited Loving Arms after I visited
Marta. I bet Dan has a copy of the guest register."

"Sucker bet." Garrett got up and started pulling his
clothes back on. "Of course he does."

Wow. Cooperation made everything so much easier,
didn't it?

Garrett drove Sprocket and me to his office, then
we walked to City Hall, a path that took us directly past
the diner. I thought about taking a detour. I didn't think
I could bear to see it, but that seemed more childish than
I wanted to be. So walk we did.

A banner hung outside of the diner. It read: "Not Under New Management."

Inside, the place was bustling.

I walked in and the entire room went silent. Megan
looked up from pouring weak coffee for Cody Moran and
saw me. She set the pot down so hard I was afraid it
might crack, and made a beeline for me. She grabbed me
by the shoulder, turned me around and marched me to
the door.

Sprocket growled. I looked around for Antoine and spotted him in a corner. I spread my feet and refused to budge.

Megan dropped my arm. "Please, Rebecca," she whispered. "Let's talk outside."

I shook myself back to my senses and said, "Certainly." Sprocket and I walked out onto the sidewalk and waited for her to join us. "So what's with the bum's rush there, Megan? And what's with the sign?"

She studied a crack in the sidewalk. "I found out why no one came to our grand opening last night."

I wanted desperately to know, too. "Why?"

Now she looked up and stared right into my eyes. "Because of you."

"Me?" I felt stung. She might as well have slapped me.

"They, uh, all are afraid you might inadvertently poison them." She cocked her head a little as if to gauge my reaction.

Understanding sunk in. "They think I might poison them because you told everyone I poisoned Lloyd McLaughlin."

She gave the tiniest of nods.

"So our joint endeavor was doomed from the start. By you." The irony of it would have made me laugh if it hadn't been breaking my heart.

She nodded again.

"So you're going right back to serving the same poorly prepared glop you've always served because then your clientele know they won't die from eating your cooking." People. Am I right?

Her eyes narrowed. "It's not glop."

I rounded on her. "You tasted the difference between

what you usually do and what we did. You know you're capable of more."

She sighed. "I get it. Yes. I just can't do it now. And I especially can't have you associated with it in any way. You're going to have to stay away."

"If I find out you're using my recipes, I will . . . I will . . ." I couldn't figure out what I'd do, so I let my words trail off.

"You can pull my hair really hard if I use your recipes," she offered. "And kick me."

I looked up, surprised. Megan looked honestly regretful. I felt tears spring to my eyes. "Deal." Sprocket and I turned to walk away down the sidewalk.

"I'm sorry, Rebecca. I really am," Megan called after us.

I kept walking.

Vera greeted me when I came in. "I didn't expect you back so soon, Rebecca. Aren't you sick of this place?"

"This side of the bars is really different," I said. "Maybe I could see Cathy a little later?"

Vera led me down the hall toward Dan's office. "Maybe. We'll see what Dan says. He just finished questioning Justin. He might have some thoughts about who gets to visit prisoners at the moment."

"What did Justin say?" I asked Vera.

She shook her head. "I'll let Dan decide what to tell you."

I picked up my pace and nearly ran her over. "So?" I asked as we burst into his office. "What did Justin say?"

"A lot." Dan leaned back in his chair.

"And?" I slipped into the chair across from him.

Dan brought his chair down with a *thump*. "He confessed to blackmailing Chris and Taylor and himself."

"Just like that? He confessed?" I was dumbstruck.

"Well, it wasn't exactly a big deal. Chris and Taylor don't want to press charges because they don't want their affair to go public. Their respective spouses would probably not be too happy about it," Dan said.

I could see that, but it wasn't Justin's only issue. "What about blackmailing himself?"

Dan shrugged. "As far as I can tell, it's not a crime."

"Could you charge him with wasting your time? Making a false police report? Something like that?" There had to be something. You couldn't run around blackmailing yourself willy-nilly and get away with it, could you?

"Sure. Or I could have if he'd ever made a police report. He gave his little press conference and that was it. He never reported it." Dan seemed remarkably calm.

I was not. "What about poisoning Lloyd McLaughlin? That has to be a crime. That's murder!"

"Justin swears he didn't do it."

"He's lying."

"It's totally a possibility. It's just . . ."

"Just what?"

Dan spread his hands in front of him. "He was pretty broken down by the time he started confessing to the blackmail. I'm pretty sure he would have admitted it if it had been him."

"It had to be him, though." I sunk back in my chair. Dan wasn't a human lie detector. He could be fooled.

"Does it? There's absolutely nothing connecting Justin to the poisoning, and he swears he didn't do it."

I sat back in my chair, stunned. "So that's it? He gets away with all of it?"

"He gets away with the stuff that isn't a crime." Dan frowned. "I actually believed him about the poisoning. He confessed to the blackmail as soon as I confronted him, but he held fast on the poisoning."

I thought that through. "So we have to find a way to tie him to the poisoning."

"I've looked at everything surrounding Lloyd's poisoning. I can't find any way to connect Justin to it except that the popcorn was originally meant for him." Dan rubbed his face. His eyes looked tired.

"What about Marta Hansen?" I asked. "Can you tie him to her?"

"Not that I know of, but I haven't looked that hard." He sat back in his chair, a thoughtful look on his face.

"How about I look? How about I start with the guest register from Loving Arms? Did anyone who's running for city council visit Marta at Loving Arms?" I asked him.

"I didn't see any candidate's name on the guest register," Dan said.

"Darn." Well, that was another avenue shut down. Or was it? "They could have signed a different name or maybe just pretended to sign in. If you come in while the receptionist is on the phone or talking to someone else, you could easily slip in without putting anything in the book."

"I suppose so," Dan said, his words slow as if he was thinking.

"There could be something there that doesn't mean anything to you, but might to me," I said. "Can I see?"

Dan pulled a file out of his desk and handed it over to me. "Knock yourself out."

Inside the file were photocopies of the desk register. I flipped through to the day I visited. After my name, I saw Olive Hicks, the Grand Lake Elementary Little Helpers, Gilberto Fowler, Joe Nguyen, Sabrina Rice and the Grand Lake First Community Church Choir.

"They don't list the names of the people in these groups." I tapped the list with my forefinger.

Dan looked over to see what I indicated. "It would take a lot of space. The choir from the First Community Church has like thirty-five people in it."

"Isn't that the church that Justin Cruz goes to? The one that he was supposedly breaking into to do good deeds?" My heart started to speed up. Maybe this was it. Maybe this was the connection.

Dan's eyes widened. "Yeah."

"Is he in the choir?" I asked.

He shrugged. "No idea."

"Could you find out?" I pressed.

"I'm on it." He dialed and in minutes was connected to Reverend Lee. They talked for a few minutes, then he hung up. "Justin's not in the choir."

"Darn." It would have been nice if the connection had been that easy to make.

Dan rubbed his face. "What reason would he have to poison Marta Hansen anyway?"

"To implicate me in the poisonings? Otherwise I don't see a link between Marta and the city council at all. Do you? When I first heard, my first thought was that someone was trying to frame me." Again. I still smarted over the rumors a certain person had started about me back when my dear friend Coco was murdered.

"No. I don't see any other connection. Someone wanted you to be blamed for the poisonings. Why you? You barely know any of these people who are running. Or do you have some grudge with someone that I don't know about?" He frowned.

"No. No grudges you're not aware of. I don't know why someone would be framing me, either." Dead end, then. I sighed. "Can I see the register again?"

"Sure." He slid the photocopy across to me.

I looked over the list again. "What about that school group? What were they there for?"

Dan smiled. "They come in and read to people. It's actually very sweet. Each kid is assigned to a particular person."

"Do we know what kid was assigned to Marta Hansen?" I asked.

"Let me call and see if I can find out." Once again, he dialed.

I busied myself combing my fingers through Sprocket's fur. Dan got put on hold a time or two, but finally was connected to the social director at Loving Arms. "Uh-huh," he said. "Really? Thanks. That's very helpful."

He hung up the phone. "Marta's assigned reader is Ada Denton, Sheri's daughter."

I froze looking directly into Sprocket's eyes. Sprocket, who Sheri had said had a beautiful aura. I looked up at Dan. "Sheri? Organic Sheri? Sheri who won't let peanuts into a classroom in case there's a kid that's allergic? Sheri who recycles other people's trash for them?"

"I know. Ridiculous. But that's the only city council connection I see." He glanced at his watch. "It's ten. The subpoena for the security tapes at Brixton Accounting should be ready. I'll see if there's anything on them that'll help us."

"Okay. I'm going to head to the library to look at old phone books."

He gave me a funny look. "Should I ask?"

"Probably not."

Fifteen

"Hi, Juanita." I slipped off my coat and brushed the snowflakes from my hair.

Juanita rolled up. "Well, hey there, jailbird. Nice to see you out and about."

I smiled. It was cold, but the light snow falling made it kind of fun. Like living in a snowglobe. "It's nice to be out and about."

"How can I help you?" she asked.

"I was hoping to look at those old phone books we talked about." I trembled a bit with anticipation.

"Right this way." She motioned for me to follow her. "Is this about that same diary?"

"It is. I think I figured out her code. It wasn't really tricky once I had a little more information. She just shifted the letters around." Still, if you didn't have some

basic information, it would have been enough to obfus-
cate certain identities.

We came to the back wall of the library. "Here they
are in all their glory." Juanita gestured to a huge set of
shelves groaning under the weight of a lot of thick old
books. "The 1950s should be down that way."

They were. It only took me a few minutes to find 1954.
I hauled the book over to one of the long tables and flipped
it open. I wanted to know who everyone was, but mainly
I wanted to know the identity of our possible secret Nazi.
I flipped to the Vs and scanned through. It took a few
minutes, but eventually I found ten people whose initials
were EV. Earl Valentine, Everett Vallins, Emmanuel Vane,
Edgar Vanwell, Eli Vaughn, Eric Vernon, Eugene Vickers,
Edwin Vincent, Edmund Vine and Elliott Vinton. One
name stood out to me. It was familiar. Very familiar.

Sheri Denton's grandfather.

Sheri who was running for city council. Sheri whose
daughter visited Marta Hansen at Loving Arms after I
had left the popcorn there. Sheri who hadn't been blackmailed or poisoned or exposed as a thief.

I shook my head. She was also Sheri who saw auras
and wanted the community to put the needs of children
as our top priority. Sheri who recycled for everyone. Sheri
whose grandfather was known for his philanthropy
around town.

Could he be our secret Nazi? If Sheri found out, she'd
be crushed, humiliated, horrified. What would it do to her
bid for city council? She was running on a platform of love
and acceptance and being good to one another and to the
earth. Would that all be undercut if people found out she
was the descendant of a concentration camp guard?

I took my list and headed toward the door of the library.

"Find what you needed?" Juanita called as I walked past the checkout desk.

"I'm not sure." I hoped I hadn't. Sprocket and I walked back to City Hall and had Vera lead us in to see Dan. Again.

"You're not going to believe who might be the descendant of Grand Lake's secret Nazi," I told Dan.

"You're not going to believe who I saw messing with Janine's panniers on the videotape," he replied.

In unison, we said, "Sheri Denton."

Then we both said, "What?"

I sank into the chair. "Sheri Denton put the poison in the popcorn?"

"I don't have definitive proof, but it's starting to look that way. And her grandfather was a Nazi?" Dan sank back in his chair.

Did I have enough to say that Edwin Vincent was a Nazi? "I don't have definitive proof, either."

Dan squared his shoulders. "Well, how about we start looking for some definitive proof."

"Where?" I asked.

"Her house seems like a good start," Dan said.

Of course it did, but it wasn't as if we could waltz in and start poking around. "Won't you need a warrant?"

"Yes. I'm going to get on that right now. What are you going to do?" he asked.

"Did anybody ever look into the anonymous note that helped the newspaper bust Cathy?" I had promised her that I would find out who had turned her in. It seemed like a good place to start.

"No. At least, not that I know of," Dan answered, but he was already distracted, making notes for his search warrant.

"What if it's one more link to Sheri?" I could be killing two birds with one stone. Or maybe it was actually one bird with two stones. Whatever. There was going to be a dead bird.

Dan looked at me thoughtfully. "Then it would be good to know."

"I think I'll work on that tomorrow."

He smiled. "Take Vera with you. Make sure she's the only one who handles whatever evidence you might come across."

The next morning, Sprocket and I walked to City Hall and explained to Vera what I wanted to do and why I wanted to do it.

"You want to go where?"

"To the newspaper to talk to them about how they got the information on Cathy."

Vera eyed me with some suspicion. "I would have thought you'd have had enough Cathy."

I had. I also had at least an ounce or two of compassion. "I made a promise to her."

Vera sat back in her chair and looked at me. "No one does anything for Cathy. Not even her husband."

"I'm aware." That was where that compassion thing came in. I'd only been locked up for a few days and I wasn't sure I would have made it without my friends.

Cathy didn't have friends. I wasn't saying that it wasn't

her own fault she didn't have friends. She was a user. That was for sure. Users don't make for good friends. I still felt bad for her.

Vera spoke into her radio and then said to me, "Hold on. I'll get my coat."

We headed out to walk the three blocks over to the newspaper office. Vera shivered as we set outside. "I can't believe it's winter again."

I glanced over at her as she wrapped her scarf more tightly around her neck. "You know it happens pretty much every year."

"And every year I dread it." She glanced over at me. "Don't you?"

I looked around. The sun had come out and the air nearly sparkled. "Nope. In fact, I can't wait for the first real snowfall."

She shook her head. "Certifiable. That's what you are."

"Possibly." I smiled.

I hadn't been sure what to expect at the offices of the *Grand Lake Sentinel*. They had not been my biggest fans. Pretty much every time I'd placed a foot wrong since I'd come home, they'd splashed it across the front page. Maybe they'd hiss at me. Or look at me with stink eyes as we walked in. I braced myself. I'd faced down plenty of people who didn't wish me well. I could handle it. I would handle it. I'd do it in pursuit of clearing up whatever was happening with the city council and clearing my name and letting Cathy face down her accuser.

The young woman behind the front desk leapt up as we walked in. "Rebecca Anderson!" she said. "Oh, my gosh. What can we do for you?"

I looked over at Vera, who shrugged. I shrugged back. "We'd like to see the publisher, if we could."

"I'll let her know you're here." She clasped her hands together over her heart and then sat down and hit a few buttons. "Ms. Sommers, Rebecca Anderson is here to see you." She paused. "Yes. In the flesh. There's a police officer with her." She listened and then hung up. "Ms. Sommers will be right with you."

I sat down wondering how long "right with you" would be. It was about fifteen seconds.

"Rebecca!" Molly Sommers strode out into the lobby. Molly was a woman in her fifties with close-cropped gray hair. She wore a pantsuit and a pair of reading glasses hanging from a chain around her neck. "To what do we owe this honor?"

I stood, feeling a little confused. "I was hoping to ask some questions about the investigation into Cathy Hanover."

"Ah," Molly said. "That explains your police escort. And this is?"

"Sorry. Officer Bailey, Ms. Sommers." Everyone shook hands. I felt like I was at some kind of bizarre dinner party.

Molly gestured for us to follow her. "Come on back to my office and we'll chat."

We walked into the bull pen and Molly stopped and clapped her hands. "Everyone, may I have your attention?"

All five employees stopped what they were doing. It wasn't a huge paper, after all.

"Everyone, this is Rebecca Anderson. I know many of you recognize her from her appearances on the front page, three of them above the fold."

There was a smattering of applause. I looked over at Vera, whose eyes had gone wide.

"She's here visiting today to find out about our investigation into Cathy Hanover, another person to whom we owe much." She then led us into her office at the corner of the room. We walked through to more slow clapping.

"Let us know if we can help," a young man called after us.

We settled into chairs. Molly leaned back in hers and asked, "So what precisely can I do to help?"

I looked around. I'd expected a little more resistance. "We were hoping you could tell us how exactly you got the tip that led you to investigate Cathy."

"I can do better than that. I can show it to you." She popped up, went over to the filing cabinet and, after rummaging around for a few moments, pulled out a Ziploc bag with a piece of paper inside it. She laid it on her desk in front of me. "This was delivered to the newspaper anonymously."

I slid the bag closer to me. It was a piece of stationery. Someone had cut letters out of magazines or newspapers and glued them to it to create a message. It was a list of five of Cathy's fake companies and then the words "Check them out."

"You have no idea who sent it?" Vera asked. "How did it arrive?"

"Someone slid it under the front door during the night. It was here when we showed up in the morning." Molly motioned for us to take it. "Go ahead. We got what we needed from it. You can have it."

"Thank you." Vera picked up the bag and we both stood.

"Yes," I said. "Thank you."

"No. Thank you," Molly said. "Your escapades have done more for our circulation in the past few months than any of the promotions we've tried. You've been better for our sales numbers than double coupons. We owe you, Rebecca. Now go out there and make some trouble!"

"That was weird," Vera said as we walked back.

"You think?" I'd been prepared for all kinds of things. For snubs or rude words or proclamations about protecting sources. I hadn't been prepared for being lauded as a heroine.

"It hadn't occurred to me that you actually sell newspapers." She smiled.

"It wasn't ever my intention." I hoped never to do it again.

"A good deed is a good deed regardless of the motive behind it, Rebecca. I think you should take the win." Vera patted me on the back.

She had a point. "Let's go show it to Dan."

Vera plunked it down on Dan's desk. He pulled out a form that they both signed, making the chain of custody official. She nodded at him and left.

"Why on earth would someone cut letters out of magazines to paste in a note like that? It's not like the old days where they might be able to match a specific typewriter to a note," I said.

Dan shrugged. "Some people are traditionalists."

"Is there anything else about it that might help us?" I peered at it through its plastic protection.

"Only if there are fingerprints on it."

"Do you think someone would go to the trouble of

cutting out letters from magazines without wearing gloves? Besides, won't that take time?" I thought for a second. "We should ask Cathy to take a look at it. Maybe she'll see something that none of the rest of us do."

"What kind of something?" Dan asked.

"I don't know. Maybe it's a little like the blackmail video and she'll know it when she sees it."

"I've heard worse ideas." He picked up the phone. "Vera, can you bring Cathy in here?"

A few minutes later, Vera led Cathy in. "Hey, Bunkie!" she said when she saw me. "I've missed your company, but at least now I get visitors."

I stood up and went to hug her, but Dan made a noise in the back of his throat. I looked over at him and he shook his head. "No contact."

I blew Cathy an air-kiss and sat down.

"So what's up?" Cathy asked.

Dan slid the note inside its clear plastic bag toward her. "Did you ever see this?"

Cathy leaned over and read it. Then she sat back in her chair. "No. I never actually saw it. That was the petard that hoisted me, was it?"

"It's what got the *Sentinel* started." Dan tapped it. "Is there anything about this note that could point to who sent it?"

Cathy's brow creased. "Why? What difference would that make?"

Dan and I exchanged a glance. "We think maybe the person who sent it might have some connection to who killed Lloyd McLaughlin."

She snorted. "Still trying to clear your name, are you?" she asked me.

I nodded. "It's probably best not to be known as the town poisoner when you run an establishment that serves food."

"Let me look again," she said. "Can I smell it?"

"You want to sniff the note? What for?" Dan's eyes narrowed.

"A hunch," she said.

"What can it hurt, Dan?" It wasn't like she could snort up any clues.

Dan sighed. "I have no idea. Go ahead. Just don't touch it."

Cathy picked up the bag, opened the top and inhaled deeply. She very carefully sealed it shut and sat back in her chair. "I can't believe it. I just can't believe it."

"Believe what?" I asked, leaning forward in my seat.

"Geraldine did it. Geraldine turned me in. The two-faced little witch." She shook her head. "Then she took all my ideas to run for the council herself. If I wasn't the one behind bars, I'd be impressed."

"You know that by sniffing the note?" Dan didn't look like he was buying what Cathy was selling.

"She put it on the scented stationery I gave her for her birthday. I was pretty sure I recognized the paper, but the sniff sealed the deal. What an idiot." Cathy shook her head.

"Smart enough to figure out what you were up to," Dan pointed out.

"True. Although considering the amount of time she spent at my house, she had ample time to snoop. I just never considered that she might betray me like that."

There seemed to be a lot of that going around.

* * *

"What does this do to our theory?" I asked Dan after Vera had taken Cathy back to her cell.

"It doesn't help it." He rubbed at his chin. "There hasn't been even a hint of Geraldine being part of any of the other instances of blackmail or poisoning.

"Does it hurt?" I wasn't sure. I'd been so sure we'd be able to link the tip about Cathy to Sheri.

"I'm not sure. I'll have to think about it a bit. I'm still going forward on getting the search warrant for Sheri's house." He looked grim. "Tree-hugging, composting, tie-dyeing Sheri. I'm not sure I can see her as a murderer. It's so not who she is, and I definitely can't see her as the granddaughter of a Nazi."

It wasn't who she was. Sheri was about the future, about hope. She wanted clean air and water for our kids. She wanted everyone to be safe. She didn't wear patchouli. "That's exactly the point. Her reputation—her personae—is so the opposite of a Nazi. Plus there's that whole thing about her being into genealogy." If it was true, if it was Sheri's grandfather who Esther was talking about in the diary, maybe there were other reasons to suspect him.

Dan leaned forward. "What whole thing?"

"Sheri did some kind of research thing about Grand Lake and her grandfather. She probably knew. She knew her grandfather was a Nazi and covered it up."

"How did she cover it up?"

"She didn't put it in her town history document."

Dan made a face. "Okay. A lie of omission. Still, it doesn't seem like enough."

"I disagree. Her reputation is, at least in part, from being part of one of the grand old families in Grand Lake. If her family wasn't so grand . . . Well, don't you think that would hurt her enough to cost her a hotly contested election?"

"Maybe."

"And if that Nazi relative had killed a teenage girl to keep his secret?" I pressed.

Dan shook his head. "You're still talking murder?"

"I think I am." I didn't like it, but it was what made sense.

"You said you were going to worry about the diary and nothing else." Dan's brow furrowed.

It was hardly my fault. "How was I supposed to know that there was going to be a murder and that I'd be involved in it?"

"Because there always is!" He threw his hands in the air.

I waited a minute for him to calm back down. "Dan, can I be there when you search?" I asked.

He hesitated. "Why?"

"I don't know. In case I see something you don't?" I just had a feeling.

He nodded.

"Okay. I'm going to go check on Carson over at my shop. Call me when it's a go, all right?"

"Will do."

I grabbed my jacket and Sprocket, and I left City Hall for the short walk over to POPS. It had been days since I'd checked in with Carson. I knew he could do whatever needed to be done without any help from me, but it felt good to start to normalize my life. Maybe Dan would prove Sheri poisoned the popcorn and my name would be cleared and I'd still have customers when I reopened the store, unlike what had happened at the diner.

I heard a buzz of noise half a block before I turned onto Main Street. Voices, maybe. Nothing more. I quickened my step, wondering what was going on.

A line of people stretched close to a block in front of the diner. Was this some kind of belated response to me helping Megan change her menu? Had I been right after all? Would people come once they knew how much better the food would be?

I stopped, trying to figure out who was in line and why they might have had a change of heart. I didn't recognize any of the faces. I did recognize some of the aromas wafting my way. I hoped I was wrong. I pulled out my phone and called Haley.

"Why is there a line at the diner?" I asked without saying hello.

"I'm not sure how to tell you this," Haley said. "Maybe you should read about it first."

"Read about it? Where would I read about it?"

"Go get a copy of the paper."

"I was just at the paper!"

"Did you read it?"

I hadn't. I hadn't even glanced at it. "Hold on." I went over to the newspaper kiosk, dug a quarter out of my jeans and dropped it into the slot. I grabbed out the top paper and read the headline:

"Collaboration between Famous Chef and Local Diner Creates a Culinary Smash"

"No," I said.

"Yes," Haley said. "I guess your idea of upgrading

Megan's cooking was a good one. It didn't work out because of your, uh, problems."

"You mean the problems Megan caused?" I swear I could feel my blood pressure rising.

"Yes. Those ones. But Antoine didn't have any of the same issues. He hasn't poisoned anyone." Haley sounded apologetic.

"I didn't poison anyone, either!" My own sister! I couldn't believe it!

"Yes, but everyone thinks you did."

I sighed. "I cannot catch a break, can I?"

"Anyway, the night that you had your Grand Opening, Antoine and Megan decided to try it themselves," Haley explained.

"And stole my idea and are making big bucks on it."

"Looks that way."

"And Antoine has a reason to stay in town indefinitely."

"That looks that way, too."

I put my head in my hand. "Does anyone want to kill me now?"

"Probably. It seems like someone in town usually does."

I hung up and shouldered my way through the line to the front door. At first there were some protests, but then I heard my name being murmured. Olive Hicks was seating people at the front. No one ever needed to be seated at the diner. There were always tables. Always. Not today. Every chair was taken. Every stool at the counter had a butt in it. "I need to speak to Antoine."

Olive shrank away from me. "He's kind of busy."

"He is not too busy to see me." I pushed past and made my way to the kitchen.

It was like I could feel the rhythm and the heat of the kitchen before I got there. My heart pounded. My breath came quicker. I swayed. I pushed through the metal doors and there it was in front of me. Antoine's kitchen.

Oh, he hadn't remodeled. The fixtures were the same as the ones I'd cooked on only days before. The counters were arranged in the same way. Nothing had moved. Yet it was demonstrably different. Somehow the air had changed. It was charged with the special electricity that Antoine brought to a cooking space. With a pang, I recognized it and rejected it all at once.

"Antoine!" I yelled.

Everything stopped. Everyone froze, knives in midair, spoons in midstir, spatulas in midflip. Then there he was, threading his way toward me through the kitchen, his smile bright and his blue eyes even brighter. My traitorous heart did the smallest of skips.

"Rebecca! You are here!" He held his arms open as if I was going to embrace him.

"I can't believe you're doing this." I gestured around the kitchen.

"Why not? You had absolutely the most brilliant of ideas, *chérie*. Why start from scratch? Mademoiselle Megan has much established here. Plus it means less competition." He smiled as if I should be glad of his good fortune.

It also meant that he would have a reason to be in Grand Lake pretty much forever. "Three meals a day, Antoine? It'll kill you. Even with staff. L'Oiseau Gris kept you hopping for twelve hours a day and that was with two dinner seatings."

"That's the beauty of this. I'm not responsible for all

of it. I will be contributing signature dishes. Over time, I might expand to take over more. Then again, I might not. We will go with the flow, as you say." He gestured for me to move out of the way and let the staff return to work.

Going with the flow was most definitely not Antoine's way. "That doesn't sound like you. You like a plan. You like things mapped out. You like things to be definitive."

He shrugged. "It's true. That was how I liked things. Then someone came into my life and captured my heart. I threw out one set of plans and made another. And then that same person left me and broke my heart into a thousand little pieces. I am still searching for a new plan. Maybe this will be it."

I knew the person he was talking about was me, and the sharp knife of guilt cut at me. I didn't buy it one hundred percent, though. "I didn't break your heart. I derailed your plan. That's different."

"We all experience things in our own way, do we not? The destruction of my plan feels to me like the destruction of my heart." He clutched at his chest.

"Fine. I broke your heart. I still don't see how this thing with Megan constitutes a new plan."

"Perhaps I will travel around to different cities and create a few signature dishes at places and help them revitalize."

"I thought you hadn't been able to come up with any new recipes. I thought you'd barely been able to cook with that broken heart of yours."

"I know! I was so pleased with what I did with Megan's meatloaf and mashed potatoes. I think it's because

I was here. Near you. Your essence permeates the town and I soak it in."

"I don't want you to soak in my essence. I want you to leave my essence alone." I put my head in my hands.

He shrugged again. "You have no control over your essence once you release it into the world."

I lifted my head and looked him in the eye. "What would it take to get you to go away?"

"More than you could ever possibly pay."

Sixteen

Everything had backfired on me. Everything. I wandered down Main Street in a daze. It had all started going wrong the second I'd come back to Grand Lake. Well, maybe not the actual second, but soon after. I made a plan to work with the woman who inspired me most in life and she was killed. I tried to get some free publicity from my ex-husband and he ended up being accused of murder. I tried to make a little money while my shop was closed and someone ended up being poisoned. I tried to make sure my ex-husband didn't have a niche to fill in the local restaurant scene and created a perfect opportunity for him instead.

In short, I sucked.

"Maybe we should move," I said to Sprocket. "Maybe we should pick up and find someplace else to go ruin. Someplace where there are fewer people I care about."

He looked up at me with that head tilt that read as quizzical.

"Yeah. I know. There would be people that other people would care about and that would spread more misery. Maybe we should become hermits." We could find a little cave someplace and only come out twice a year to buy supplies. I could stop shaving my legs. There were all kinds of potential benefits.

We got to POPS. There was music, but the thump was pretty quiet. I wasn't sure what that meant. Sprocket and I pushed through the front door and I almost needed to sit down.

All the smoke damage had been scrubbed away. The dust had been cleared off the glass shelving. The counters glistened. Tentatively, I walked into the kitchen. Then I really did need to sit down. I grabbed a chair and sank into it.

"Girl." Carson rushed over to me. "You okay?"

I pointed around the room at the new shining stove, the gorgeous cabinets, my old French-country table holding court in the center of the room, albeit with a few scorch marks, but still holding court. The scorch marks just gave it character.

"Yeah," he said, smiling. "It's almost done. I figured I'd spring it on you in a day or two. You seemed busy."

"Oh, Carson," I said. Those were the only words I could get out because the feels were so strong. They broke over me in waves. The feeling when I signed the lease on the place with Coco by my side. The feeling when Carson and I finished the renovations the first time and I knew I had created a new happy place for my heart. The feeling when I made my first batch of Coco Pop Fudge and knew my store would be okay.

Yes. Things had gone wrong. Terribly wrong on occasion, but things had gone right, too. I had held my little niece hours after she was born. My nephew counted on me for his Friday night bath and fun times at the park. My sister knew I would always be there for her. My best friend trusted me and relied on me. My boyfriend had proposed.

I sprang up, threw my arms around Carson and said, "Thank you. Thank you for this beautiful kitchen."

Before he could reply, my phone rang. It was Dan. "I've got the search warrant. It's on."

Searches look exciting on television. Crowds of law enforcement officials race through the house, empty out drawers, check under cushions, rummage through closets. Then somebody yells, "Got something!" Everyone races over and the case is solved.

The reality? Not so thrilling.

In reality, a small group of people slowly and carefully make their way through a place wearing plastic booties on their feet so as not to track in mud. Nobody yells anything, because Sheri's house is neat and tidy and nobody's finding anything except the occasional Lego under the sofa and a tiny hand-knitted sock stuffed between the couch cushions.

Sprocket and I stood next to Dan out by his cruiser. "We're not finding anything," he said. "Not anything to link her to the poison. Not anything to link her to the diary."

"Can I go in?" I asked.

He sighed. "It's not like there's any evidence we've collected that you could taint. I suppose it couldn't hurt."

I went in through the side door into the kitchen, leaving Sprocket outside with Dan. Her kitchen was set up much the same as mine was at POPS. It made sense; the houses had been built at about the same time. Of course, her kitchen wasn't as fabulous as mine was currently. It was then that it struck me. Her dishwasher was in the exact same place as mine. I rushed out the door. "Dan, you should look under the counter."

"What do you mean?" He looked up from where he'd squatted down to pet Sprocket.

"In the corner. Next to where the dishwasher is. There's nothing but empty space back there. It would be the perfect place to hide a body." I knew I was babbling, but I couldn't slow myself down.

Dan straightened up. "And you know this how?"

"Because when Carson pulled my dishwasher out, I could see under my counter and that it was a big old empty space perfect for hiding something. Ask Evan. He thought it was a super fun cave to play in until he saw a spider."

"Ain't that always the way?" He shook his head. "So I'm getting tips for crime-solving from my four-year-old son?" He strode into the kitchen with me at his heels. It took a few minutes to call the team together and get all the tools they needed.

They slid the dishwasher out. I could only see darkness behind it. Huerta strapped on a headlamp and crawled into the space and for a few minutes all I could see was his khaki-covered behind. It's not that the view was bad, it just wasn't what I wanted to be seeing.

"What do you see? Is something there?" I craned my neck to try to see around him.

Sprocket whined.

Dan put his hand on my shoulder.

Huerta backed out, sat down heavily, and snapped off the headlamp.

"Well?" Dan asked.

Huerta shook his head. "Nothing. Some spiderwebs. A lot of dust. Maybe some mouse droppings. But mainly nothing."

Sprocket barked. We all looked at him and then back at one another.

"Look again. Take your time," Dan said.

Huerta went back in. This time when he came out, he was holding something.

It was a tooth.

In the end, they found three teeth and a finger bone. There was no DNA to match it to, so there was no real way to know if it belonged to Esther Brancato. The age of the bones was about right, but that didn't mean much. What did mean something was the rest of the skeleton that they found underneath Sheri's compost pile and the small bag of pesticide that they found hidden under a loose floorboard in Sheri's garden shed, the same kind of pesticide she'd gotten them to stop using at the school and the same kind that had been used to poison Lloyd McLaughlin and Marta Hansen.

Later that evening, Garrett and I were back at my apartment. "I'm still confused," he said.

"Because it was confusing. We'd been looking at it all wrong." I stood there with the wooden spoon stuck up in the air. I was making a béchamel sauce, one of my specialties and the base for quite a few of my sauces.

"I don't think there's a wrong way to look at your béchamel. It's delicious from any angle," Garrett said, sneaking in and taking a taste.

"Not the béchamel. The city council. The poisoning and the blackmail and the anonymous tips to the newspaper. We'd been looking at it like it was all one chef, like there was one person responsible for all of it." It was a muddle, a mess, a mad, mad mishegoss, just like the beer cheese soup that Megan and I had tried to serve at the diner. There had been too many chefs, literally in the case of the soup, but metaphorically in the case of what had been happening around us.

"There's not one person behind it all?" Garrett scratched his head. "It seems like Sheri's at the center of a lot of it."

"Yes and no." I turned around to face him.

"Maybe you better put down that spoon and explain it to me." He wrapped his arms around my waist and pulled me closer.

"We kept looking for one person to be responsible for all of it, but they were all crooked. None of them were the people that Allen thought they were when he made his big speech to them." Poor Allen. He had to call off the election since none of the candidates were left standing. I'd thought he was going to cry when we told him.

Garrett kissed my neck. "Poor Allen."

"What I don't understand is why Sheri felt she had to poison anyone." I tried to reach over my shoulder to stir the béchamel.

"Don't worry about it. Dan will get her to talk." He reached over and turned the heat off from beneath my saucepan.

I started to protest then decided I could always make another béchamel.

"I couldn't get her to talk," Dan said the next morning, head resting on his pillowed arms on the kitchen table. "Not a word."

"You're kidding." I poured him a cup of coffee and set it in front of him.

"Nope. Well, she did say a couple of words."

"What were they? That she wanted a lawyer?" Sheri wasn't stupid. Maybe she'd try to hire Cynthia. I would if I were her.

"Nope. She wanted you." He looked at the cup of coffee like he wanted it, but didn't have the energy to pick it up.

I sat down across from him. "Me?" That made no sense. I wasn't a lawyer. I supposed I could bake a very nice cake with a file in it, but having been locked up, I still wasn't sure how that would help in any way.

"You. So will you come downtown?" He sounded so miserable.

"Of course." I got out my mother's old waffle iron. He looked like he was going to need some real sustenance to get through the day. Pancakes weren't going to cut it.

"You were right about her grandfather, I think. Huerta started checking back through his records and the guy basically didn't exist before 1949. The crazy cousin might have been right all along. He might have been a guard at a concentration camp who escaped from Germany in the chaos at the end of the war, assumed a new identity and settled here." He finally took a sip of coffee.

"Wow." I looked in the refrigerator. Haley had no buttermilk. Whatever. I'd make my own. "I still don't understand why she would poison Justin, though. What did that have to do with anything?"

"If she doesn't talk, I don't think we'll ever know."

Two hours and quite a few waffles later—Haley and Evan needed sustenance, too—I was seated across from Sheri in the same old interrogation room down the hall from Dan's office. I had to admit, I liked the view from this side of the table a whole lot better than I did from Sheri's side. Looking at her, I could almost feel the scratch of the orange jumpsuit against my skin. I hoped never to be locked up again, never to be shackled, never to be forced to be without decent hair conditioner.

"Here," I said, pushing some magazines across to her. "I wasn't sure what you liked to read, but these might help you pass the time."

She looked at them, but made no move to accept them. "You think this is enough?"

"Enough to entertain you forever? No, but it'll get you through the day. If you tell me what you like to read or do, I'll see if I can get something more long-lasting." I hadn't expected effusive gratitude, but a thank-you wouldn't have been out of place.

"Do you think it's enough to make up for what you've done to me?" She spit out the words like peas hitting a hot frying pan.

I pushed back in my chair. "What I've done to you?" I had no idea what she was talking about.

She gestured down to her orange jumpsuit as best she could with her hands handcuffed to the table. "You realize this is your fault, right?"

"What?" That made no sense. None at all. "What does this have to do with me?"

She snorted. "Only everything."

"How did anything I did make you try to poison Justin Cruz?" My brain was scrambling for an answer.

Sheri shook her head. "I wasn't trying to poison Justin Cruz. Well, not really. That was just a side benefit."

"A side benefit to what?"

"To getting rid of you."

Now I really was confused. "You thought I was going to eat the popcorn and die? How? I'd already sent it out."

"No. I thought you'd get blamed for poisoning the popcorn. Then you'd be too busy worrying about that to spend any more time looking at that stupid diary from that stupid girl that my stupid grandfather killed and stowed under my stupid kitchen counter."

I couldn't have felt more stunned if I'd dropped a cast-iron skillet on my own head. "So you knew about that all along?"

Sheri laughed. "You really think I wouldn't notice the corpse of a girl under my counter? And that if I did notice it, I wouldn't do anything about it?"

None of this was making sense to me. "She stayed hidden for more than sixty years. Why wouldn't you think she could just stay hidden?"

She turned away from me as if she was dismissing me. "You're insane."

That was rich. "I'm not the one who poisoned two people."

"No. But everyone thinks you are, don't they?" That thought apparently made her smile.

She had a point. "Okay. I think I'm beginning to see what you're saying. You poisoned the popcorn so I'd stop trying to figure out who the secret Nazi in Esther Brancato's diary was."

She clapped her hands, making her chains clank. "Bravo. You aren't as stupid as you look. But then it took you and Sheriff Dan too darn long to figure out that the poison had been in the popcorn because of stupid Justin Cruz and his stupid nut allergy."

I paused for a second to appreciate the irony of her being undone by an unknown nut allergy after trying to make the entire elementary school nut-free in case of just such a thing. She didn't seem to notice.

"So then I had to poison Marta, too, to make sure people would suspect you. I thought I was totally home free when Dan locked you up. What damage could you do from there?" She shook her head. "Apparently plenty with all your little minions running around town, signing petitions to free you, protesting, asking questions for you. Unbelievable. The nightmare wouldn't stop."

A smile quirked at my lips. It felt good to know people had my back. Or had had my back for a little while at least. "But, Sheri, you were the person who poisoned the popcorn. Why would investigating that instead of the diary take the heat off you?"

"I didn't think you'd investigate the poisoning! I thought Dan would keep you out of it. Then your business would fail because no one wants to eat potentially poisoned popcorn and you'd be gone and no one would remember the moldy old diary you found in the wall of your failed store." She slumped back in her seat.

She'd been right about the effect of the poisoned popcorn. Look what had happened to Megan's and my diner experiment. "What made you think Dan wouldn't figure it out?"

"With everything else everyone running for council was pulling? He'd have too many suspects. It would take him forever to sort it out. He'd still be investigating it as a deliberate murder of Lloyd McLaughlin if it wasn't for you." She made a shooing gesture as if she could get rid of me like a fly.

Sheri's motives were never going to make sense to me. "How long have you known your grandfather killed Esther Brancato?"

"I found the bones there when I was painting back when I first moved into the house. I wanted to get all around the dishwasher, so I pulled it out. It was so filthy in there. So dirty. I couldn't stand it." Sheri shuddered. "I crawled in to clean and there they were."

"And you didn't tell anyone? Didn't call the authorities?" I was pretty sure that would be my first call if I found human remains under my kitchen counter.

"And let everyone know my grandfather was a murderer? I mean, not just a Nazi, which would have been bad enough, but the murderer of a young woman in this town? Don't be insane!"

I actually grabbed hold of the table. I felt so at sea, I thought the room might actually be moving. "Wait. You already knew your grandfather was a Nazi?"

She rolled her eyes. "Of course I did, Rebecca. When

I started doing my genealogy research on him it became clear pretty quickly that there was something fishy. It was as if he didn't exist at all before 1949. Then when I was going through some of his things, I found a pin. It had what looked like two lightning bolts on it. It didn't take a lot of research to figure out it was an SS pin, the kind a Nazi officer would have worn."

I gasped.

"Don't get all dramatic about it, Rebecca." Sheri rolled her eyes.

"No need to get all snippy with me, Sheri. I'm not the one who killed someone to cover up the fact that my grandfather had killed someone to cover up the fact that he was a Nazi." I rolled my eyes right back at her. No one out eye rolls me. No one.

"No. You're not. You're the one who's constantly sticking her nose into everyone else's business. You're the one who's always asking questions about things that have absolutely nothing to do with her. You're the one who was going to start digging into that stupid diary you found and eventually figure out who the Nazi was and what happened to Esther Brancato."

"So you poisoned Lloyd McLaughlin? How does that make any sense whatsoever?" I still couldn't see the connection.

"You are such an idiot. No one was supposed to die. He was just supposed to get sick. And I'm not talking about Lloyd. I'm talking about Justin." Sheri shook her head.

"Why Justin?"

She shrugged. "I figured a little pesticide would wipe that smirk right off his face and I was hoping it would make him sick enough that he wouldn't be able to campaign for a while. We were neck and neck in the polls, you know."

I did know. I'd been one of the people planning to vote for Sheri. That made me feel a little ill.

"Justin kept saying those pesticides were so harmless, so I thought he wouldn't mind eating some. I thought it would take care of you, too. If everyone thought you'd accidentally poisoned someone, POPS would go under and you'd leave again."

"How did you even know about the popcorn?"

"You told me. That day at the park. I saw you there with your nephew and wanted to find out what you knew already. You practically sketched out the plan for me to frame you right there and then. You told me about the popcorn. You told me about Marta Hansen. You might as well have given me a blueprint."

"Weren't you worried the poison would be traced back to you?" I asked.

"Not really. I mean, you didn't actually trace it back to me, did you? It was the stupid diary about my grandfather that did me in," she said.

She had a point about that.

"And why Marta Hansen?" I asked, although I suspected I knew the answer.

"Serendipity again, with my daughter being assigned to read to her, but I would have found a way to get into her room. It's not that hard. Everyone's so happy to have visitors over at Loving Arms, they'll let you in anywhere. I figured if it looked like you had poisoned Marta, too, it would seal the deal."

There it all was. I stood up and knocked on the door. "Huerta," I called. "I'm done here."

So was Sheri. The difference was that I got to leave.

Except I didn't. Huerta came when I called. He's good about that. He came especially quickly that day, though. And he had a spring in his step that I hadn't seen in a while. "What's different about you?" I asked.

He looked down at his uniform, touched his hair, rubbed his chin as if to check to see if he'd shaved and said, "Nothing that I know of."

"No. There's something." I kept looking. I couldn't figure out what it was, but something was definitely different.

"He's been whistling all morning," Sheri said from behind me. "So irritating. Whistlers are the worst. Worse than hummers."

Whistling. When had I heard someone whistling recently? I froze. Garrett. Garrett had whistled. He'd whistled after I set the frittata aside and he'd whistled after he'd turned off the heat under the béchamel, but turned up the heat in my bedroom.

"You called Cynthia, didn't you?" I punched him in the shoulder.

His cheeks went red, but a grin spread across his face. "I may have arranged to see her."

"You saw quite a bit of her, didn't you?" Sheri asked with a giggle.

Huerta got redder.

I clapped my hands. "Good on you, Huerta. Good on you."

Sprocket yipped.

"Did you want something else, Rebecca?" Huerta asked. "Or was embarrassing me in front of a prisoner all you needed?"

"I'd like to see Cathy, if I could," I said.

"No one visits Cathy," Sheri said. "No one. Not even her husband."

"I'm aware," I said to her. Then I turned back to Huerta. "Please?"

"As you wish." He went into the room, unlocked Sheri from the table and led her out. "Wait here."

Sprocket and I did as we were told. We'd learned to be a little more obedient during our time in the big house.

We settled ourselves in the interview room and Huerta brought in Cathy.

"What the hell are you doing here?" she asked as Huerta cuffed her to the chain in the table.

I pushed my offerings across the table to her. "I brought you some books and some popcorn."

She fanned the books out. "Thanks." She gestured with her chin toward the tin of popcorn. "That's poison-free, right?"

I opened the tin, took a chunk out and ate it. "We're going down together if it isn't."

She laughed and took some herself. "This is good. I guess I should be relieved I didn't get a chance to run for city council. I would have gobbled the whole tin down and died instantly."

"How are you holding up?" I asked.

She shrugged. "The new roommate isn't as fun as you were, but she's certainly got an interesting story to tell."

"Okay, then. I should go. See you in a few days?" I stood and knocked on the door again for Huerta.

"Why?" Cathy looked surprised.

I shrugged. "Because everybody needs friends, Cathy. Everybody."

I had one last set of tasks to accomplish, one more person with whom to set things right. Garrett was in court on Monday morning over a small matter. He was representing Step Right Shoe Repair. Dixie Pratt was suing them for allegedly having resoled her favorite pair of boots in a way that made her fall. Garrett had been feeling confident of a win because of eyewitness testimony to the four margaritas Dixie had consumed before the alleged fall.

I met Faith in the hallway outside the courtroom with her two daughters. Annie was there with two baskets of flower petals. "Everyone ready?" I asked.

Everyone nodded.

I pressed my ear to the courtroom door. I heard Judge Romero's gavel bang and said, "Here we go."

I opened the door to the courtroom. Annie marched in strewing flower petals around her. Faith's daughters followed playing "Mary Had a Little Lamb" on their recorders. I had been hoping for something more romantic, but it was the only song they both knew and felt they could play by heart.

I pressed my hand against my chest, hoping that would still the over-rapid beating of my heart, and walked in behind them. Everyone in the courtroom was staring. The photographer from the *Sentinel* was there. Judge Romero was there. Phillip Meyers was there.

It was all set. Flowers. Music. Now it was my turn. I

got down on one knee in front of Garrett and said, "Garrett, will you marry me?"

He shook his head and for a second I thought he was going to say no. Then he held his hand out to me. I took it and he pulled me to my feet and kissed me.

RECIPES

S'MORES POPCORN BARS

GRAHAM CRACKER CRUST
1½ cups graham cracker crumbs
6 tablespoons butter, melted
⅓ cup sugar

Mix together the crumbs, melted butter and sugar. Press into a foil- or parchment paper–lined 8-by-8-inch pan. Bake at 350 degrees for 7 minutes or until it starts to brown.

FILLING
1 (10-ounce) package chocolate chips
1 (7-ounce) jar marshmallow crème
3 cups popped popcorn

Melt the chocolate chips in microwave or in a double boiler. Pour over the graham cracker crust. While the chocolate chip layer is still warm, microwave the marshmallow crème for 30 seconds at 50 percent power. Watch closely so it doesn't go full Vesuvius on you. Pour the crème over the chocolate chip layer. Press the popped popcorn into the marshmallow layer. Refrigerate for 30 minutes.

To serve, let it come to room temperature, then cut into squares.

POPCORN WITH
SHIITAKE CRISPS

1 (8-ounce) package shiitake mushrooms
¼ cup olive oil
1 tablespoon kosher salt
4 cups popped popcorn
⅓ cup shredded Parmesan cheese
2 tablespoons fresh rosemary

Remove and discard (or save for another use) the mushroom stems. Slice the mushroom caps into thin slices. Toss the sliced caps with the olive oil and salt (add more salt if you're like me and would probably fight off a deer to get to a salt lick). Bake on a parchment paper–lined jelly roll pan for 15 to 20 minutes at 375 degrees or until they start to shrivel and turn black. Allow to cool. Combine with the popcorn, Parmesan and rosemary while the popcorn is still hot.

ABOUT THE AUTHOR

Assault and Buttery is **Kristi Abbott**'s third book with Berkley Prime Crime. She has been obsessed with popcorn ever since she first tasted the caramel-cashew popcorn at Garrett's in Chicago. If you've never had it, you might want to hop on a plane and go now. Seriously, it's that good.

Kristi lives in northern California, though she was born in Ohio like the heroine of the Popcorn Shop Mysteries. She loves snack food, crocheting, her kids and her man—not necessarily in that order.

Ready to find
your next great read?

Let us help.

Visit prh.com/nextread

Penguin
Random
House